# JET XIV

†

Dark Web

Russell Blake

First edition.

Copyright © 2018 by Russell Blake. All rights reserved. No part of this book may be used, reproduced or transmitted in any form or by any means, electronic or mechanical, including photocopying, recording, or by any information storage or retrieval system, without the written permission of the publisher, except where permitted by law, or in the case of brief quotations embodied in critical articles and reviews. For information, contact:

Books@RussellBlake.com

ISBN: 978-1793435606

Published by

**Reprobatio Limited**

# Chapter 1

*Oulad Terna, Morocco*

The beige parapets of the walled city of Taroudant jutted skyward in the near distance, distorted by late morning heat waves rising from a dry riverbed that stretched east as far as the eye could see. The valley floor between, rimmed by foothills to the south, was a patchwork of verdant green where persistent farmers had managed to win an ongoing fight against the elements, and to the north the peaks of the High Atlas mountains shimmered white in the blinding sun.

A small crowd had gathered around a new building on the outskirts of the farming town, and the hard-packed dirt parking lot was filled with official vehicles. A half dozen troop transports brooded at the perimeter, and the soldiers they'd carried were now stationed around the structure, where a small stage had been erected at the entrance. A pipeline ran from the building, to the south, supported by regularly spaced concrete stands that allowed wildlife to pass beneath it, its length painted dark brown.

A plump man with a gleaming bald pate addressed the assembly from a podium at the front of the stage, behind which sat five other functionaries sweating in their suits.

"Today marks an important point in the progress of the Friendship Pipeline," the man said, his voice booming through amplified speakers at either end of the building. "This compressor station is one of two in Morocco that will serve as a maintenance hub for the installation, which will provide over two hundred local jobs!"

The crowd cheered and the speaker paused for effect, soaking in the smattering of applause in the manner of a practiced orator. When it died down, he motioned to one of the seated figures behind him and dipped his head deferentially.

"It is with great honor that today we host the head of the Moroccan oil and gas agency that is responsible for overseeing the project. Ladies and gentlemen, please welcome François Jaubert."

Jaubert rose, approached the podium, and shook hands with the plump mayor, who lingered like an unpleasant smell until Jaubert threw him a look that indicated his time in the spotlight was done. The mayor retreated to his seat, and Jaubert adjusted the microphone higher before clearing his throat and commencing his scripted comments.

High above the valley floor, on a water tower at the edge of the agricultural plots to the north, a figure shifted on the metal platform where he'd been hiding since dawn. He squinted through a high-power SCROME J8 scope attached to a French-issued FR F2 sniper rifle and watched as the mayor left the stage. The rifle had been sanitized and its serial number filed off, but even if it were traced, it would only lead to an armory near Lyon where a substantial number of weapons had gone missing in the 1990s. Still, the shooter was a professional and meticulously careful through force of habit, and had only handled the weapon and ammunition while wearing latex gloves. It was a favorite model, familiar and efficient, and he couldn't help but grin as he chambered one of three custom-loaded 7.62mm cartridges he'd prepared for the event, never taking the reticule off the target's chest.

Jaubert glanced over his shoulder at a red satin ribbon draped over the pump station's entrance, and allowed himself a satisfied smile as his eye traced along the pipeline, as though if he tried hard enough, he would be able to see all the way to where it began in Nigeria. He was responsible for the Moroccan stretch, which, with any luck, would be completed by the end of the year. Workers were laboring around the clock to lay pipe from the northern coast, where it would connect to an underwater section that would run beneath the Strait of Gibraltar – which in turn would feed African natural gas to Europe much more economically than current delivery systems, and which would alter the balance of power in the region.

He returned his attention to the hundred or so spectators there for the station opening. Four cameras were filming from the rear of the group, memorializing the event for the international news. The compression station itself was insignificant in the scheme of things, one of countless pump stations situated every sixty miles along the pipeline, but it was a powerful representation of progress in a nation that was considered largely undeveloped by first world standards. Jaubert had succeeded in spearheading the construction in spite of strikes, union problems, and terrorism – the latter always a concern given that fragments of Daesh were active in areas of southern Morocco.

"Many thanks for the greeting," Jaubert said, his voice rich and measured. "It's a sincere pleasure to be here, putting another link in an important chain into place. The Friendship Pipeline will transform the economics of all the countries it runs through, and we should see a surge in prosperity in Morocco once it goes online. For now, it's humbling to be welcomed with such warmth and sincerity. Without further ado, let us move to the ribbon cutting. I'm sure we'd all like to get out of the heat, *n'est-ce pas?*"

The sniper slowed his breathing as he eyed the target through the scope. The laser range finder he'd brought had confirmed the distance as 550 meters, easily within the accurate reach of the rifle, especially with his hot-loaded ammunition. There was little breeze, even at the higher elevation of the tower, so he was assured of a clean shot. His focus compressed to the single point on the target's chest, and he fleetingly noted the man's tie was Hermès as he gently squeezed the trigger, exhaling as he did so.

The rifle bucked against his shoulder, the report a sharp crack that echoed across the valley, and he was already automatically chambering another round, his movements fluid and practiced, as he observed the result of his first shot through the high-magnification scope.

Jaubert crumpled forward when the sniper's round struck him in the center of the sternum, shattering the bone and continuing through his heart before the fragments skittered around in his rib cage like Pachinko balls, shredding his organs as they went, the damage a testament to the shooter's skill in honing a round that ensured maximum injury with a single shot. A woman at the front of the stage shrieked at the crimson blossom spreading across Jaubert's shirt as he fell to the floor, and then the throng was stampeding in panic, rushing away from the station as the shocked bureaucrats sat with mouths agape.

A moment later the mayor was on his feet. A combat veteran in a prior life, he moved to where Jaubert lay dying, his expensive suit, silk tie, and starched shirt ruined by the blood seeping from his wound. His appendages twitched, the light already fading from his eyes even as the mayor knelt by his side, and then he was still.

The sniper didn't take a second shot, even though he could have – he had a clear line of sight, and to put another round in the target's head, or into one of his companions, would have been child's play. But time was working against him, and he needed to get clear of the water tower before the stunned soldiers could pinpoint him. He rolled away from the rifle, leaving it for the homicide inspectors, and crawled to the far side of the tower, where a length of rappelling line lay neatly coiled in the shade.

He pulled a pair of heavy gloves on over the latex, dropped the rope over the side, adjusted his rappelling harness and snapped the locking binder in place, and glanced down at the ground, where the line was brushing the hard-packed dirt at the base. He tested the brake end of the line out of habit and then lowered himself through the walkway opening, allowing the cord to take his weight.

Shots rang out from the pump station, and he cursed under his breath – he'd hoped for a few more seconds before they spotted him.

The soldiers had little chance of hitting a moving form at that range, but he still felt exposed and began feeding out brake line as quickly as he dared.

He dropped like a stone, far faster than he could have negotiated the metal ladder that ran the length of the tower, and resisted the urge to accelerate faster; he knew from experience that with the smallest error in judgment, he could lose control. He reached the ground after seven tense seconds and freed himself from the harness as he felt in his beige tactical vest with a gloved hand.

More shots barked from the pump station. His fingers seized the object he'd been searching for – a small transmitter with a pair of buttons covered by a transparent plastic lid. Sprigs of dirt fountained six yards away from rounds pocking the ground, reminding him to keep moving, and he rolled as he flipped up the cover and depressed first one button and then the other.

A series of explosions from the pump station and pipeline rocked the valley as charge after charge of C-4, placed along the run the prior night, detonated. The blasts had the desired effect: sections of the pump station walls blew outward, sending shrapnel and debris cutting through the crowd in a fireball.

He was up and running toward a slight rise before the last of the explosions' roar had faded, and was safely out of range within thirty seconds, the rifle fire from the soldiers a staccato chatter in the distance, the bullets thumping into the ground well behind him.

A battered Renault sedan sat with its engine running on the far side of the rise. The shooter made for it, zigzagging as he sprinted for the vehicle. He threw himself into the passenger seat, and the driver, a swarthy young man with four days' growth of stubble on his gaunt face and a curtain of oily black hair hanging over his brow, smirked, drew a long drag from the cigarette that dangled from his mouth, and floored the accelerator, sending a spray of gravel flying.

"Everything go as expected?" he asked over the revving engine.

The shooter nodded, his eyes locked on the road. The driver worked through the gears, and the little car practically flew along the track until it slowed at a paved road. He twisted the wheel and stomped on the accelerator again, and the Renault labored to gain speed. The sniper twisted in the seat and stared through the dusty rear window, sweat coursing down his face.

"Don't worry. No way they'll catch us now," the driver said.

The sniper frowned at the younger man's assurance. While the troop carriers were slow and ungainly, he knew that it was just a matter of time until helicopters were dispatched and roadblocks set up – there was no outrunning a radio.

He stripped off the gloves and tossed them in the back of the car, but kept the latex on in spite of the perspiration coating his hands. "How many minutes to the plane?" he asked. A single-engine Cessna was waiting for him at a dirt airstrip north of Oulad Aarfa, with a full tank of gas and no pesky locals to demand formalities like a flight plan.

The driver shrugged. "No more than ten minutes."

The sniper sat back and relaxed in his seat as the car bucked along the potholed road. Another day, another job executed flawlessly. He didn't know – or care – who the target had been, or why he'd been hired to execute him and destroy a section of the pipeline. That was none of his business. With any luck at all, he'd be enjoying the company of a young escort in Casablanca for dinner, his account in Vienna two hundred thousand euros fatter, while the Moroccan authorities chased their tails looking for a ghost. Not a bad payday for forty-eight hours of work, even when the cost of the equipment and arrangements were factored in.

"Slow down. We don't want to attract any attention," the sniper growled.

The driver obeyed, the shooter's demeanor making it clear he was in no mood to have his orders questioned.

"Whatever you say," the young man snapped, and instantly regretted his tone as the sniper's eyes narrowed to slits.

The shooter's right hand slid to the slight bulge of the compact 9mm pistol in his tactical vest for an instant and then felt for the seatbelt behind him and snapped it into place. The kid was just nervous, he reasoned. Probably the first time he'd ever been involved in something this big.

And the last. The sniper couldn't afford any loose ends. He was one of the top men in his field, a former special operations soldier who'd set down roots in Morocco and who only took on contract work that couldn't be traced back to him.

The driver had seen his face, sealing his fate, although he had no way of knowing what awaited him at the end of the short drive.

# Chapter 2

*Ramla, Israel*

Moonlight illuminated the exercise yard of Ayalon Prison, where a pair of seagulls were picking at the dirt in an effort to locate edible scraps. The large complex was quiet; the prisoners were locked down for the night, six to a cell in facilities designed to house two.

A scattering of guards patrolled the grounds, most the night crew comfortably ensconced in towers. Spotlights randomly swept across the building exteriors, revealing snatches of gray concrete. Gleaming coils of razor wire topped the high perimeter walls, and only a few vehicles moved along the adjacent road at the late hour, traffic having long before slowed to a trickle.

Inside the cell blocks, the halls echoed with snores and farts and moans, the air sweltering in the poorly ventilated bunkers. Most of the incarcerated were Palestinians convicted of terrorism or insurrection or violence, with the run-of-the-mill criminals of Israeli descent separated from the majority to minimize racial strife that was endemic to the prison population – a microcosm of the world outside the walls.

The corridors were dark, the only light coming from a pair of ancient fluorescent bulbs at either end of the building, their glow a white flicker accompanied by a faint hum of the air-conditioning compressors that cooled the guard areas and an occasional whine from one of the electric water pumps that fed the compound.

The clank of the cell door locking bolts snapping open shattered the silence inside, the sound as loud as the cocking of a .50-caliber machine gun as the twin lights blinked out and darkness settled over the central walkway. Groggy prisoners stumbled to the doors and pushed them open, wary of some sort of trick. Puzzled shouts filled the air, and then the men streamed from the cells, making for the main doors at the end of the block.

The guards in the towers fumbled with the searchlights, and the voice of the night watch commander sounded from the radio.

"What the hell's going on?" Superintendent Gidoni barked.

One of the guards felt for the handheld on the desktop and raised it to his lips. "Power's down. Whole place is dark."

"Transformer?"

"Don't know."

"Who is this?"

"Ben Rafi, sir."

"Ben Rafi, get some men with flashlights and figure it out."

Ben Rafi hesitated. "Sir? Is…what about the cells?"

"Don't worry. They default to locked in the event of an outage."

Figures running through the shadows at the exterior of one of the buildings drew Ben Rafi's attention. "Sir? Some of the prisoners are loose. At least a dozen are in the east yard."

Gidoni hesitated for a beat. "That's impossible. Are you sure?"

Gunshots rang out from near the administrative buildings, and Ben Rafi gave the others a panicked glance before answering, "You heard that?"

The superintendent's voice hardened. "All hands, we have a prison break. Repeat, we have a prison break. All personnel are authorized to use lethal force."

"Yes, sir!" Ben Rafi said, and turned to where his companions stood frozen near the window openings. "You heard the boss. It's a break."

More shots echoed through the yard, followed by screams of agony. The guards began firing at the running figures, who vanished into the darkness after the first volleys.

The jailers down in the cell blocks had been overwhelmed by the press of humanity that had rushed them before they could process what had happened. Their corpses lay twisted on the cold floor in pools of blood, their weapons confiscated by the prisoners, who were making for the main entrance. Gunfire erupted from the main-level guard station, and the prisoners quickly answered it with fire of their own. Dozens of the escapees collapsed, clutching wounds, but the guards were outnumbered hundreds to one, and the prisoners with rifles cut them down. Still more convicts poured through the doors and snatched up their dropped weapons; and then the tide of humanity spilled from the prison entrance, and escaping men ran through the darkness with all the speed they could manage.

A score of the Palestinian convicts made their way to the segregated area, and a battle began between the Israeli criminals and their Palestinian counterparts, armed with pipes, metal chairs, handguns, and anything else they could use to exact revenge on their hated enemies. Within minutes the floors were clogged with the bodies of the dying, the air redolent with the copper stench of blood. Years of accumulated hatred erupted as the carnage continued, and by the time the guns were empty and the stragglers who hadn't run for freedom had been found, over a hundred had been butchered.

The guards in the towers sniped at the escaping men, but the sheer number was overwhelming, and for every prisoner they shot, twenty more made it out of range. Soon they'd exhausted most of their ammo and prudently elected to barricade themselves in the towers and reserve their last magazines for self-defense.

Ben Rafi lifted the radio to his mouth during a lull in the shooting, his eyes roving over the prison. "Status check. All units, call out starting with tower one. We've got six here, all fine."

The other towers checked in. Most hadn't suffered any casualties, although two of the guards had been wounded.

"Superintendent, are you safe?" Ben Rafi asked.

The radio answered with static.

"Repeat. Superintendent, confirm your status. This is Ben Rafi in the south tower."

Ben Rafi's gaze drifted across the yard, and he slowly lowered the radio and turned to the others. "Hopefully he got a distress call out to headquarters. In the meantime, we–"

The window behind him blew inward with an explosion of glass, spraying the guards with shards. Ben Rafi threw himself to the floor, and the others did the same. Ricochets whined and whistled as bullets tore chunks out of the ceiling.

When the shooting stopped, Ben Rafi strained to see in the near total darkness.

"Should we return fire?" one of the men whispered.

"No point," Ben Rafi said. "We'd just waste ammo we don't have. We should wait for help."

The man responded forcefully, but Ben Rafi, suddenly dizzy, couldn't seem to make out the words. Warmth spread across his shoulder, and he reached up to his neck, puzzled. His fingers came away sticky and wet, and his brow furrowed in confusion as he drifted into unconsciousness, his final thought that this couldn't be happening – that it had to be a mistake, that his life couldn't just end like this, from a fluke. The wound in his neck pulsed blood with each beat, and then darkness replaced his awareness and everything went black.

By the time helicopters reached the prison, the convicts were long gone, all but a handful having disappeared into the surroundings like cockroaches exposed to light. The grounds outside the prison walls were littered with dead and wounded prisoners, their bodies sprawled where they'd fallen, most shot in the back as they ran.

Too little, too late, emergency vehicles formed a perimeter and sealed off the area, their roof lights strobing red and blue across the walls and nearby fields. Paramedics ignored the fallen convicts and concentrated on locating wounded guards. By the time the sun's first glow was brightening the eastern sky, sixteen members of the security detail had been confirmed dead, with another six seriously wounded. Box vans from the coroner's office drove away filled to capacity, and more took their place.

The IDF barricaded the roads and began a manhunt for the escapees, but with little hope of success – too much time had passed under cover of darkness, and most had probably made it out of the area, judging by the rash of car thefts reported in the morning. Given that many were members of groups considered to be terrorist organizations, their successful escape boded ill for attacks in the coming months, and should all the details leak, the state's ability to maintain order would be thrown seriously into question.

The media was barred from getting anywhere near the prison, and a gag order went out prohibiting any mention of the breakout other than to say an unspecified number of prisoners had escaped and were to be considered armed and dangerous. A door-to-door search of neighboring homes yielded nothing but the grisly discovery of several murdered residents, prey to the worst of the escapees who'd happened upon them in the dead of night.

By the end of the day, only a few dozen prisoners had been caught. The authorities had imposed a curfew, and patrols roamed the streets and helicopters swept grid searches, but it was largely for naught; nearly a thousand of the most dangerous miscreants in Israel had vanished like morning mist, their escape a body blow whose ramifications would be felt for a long time by the government.

Ben Rafi and the rest of the dead would be buried in unmarked graves, their families sworn to secrecy in the name of national security, but even so, everyone involved knew that it was just a matter of time before word leaked and a public outcry would be raised by a frightened and angry citizenry.

# Chapter 3

*Tel Aviv, Israel*

Jet entered the warehouse where the director's driver had deposited her and looked around the empty space. Stacks of pallets dotted the floor beside old forklifts rusting in place, the interior quiet except for the tapping of rain on the roof and the steady dripping of water peppering the loading docks. She glanced up at the corners of the cavernous room, where motion detectors and cameras tracked her every step, and wondered where the security contingent that protected the old man was hiding.

She had no doubt they were there. He was never exposed, no matter how hard he tried to make it appear that he had little concern for his own safety. But if it pleased him to put on an act, she was fine playing along. With measured steps she walked toward the rear of the building, her footfalls muffled on the concrete slab.

"Are you in there?" she called, head cocked to the side. Her nose twitched at the rank odor of stale cigarette smoke that pervaded the area near the offices.

"Yes, yes. Come in," the director's voice called, the final word truncated by a spasm of coughing.

Jet entered a long hall. She proceeded to the end and poked her head through the open doorway. The director looked up from behind a heavy wooden desk and waved a cigarette at her, the smoke leaving a pattern hanging in the air before fading to nothingness. He coughed again and indicated a chair in front of the desk.

"Sit."

Jet was used to the director's unusual mannerisms and sat, waiting wordlessly for him to tell her why she'd been summoned.

"How's the family?" he asked.

She was surprised by the question, although she didn't show it. "Good," she said, aware that the inquiry was a not-so-subtle reminder that their well-being was entirely in his control, and that she was obligated to the Mossad for their safety.

"Glad to hear it," he said, and stubbed out the cigarette in a half-full ashtray.

"You rang?" she asked, hoping to move the meeting along.

"Yes. Thank you for coming on such short notice." He paused, his hound-dog eyes watching her without emotion. "We have a project we need your help with."

"It's only been a couple of months since the last one," she said. "I thought I made it clear that I wanted some time for my family."

The director nodded. "You did. But something's come up, and we require your unique skills for an operation. An important operation, believe me, or I would never have called you in."

She didn't blink, waiting for more information.

The director leaned back in his chair. "You've no doubt heard about the prison break?"

"It's all over the news. Although with surprisingly little detail."

He nodded again. "My doing."

"Why?"

He pushed a file across his desk. Jet opened it to a dossier with several photographs of a handsome man in his late fifties, strong of jaw and thick of hair, his face radiating strength. She scanned the summary quickly and tossed the file back on the desk.

"Nicolai Karev," the director said. "Russian. Multibillionaire with his fingers in more pies than I can count. Energy. Arms. Technology. Banking. A real renaissance man who spends his time between nine homes scattered across the globe when he's not in Moscow." He held Jet's stare. "We need you to take him out."

It was her turn to nod. "I figured. But what does this have to do with the prison break?"

"That was a week ago. The following day we received a demand for four billion euros by the group claiming responsibility. Karev's group."

"I don't understand."

"The prison was an example. Apparently malware was planted in the power delivery system for the entire area, and at a predetermined time, it shut down electricity to the prison and overrode the failure safeguards. All of the security doors were opened, letting out some of the worst scum on the planet, who murdered any guards they could get their hands on before they escaped, presumably to Gaza or the West Bank." The director lit another cigarette. "The demand for the money spelled out that no element of Israeli infrastructure was safe from a prolonged shutdown that would make the prison failure look like a road bump. We've been running outcome scenarios ever since, and the reports aren't good. If they shut down our grid, it would be disastrous. The airports, the hospitals, the ports…the economic damage would be catastrophic. Tourism would be impacted, but so would virtually everything you can think of. The supply chain. The ability of the military and emergency services to respond. Mundanities like gasoline pumping from underground storage tanks. Nothing would be safe."

Jet digested the information. "And Karev is responsible?"

"Yes."

She studied him as he inhaled deeply and blew smoke at the ceiling. "What is it you're not telling me?"

"We stalled for time. It's not like we keep four billion lying around to pay off blackmailers. It takes some doing, even for a nation-state, to free up that kind of gelt. We bought ourselves a week, but…regrettably, the mission we fielded to neutralize Karev didn't go off as planned."

"What mission?"

"We attempted to blow up his vehicle in Paris. But our intel was faulty, and he wasn't inside when the bomb went off."

Her eyes widened. "I saw that on the news. A terrorist attack, wasn't it?"

He nodded and took a long drag on the cigarette. "We framed it to look like anything but a deliberate sanction. But we can't be sure he didn't figure it out, even with the media disseminating our story."

"I sense there's more."

"That's right. We received a communication the day after the bombing, demanding the money. We had no choice but to commit to delivering it by the end of the week."

"How?"

"Cryptocurrency. Bitcoin." He tamped out the cigarette. "Hell of a world we live in. Used to be kidnappers wanted briefcases with cash. Now it's all done with the tap of a few keys."

"What's the setup for the hit?"

"He's going to be at a wedding in your old stomping grounds. Monaco. Tomorrow evening. We've got decent G2 on the wedding location, the catering company, the works, so we can get you inside his perimeter as an employee." The director's tone hardened. "I want you to take him down, no fuss, no mistakes. We can't afford another screwup like Paris. Which is why I need you instead of one of our usual contractors. You've more than proven you can think on your feet. Because of the short notice, that might come into play. Obviously we hope not, but if so, I have ultimate faith in you."

"Logistics?"

"We'll have a sniper rifle stowed for you. All you have to do is get to it. Should be trivial for someone of your experience. A quick in and out, one shot across the water at a distance you can't miss. There should be no complications, and you'll be back home by the following morning. We already have assets on the ground there preparing for your arrival. Everything's in place. It'll be a milk run."

A line formed in the center of Jet's brow. "I work alone, remember?"

"How can I forget? You'll have complete control over the field personnel. Anything you want, you have. They're only there for support. You'll be autonomous."

She considered the request for a long moment. "How can you be sure that the Russians won't trigger the malware once Karev's dead?"

"Our analysts are confident that his organization will be in turmoil without a leader. He's a strong personality. Very hands-on. It's unlikely he would have delegated a four-billion-euro heist to one of his adjuncts. The recommendation to terminate him came from our analysts as the best possible solution. I don't second-guess them when there's consensus on something like this." The corner of his mouth twitched. "A high-profile assassination will also send a clear message not to screw with us. If we can get to one of the most protected men in the world, what chance would his subordinates stand? Our bet is that nobody would want to roll the dice once Karev is dead." He shrugged. "Cut the head off the snake, the body withers."

"If you're wrong…"

"That isn't your concern," he snapped, and retrieved another file from his desk and tossed it onto Karev's. "All the wedding details are in there. There's a flight to Nice this afternoon. I'd like you to be on it."

"What identity?"

"Spanish. You're to be a nanny."

That brought a smile. "You have a clean passport?"

"It's already being processed. Should be done within the hour."

Her green eyes bored into his. "You seem sure I would accept."

"I know your loyalty to me, and your desire to protect your family. If Karev shuts down the grid, we can expect that all of our enemies will seize the chance to attack us. It wouldn't take long for word to spread. Israel wouldn't be safe, even for you. So it's in your best interests to accept."

Jet held his gaze without flinching. "I'll need to review all aspects of the mission. If I don't like anything, I either change it or I don't take the assignment."

The director glanced at his watch. "You have three and a half hours until your flight departs. I'm sure you'll want to say goodbye to your family. You can review the file on the way home. I'll have my driver take you. And you have my word that you have complete control over the operation. I didn't bring you in to have it fail. You're the best we have. I'd be a fool to get in your way or try to second-guess you."

"We agree on that." Jet pushed back from the desk and collected the files. "Anything else I need to know?"

"Your passport, identity package, and cash will be delivered to your home in ninety minutes. The same car will take you to the airport, where you're booked on the afternoon flight." He paused. "I can't stress the importance of a successful conclusion."

Jet brushed a lock of hair from her forehead. "You don't need to."

Something that passed for a smile crossed the director's face, although the effect was anything but friendly. "I know. I'm sorry to drag you into the field again on such short notice. It was unavoidable."

"I just hope your advance team's up to snuff and that your intel's correct. You know how I feel about last minute ops."

"You'll have all day tomorrow to look over the site." He retrieved a cell phone from beside his computer monitor and tossed it to her. She caught it with an audible snap of fingers on metal, never blinking. "Call me if there's a problem. Whatever it is, I'll fix it."

"Will do."

She spun and headed back down the hall, files and phone in hand, annoyed at the abrupt timing but unsurprised – the director had rarely handed her a mission that wasn't critical, which usually meant that all other alternatives had been exhausted, burning valuable time in the process.

The driver was waiting at the warehouse entrance. Jet climbed into the back seat of the unremarkable car, and he wordlessly pulled away while she studied the dossiers, already lost in the upcoming mission, mind poring over possible ways the entire thing could go sideways.

# Chapter 4

*Tallinn, Estonia*

A slight man stood in the center of a sound stage wearing a motion-capture suit covered with active LED markers, sipping a cup of coffee while waiting for a gaggle of camera operators and lighting technicians to finish their preparations. The operators joked with each other as they made adjustments to the gear, but the lighting crew was deadly serious and worked in determined silence.

The actor yawned, stretched, and called to one of the grips. "Got any cigarettes?"

The lead camera operator shook his head. "Can't smoke in here. Sorry."

The actor muttered and considered his skintight, flexible suit with ill-disguised disdain. "I can't very well go outside dressed like this, can I?"

"You're being paid well. You can suffer for a few hours."

The actor made a face and took another pull on his coffee. "I want my agent!"

Everyone laughed, but the tittering quickly died when a door at the far end of the sound stage opened and the high-pitched whining of an electric motor filled the room. A mountain of a man on a motorized cart, the heavily built conveyance fitted with oversized wheels in order to accommodate the occupant's massive bulk, rolled toward the soundstage. He slowed as he neared and stopped near the first camera, his sunglasses reflecting the boom lighting.

"How's it coming?" he asked. His porcine face had a light sheen of sweat in spite of the frigid air, and his jowls jiggled as he spoke.

"We're close. Should be ready fairly soon," the operator answered. "Whenever Oskar arrives, which should be any minute."

"Take your time. This has to be perfect. I don't want to have to contend with artifacts after the fact."

"That's the idea."

"The new equipment check out? It cost a small fortune."

"Yes," the operator said, patting the camera. "It's a real pleasure working with it."

"Latest generation. We jumped to the front of the line, ahead of three Hollywood production companies, after a few well-placed tokens of our appreciation." The big man laughed. "So they'd better live up to their reputation."

"I have no doubt they will."

The fat man swiveled his cart around and rolled to the edge of the stage, inspecting each of the expensive cameras with a practiced eye. The actor avoided staring at him until the cart pivoted toward him and stopped in front of him.

"You clear on the script?" the big man asked.

"Yes, Mr. Kalda, sir. I'm a professional."

The fat man waved his hand. "Please. Oliver. I abhor formality."

"Of course, Mr. Oliver."

"No Mr."

"Yes, sir. Oliver."

"Everything okay? You want more coffee? A snack?"

"No, sir. I mean, Oliver. Thank you. Everything's fine."

"You understand what you're to do?"

The actor nodded. "I memorized the script. It's pretty straightforward. I understand it's not supposed to seem staged or theatrical. More on the amateur side."

"Exactly. And it was explained to you about the confidentiality clause? You can never discuss this with anyone. You must take it to your grave. No exceptions."

"I understand. It was quite clear. This never happened." He looked away. "Never."

"Just so."

A beep from the cart interrupted them, and Oliver pressed a button on one of the armrests. A screen attached to a thin arm rose from a slot, and he positioned the monitor so that he could see it. He tapped at a menu and peered at a message notification before grunting and looking away at the entrance, where a short man with spectacles and a bald pate approached with a leather satchel.

"Ah," Oliver said. "Oskar, you're finally here!"

"Sorry. Traffic from the airport was crazy."

"The important thing is that you're on the ground. Everything looks ready. Your crew has done a good job, as usual."

"Thanks. Let me get busy."

"Perfect. You'll have to excuse me. I have to go attend to some breaking issues." Oliver took a final look around the set and gave the newcomer a fleshy grin. "I'll leave you to it."

A commotion sounded from the door, and a stern woman entered with two prepubescent girls in tank tops and skimpy shorts. A makeup artist approached them with a makeup kit, and Oliver watched as she began her preparations, applying a light dusting of base before going to work on them with blush. Oliver's tongue darted over a pair of wormy lips, and then he tore his eyes from the girls and activated his cart using the contrivance's joystick.

The motor whined, and he reversed, then did a slow turn, and trundled back toward the door, trailing the faint odor of expensive cologne and perspiration as he went. Once he'd departed, Oskar began to bark orders at his crew.

"Come on. I want to get this over with. Let's do a camera check, and if everything's operational, try a first take." He looked over at the girls. "How long till they're ready?"

"Maybe five more minutes," the makeup artist said, never looking away from where she was tracing eyeliner beneath a wide eye.

Oskar nodded in satisfaction. "Okay, people. You know what to do. I'm going to hit the john, and when I get back, I want to do the system prep."

He laid his satchel on a director's chair near the first camera and went in search of a bathroom, leaving the actors and crew to complete their preparations, Oliver's visit having reminded everyone of the seriousness of getting the shoot right the first time. The girls stood woodenly as the artist completed her work, their angelic faces expressionless and their eyes dead, body language that of survivors in a war zone after a protracted battle.

# Chapter 5

*Tel Aviv, Israel*

Hannah greeted Jet at the door with a hug. Jet returned the embrace for several beats before looking up at Matt, who was in the dining room, pecking at a laptop computer.

"How'd it go?" he called.

"Mama's gotta pack. I'll be gone for a couple of days."

Matt rose and walked over. "Anything you can tell me?" he asked in a low voice.

Jet looked away. "You know how it goes."

"How about level of difficulty? One to ten?"

"Sounds like a three or four. But he always makes them sound that way, doesn't he?"

Matt frowned. "I thought this was only going to be occasional. Like once a year."

"So did I. Apparently if you have something that works, you're tempted to use it more often."

"I don't like it. No offense, but even the best baseball players strike out."

She cocked an eyebrow. "A charming American metaphor."

"I'm serious."

Jet smiled. "So am I." She sighed. "I've only got an hour, Matt, and I have to pack." She looked to Hannah. "Want to help?"

"You're going now?" Hannah asked.

"In a little while."

"Why? I thought you were coming to school Tuesday."

Jet bit her lip. "Damn. That's right. I'm sorry, honey, but Mama's got to work." Jet would miss the first recital of the year. She knew that Hannah wouldn't even remember it, but remorse still twisted in her gut at having to miss it. "Matt will be there, though, won't you?" she offered.

"Of course. Wouldn't miss our little bumblebee for anything," he said. Jet had found a bee outfit for the performance, and Hannah had been ecstatic when she'd tried it on. They'd taken at least fifty photos of her in the costume, each one cuter than the last.

"Well, come on, then. Let's go pick out some clothes," Jet said, her tone light. She reached out to Hannah, who took her hand, and they walked together to the bedroom, Matt behind them.

"What kind of stuff are you taking?" Matt asked.

"Simple clothes. And one semiformal outfit. The kind of thing you might wear for a daytime wedding if you were a worker and didn't want to stand out."

"Ah. Someplace warm?"

"This time of year, probably gorgeous."

"Tropical?"

Another smile as she pointed at the ceiling to remind Matt that the condo was wired. "Nope."

"Phooey."

She busied herself with removing underthings and tops from a dresser, handing each item to Hannah to pack in her lightweight nylon duffle, and then crossed to the closet for a pair of navy linen slacks and a tobacco blouse – clothes that would be appropriate but wouldn't be remembered by most on the day of the ceremony. Jet finished her chore and ruffled Hannah's hair. "You know what sounds good right now? Ice cream."

The little girl's eyes lit up. Jet tossed a few more items into the duffle and carried it to the dining room.

Matt closed the laptop. "I ate most of the chocolate," he confessed as she opened the freezer door. "But there's still a lot of vanilla left."

"Matt," she scolded, "I got that for Hannah, not you."

"I have no self-control," he said, deadpan.

Jet withdrew a carton of vanilla and set it on the counter. "I've always liked that about you."

Jet spooned out two scoops of ice cream for Hannah and a small one for herself and then put the carton back. Matt frowned theatrically as she carried the bowls to the table and sat.

She smiled at him. "I figure you can help me with this one," she said. "Tubbo."

"I resent that," he replied, pinching his waistline. Matt ran an hour each morning and did another hour of extreme workout later in the day, and his physique was that of a man half his age. Which didn't prevent Jet from teasing him relentlessly, although with obvious affection.

"Own it, Mr. Chocolate."

"Ouch."

"Not like anyone forced you to wolf it all down."

"Touché."

They finished their treat, and Jet was rinsing out the bowls when the intercom buzzed. Jet glanced at the wall panel and then at Matt before kneeling in front of Hannah and wrapping her arms around her.

"I love you, my little bee. I know you'll do great. Matt will film you, so I won't really miss it," she said.

Hannah pouted and looked away. "I wish you didn't have to go."

When Jet stood to face Matt, moisture was brimming in her emerald eyes. "Me too, sweetheart."

"I'll add my vote to the wish-you-didn't-have-to-leave poll," Matt said.

She hugged him close and kissed him, her lips on his for several seconds. When she pulled away, she took a deep breath and steadied herself. "All right. See you both in a few days."

"Plan on it," Matt said, and exhaled heavily. "Please."

"Don't be so dramatic. This will be a milk run. His words."

"That's even more worrisome."

She nodded, hoisted her duffle, and made for the door. "Tell me about it."

"I won't say be careful."
"Maybe break a leg?"
"Just come home in one piece."
"I'll try."

# Chapter 6

*Monte Carlo, Monaco*

Jet studied the harbor of the world-famous marina through the taxi window, the setting familiar from the last time she'd been in Monte Carlo, although her appearance was so different from that visit that her own mother wouldn't have recognized her. The cab wound its way along the final stretch of the famous Boulevard des Moulins and rumbled through the town, jockeying for position among Lamborghinis and Rolls Royces and Ferraris. Jet remembered the incredible amount of wealth concentrated in the small principality from her last visit, the spot a perennial favorite for Arab billionaires, Russian oligarchs, and Hollywood celebrities, all happy to flaunt their prosperity in the privileged enclave.

The sun was sinking into the Mediterranean by the time they reached the hotel. It was one of the lesser establishments on the water, but with a direct sight line across the most famous marina in the world to the Rainier III Nautical Stadium, with its elevated Olympic-sized saltwater swimming pool and party deck, where the wedding was to take place. Her cover had her working as a nanny for the children of the rich who would be attending the wedding of one of Karev's friends – a playboy Russian industrialist and a supermodel from Siberia a third his age who favored lavish parties and all-night events in Paris and London.

Jet knew from the dossier that the hotel was 320 meters from the stadium, an easy shot for her in any weather, but especially in clear skies, which the weather report predicted for the following evening.

The taxi braked in front of the hotel, and she paid the driver and retrieved her bag from the trunk, ignoring the man's lecherous gaze. She'd deliberately applied her makeup so she looked harder and older than she was – at least in her early thirties – but even so, apparently she could draw the wrong kind of attention.

The reception desk checked her in, and a bellboy escorted her to her room, where she tipped the man a small amount in keeping with her humble station in life. Once inside, she methodically went over the room, searching for hidden cameras or bugs. When she was sure it was clean, she removed the cell phone the director had given her, slid the battery into place, powered it on, and selected the second speed-dial number.

A male voice answered on the third ring. "Yes?"

Jet walked to the window and looked out over the marina. "I'm here. Where do you want to meet?"

"There's a Portuguese restaurant by Square Chiabaut. Can you find it?"

"What time?"

"Forty-five minutes from now."

"See you there."

Jet disconnected and removed the cell battery again. She didn't trust anyone, expected no calls, and saw no reason to carry a device that could pinpoint her location to within a few meters. She pocketed the phone and battery in her windbreaker and slipped a wallet with three credit cards for her alias of Gabriela Mendez into her back pocket.

The director's mission package had included a passport, the wallet and cards, and five thousand euros in well-worn notes, as well as a smattering of photographs of a young boy who was purportedly her three-year-old son. Conspicuously absent was any photo of her husband, whom she'd divorced the prior year, according to the file planted with Interpol.

Jet checked the distance to the park on her new tablet and saw that it was only slightly over a half kilometer from the hotel. She opened her window and inhaled the salt air. The temperature was cool, the wind off the sea mild, and she saw no reason not to walk to the restaurant. She took a long look at the stadium on the other side of the marina and then closed the glass. There really would be nothing to the task, assuming she wasn't missing some important piece of information.

Jet emerged from the elevator, strode out the door, and found herself on J. F. Kennedy Avenue, which ran along the waterfront and was bustling with well-heeled tourists. She picked up snatches of French, German, Italian, and Russian within the first long block, which was strangely reassuring to her. In a tourist town nearing the end of high season, she would blend in seamlessly. Jet knew from experience that a working-class woman like she was pretending to be was all but invisible to the moneyed class, who no more would notice her than a group of teenage girls would notice a septuagenarian at the mall.

She made a right, crossed Avenue d'Ostende, and continued up the hill, past endless apartment buildings where a humble abode the size of her place in Tel Aviv would run in the multiple millions of dollars. Monte Carlo had the strictest residence regulations in the world and required a bank balance of at least a million euros as the baseline to live there. The message was clear to even the dimmest: the wealthy had no interest in commoners sullying their playground, and the bar was deliberately set high to keep the riffraff limited to day trips from cruise ships.

There were police on every corner, as she remembered from her last visit, their uniforms neat and well pressed; if you intended to misbehave, you'd best do so elsewhere. She walked slowly, enjoying the night air, secure as if surrounded by a retinue of private bodyguards.

The exertion of climbing the steep hill felt good, and she paused occasionally to marvel at the city lights spread out below her, as well as the carnival glow from the mega-yachts moored in the harbor.

She arrived at the restaurant fifteen minutes early and asked the hostess for a table in the rear, well away from the entrance. When she was seated, she did a slow scan of the other diners, who were mostly locals of a certain age – older couples speaking French in hushed tones with bottles of middling red wine on their tables. Her antennae didn't pick up anything out of kilter, but she turned her attention to the wait staff, who were obviously related, the familial resemblance as clear as a brand.

A tall man wearing a rumpled brown jacket pushed through the doors and looked around the restaurant. Jet recognized the red scarf that hung from his neck from her briefing document and waved. His face lit up and he made his way to her, an easy smile in place. She rose and he kissed her cheek in the European way, and they sat across from each other, he making small talk in Spanish about his day until a waiter arrived with menus.

When they'd ordered and the waiter had disappeared, he leaned forward as though confessing a secret. "Well, Gabriela. Lovely to see you."

"Thanks, Giancarlo. Anything I should know?"

"No. Everything's set. We've got you working the event tomorrow as planned; that will allow you access to any of the areas you need to go. The daycare will be at your hotel, which is one of the reasons we chose your cover. Security will be tight, and the wedding party has booked all the rooms except those reserved for the staff – which is how we got you in there."

"And the target?"

"He'll arrive on his yacht tomorrow afternoon. We don't know when, but probably late morning."

"Why don't I neutralize him then?"

Giancarlo shook his head. "There's little chance he'll show himself before the main event. He's reclusive, so it would mean hoping against hope that he does something like sunbathe on deck, which is unlikely. Whereas at the wedding he'll be forced to stand fully exposed for a prolonged period, so you can pick your shot. That, and there's no way you can just disappear all day and take up a firing position without being discovered by the security force. They'll be searching all the public areas of the hotel, and there will be metal detectors at the exits."

"Which isn't a problem for you?"

"Not at all. The weapon's already in place, in the building next door."

"Next door?"

"That's right." He slipped her a tiny USB drive, which she palmed without comment. "It's all on the drive: assembly instructions, location of the ammunition, the works. A shell company rented an office for a week there. A key is in your night table at the hotel. At the appropriate time, make your way to the office. The rest will be simple."

"Impressive that you were able to secure it on such short notice."

"Life is filled with serendipitous events."

"Indeed."

Their meals arrived and they ate without enthusiasm, the fish lackluster, the sauces bland. When they were done and their plates had been cleared, they resumed their discussion in hushed tones.

"Will you be around tomorrow if I need anything?" she asked.

"Of course. I'll also be standing by to take you to Nice after you're done. I'll be in a car up the road with the engine running. You can leave everything but your bag in the office. By the time anything's detected, we'll be long gone – and the police are unlikely to search a locked, vacant office. Even if they do, if you replace the weapon exactly as you found it, they'll never spot it."

"I'm not sure I understand. How do I get into the office building if there's going to be such heavy security around it and the hotel?"

"You'll go from the hotel roof to the office building roof and enter through the rooftop access door. The security on the ground will never see you, so they'll verify the building is empty before the wedding starts. That will help after you're finished, because they'll be unable to determine where the shot came from." He looked around. "Use the rear exit to get out of the building. They'll be watching the front. The rear opens only from inside – it's just a metal slab, so they won't suspect it."

She nodded. "Sounds like you've thought of everything."

"Look, we were told you run the show, and there could be no screwups. We've covered all the bases we could, given the timing. But we both know that only narrows the odds — it doesn't guarantee anything."

Jet smiled and rose. "It was lovely seeing you again."

"Call me if you need anything. If not, reach out before you do it so I know to get into position." He hesitated. "My biggest fear is the local cops shooing me away while I'm waiting."

She blinked once. "If that's your biggest fear, you haven't been paying attention."

Giancarlo followed her to the front door and kissed her cheek again in the foyer. "I need to find the restroom. Nice seeing you."

"You too."

Her eyes darted over the diners, and she was reassured that nobody seemed interested in her. Giancarlo was going to keep an eye on the crowd when she left, to ensure nobody made any phone calls or was in a hurry to leave — standard tradecraft. She stepped onto the narrow sidewalk and glanced around. Fog was beginning to roll in off the harbor, and the air was heavy with moisture. The street was empty, the asphalt already slick from condensation.

The walk back to the marina took half as long as her trek up the hill, and when she reached the esplanade, she ambled along the water, admiring the yachts, one of hundreds of pedestrians out for an evening stroll. The stadium loomed over her as she continued toward the southern end of the harbor, and then she was past it and nearing the waterfront restaurants and bars that featured one of the most rarefied views in Europe.

After completing her stroll, she looped back around and continued to her hotel, slowing to consider the building next door, which appeared to be undergoing a renovation, judging by the trash chute running from the roof and the weathered appearance of the façade. All of the windows were dark, unlike the hotel, which was lit up like the largest boats in the harbor, glowing with megawattage from every angle.

The sight of the casino farther up the coast spurred a memory of her prior adventure in Monte Carlo, a lifetime ago, before Matt and Hannah and her slog across multiple continents, when the only thing she'd lived for was revenge. Now here she was again, this time risking her life to target a different Russian oligarch, returned to the employ of the Mossad, but doing it to ensure her daughter and Matt had a safe future.

The doorman looked her over as she approached, and seemed reluctant to admit her, but she mumbled that she was a guest and held up her key card. He swung the oversized door wide and she stepped inside, where she spotted several obviously Russian security goons stationed around the lobby. The precautions made sense – the guests were arriving for the fete the following day, and even at a less opulent hotel than this one, there would undoubtedly be those for whom safety was a concern, notwithstanding that they were on the most secure plot of land in Europe.

She waited for the elevator and sensed the security guards' interest moving from her back to the door. When the elevator opened, she stepped in and swiped her card and then stabbed a floor button with her thumb, her face unreadable as the door closed.

There was no evidence that anyone had searched her room, and after checking the two hairs she'd placed across the closet and bathroom doors, she relaxed and shrugged out of her clothes. Once in bed she wished she could call Matt, but knew that it would have been immediately detected by the director's watchers, and would have signaled a weakness in her character she couldn't afford to alert them to. Instead she stared at the ceiling and focused on her breathing, until her awareness gradually slipped away and was replaced by the awkward embrace of restive sleep.

# Chapter 7

*Barcelona, Spain*

Roadblocks stopped traffic on the Avenida Diagonal, where police lounged around the barricades as the leaders of a protest march attempted to organize the throng that had gathered at the Plaza Francesc Macià.

A scrawny man with dreadlocks yelled instructions through a bullhorn while a pair of female assistants passed out flyers describing the reason for the march. Many of the gathered carried signs, the most plentiful stamped with the distinctive hammer and sickle emblem of the Socialist Students for Change.

The crowd was largely younger, university age, with a scattering of older hippies, their beards and hair threaded with gray. Pungently sweet marijuana smoke drifted in the air, and the mood was festive. The sun was high in the sky, warming the boulevard down which the march would proceed. A group of ragged young men thumped and pounded a polyrhythmic beat on handheld drums while several young women with brightly colored summer dresses and long tanned legs danced to the entrancing rhythm.

A van pulled to a stop in front of the barricade, and a news crew spilled out. The cameraman wrestled with a shoulder-carried camera while a female reporter and an audio tech fiddled with a wireless microphone and receiver. A sedan stopped next and two more journalists stepped out, their light windbreakers emblazoned with the call letters of a local radio station. A network helicopter hovered high overhead, its blades thumping dully in the background as the organizer's amplified voice blared from the bullhorn.

"Five minutes, everyone! If you don't have a sign and you want one, ask one of the coordinators. There are plenty to go around. Once we begin the march, I'll call out the chants, and everyone repeat them with me!"

A murmur went up from the group when they spotted the media closing on the plaza, and more stragglers joined the assembly from the sidewalks. Many wore all black in spite of the heat, and few looked like they'd ever held a job – not surprising in a country with nearly thirty percent unemployment and a nightlife that routinely stretched well into daybreak.

A riot transport arrived and disgorged a dozen police in full battle gear, replete with Plexiglas shields. The protestors jeered at the cops, whose presence was typical at large protests, the helmeted figures representations of an oppressive state eager to clamp down on anything that hinted at insurrection. Another transport joined the first, and soon there were over fifty troops waiting on the other side of the barricade while the protestors grouped into a rough column in preparation for the march.

More protestors joined the main body, and by the time the organizer blew a whistle to signal the commencement of the march, there were at least two thousand protestors assembled along the plaza and the wide avenue. The organizer's voice blared over the bullhorn and the protesters began their trek, the promised chants rising from their midst.

"Jobs, not corporate plunder! No pipeline, no poison! Down with gas profiteers!"

Good-natured taunts and jeers hurled at the police who followed the last of the marchers went unchallenged; the riot squad was well versed in city protests and too savvy to allow themselves to be provoked into action they'd later regret, especially in front of the cameras. This was a small protest, as Barcelona went, one of scores that shut down streets most weeks from a citizenry vocal about their disapproval of government actions. For their part, the cops were ordered to stand down unless attacked or unless the event became a riot, which today seemed unlikely, given the environmental nature of the protest. Usually the troublemakers stayed home unless they were railing against the government, and those gatherings drew tens of thousands, not handfuls.

The marchers passed the first long block in their two-mile journey, fists raised, signs waving, voices loud and rebellious. Some of the drummers beat their skins in time with the chanting, increasing the volume as still more protestors fed into the main column from side streets.

"Looks like a slow day," the female journalist commented to her cameraman. "We'll be lucky to get ten seconds of airtime out of this."

"That's why they pay us the big bucks. At least you don't have to haul this beast around in the heat," he said, tapping the camera with his hand.

"And you don't have to worry about melting on air," she volleyed, her smile rueful as she dusted her face with fresh powder.

A commotion broke out near the front of the protest, and a high-pitched scream cut through the air like a knife from the edge of the column. The glass façade of a bank exploded in flame, and the display window splintered and collapsed onto the street. One of the marchers, a black-clad man with his face covered by a bandana, lit a second Molotov cocktail and hurled it at another storefront. The bottle detonated in a blast of flame and glass, and two more homemade bombs followed it, sailing through the air before exploding against the front of an insurance company and a high-end clothing store.

More screams joined the first as the crowd panicked. The press of humanity tried to reverse course, trampling those who weren't quick enough to get out of their fellows' way. The organizer yelled in an attempt to take charge, but it was too late – more thugs were lobbing Molotov cocktails and rocks over the rear of the protestors, directly at the police. Blood streamed down the face of a woman who'd been struck by a sign when its holder had spun to avoid being run down, and she held her hand to the gash in her head as though perplexed by where all the red was coming from.

"You getting this?" the journalist cried to the cameraman.

"Yeah. Trying. But we should get out of the main body. The cops are advancing."

"Who's throwing the bombs?" she demanded.

"I'm trying to get one on camera, but I don't see anyone. They're staying in the thick of it."

"Smart."

Sirens whooped from behind the advancing riot brigade, their shields raised. An officer gave an order, and six tear-gas launchers fired at the crowd. The smoking canisters thumped into the midst of the marchers, adding to the pandemonium. A shower of Molotov cocktails greeted the police offensive, exploding in the cops' ranks and sending them scattering.

Shotgun blasts boomed from the blue line. The police had escalated to using rubber bullets and high-power water cannons on the crowd, the majority of whom weren't charging the line but rather trying to run from the bomb throwers in their midst. But to the cops it looked like an out-of-control riot approaching, and they instinctively doubled down with more tear gas and shotgun fire.

The cameraman pulled the journalist into a doorway as the throng swept by, still filming even as the gunfire from the police barricades intensified. The audio tech gave her a thumbs-up, and she began live coverage, describing the mayhem that the camera was capturing over the protestors' bloodcurdling yells of fear and anger.

Fifteen minutes later, hundreds of police were cuffing anyone they could find, though the bomb throwers had melted away once the shooting started, leaving many of the protestors injured from trampling or from gas and rubber projectiles. The street was painted with blood and vomit and broken signs, and the organizer sat on a bus stop bench in a daze, still clutching his bullhorn, in shock at how quickly the peaceful march had spiraled into pandemonium. He barely registered when a helmeted cop slammed him in the head with a truncheon, and he slumped to the ground as the man was cinching restraints around his wrists, all filmed by the crew.

That night the riot was the lead story on all the networks, and the crew's footage showed the savagery of the police response in vivid detail. Over three hundred marchers had been arrested and thirty-nine injured, four seriously, two of whom were police.

Nobody could pinpoint who was responsible for the Molotov attack, and the marchers were generally described as an unruly mob that had come looking for confrontation. That no incendiaries or bomb-making material was found on any of the arrested didn't slow the narrative, nor did eyewitness reports that those who had initiated the rioting had been strangers nobody recognized, who'd kept their faces covered.

The reports all highlighted the growing public outcry against corporate greed, government corruption, and gestapo-like tactics that harkened back to the fascist days of Francisco Franco, and most predicted more unrest and possible violence in the weeks to come.

# CHAPTER 8

*Monte Carlo, Monaco*

Jet sat at a café on the waterfront, sipping an espresso from a tiny cup and watching the late morning sun glint off the blinding white hulls of the yachts. The surface of the harbor was still, reassuring Jet that her shot that evening would be an easy one, with virtually no breeze to contend with. She sat back and scanned the larger boats for the Russian's, but it hadn't arrived yet. There were several large open mooring slots on the far side of the harbor, which to her eye were the only ones big enough to accommodate a sixty-eight-meter yacht. While anywhere else in the world, that would have been a super yacht, in Monaco it was merely at the larger end of the spectrum, with at least a score of larger boats in the marina.

Her job as a glorified babysitter would begin at five that afternoon, with the ceremony scheduled for seven. She'd already gone to the hotel roof and studied the two-and-a-half-story drop to the adjacent building, which she didn't see as being a problem. The trick would be to evade any security the Russians might position on the hotel roof deck – a long shot, she knew, as any danger would be expected to enter from the street, and thus the bodyguards would be stationed there – and she hoped her assessment was right. If not, she'd have to take out whoever was sharing the roof with her, which would compress her timeline unacceptably; once the body was discovered, any security contingent worth its salt would shut the wedding down, suspecting a sniper, and it would be a miracle if she got out alive.

She glanced over at the stadium, where trucks were unloading sound equipment and collapsible tables for the banquet that would follow the nuptials. Jet intended to check in with her employers after her coffee, her only reason for doing so to obtain an event pass so her coming and going from the hotel wouldn't set off any alarms. She'd already decided that once she spotted the Russian's boat, she would begin to fake food poisoning and would time her final bathroom visit near the start of the ceremony, when Karev would be immobile and in easy range of her weapon.

Jet had checked an online almanac and confirmed that the sun would set at a few minutes after seven, which would ensure that it was dark when she was bolting from the office building to where Giancarlo would be waiting. Her bet was that the combination of the darkness and the confusion caused by the assassination would buy her the precious seconds she would need to slip out the back of the building without being seen.

The waiter came when Jet signaled for him, and she paid for her coffee and stood. She used the bathroom, checking to ensure that her makeup still made her look older, and then set off for the stadium at an unhurried pace along the waterfront promenade. A cruise ship floated at the dock that served as the marina breakwater, and the path was clogged with cruisers waddling in the opposite direction, stopping in clumps to take photographs of each other with the harbor for their backdrop. By the time Jet made it to the stadium lower service entrance, she was annoyed, but her face showed nothing, and she breathed deeply as she neared the guards at the door.

A man with a clipboard watched her approach. She stopped in front of him, and he looked her up and down. "Yes?" he asked.

"I need to check in and pick up my badge."

"Name?"

"Gabriela Mendez."

The man flipped a page and traced down the sheet with his finger, and then nodded, slid a pencil from behind his ear, and checked off her name.

"Go to the first office on the right and show them your ID."

Jet did as instructed and found herself facing a pair of heavyset men seated in front of a computer. She handed them her passport, and one wordlessly ferreted through a basket of badges while the other regarded her with frank interest.

"So. You're one of the childcare people?" he asked in French colored with a heavy Russian accent.

"That's right," she said.

"Do you live here?"

She shook her head. "No. I'm with the agency. They brought us in for the event."

"Ah, like us, then. Just here to see how the rich and famous live."

Jet offered a small smile. "It's amazing, isn't it? Hard to believe until you've been here."

He returned her smile, his eyes never leaving hers. "Maybe after the reception you'd like to have a drink?"

She calculated how to play it for the least headaches and opted for flirtation. "Maybe. Depends on how much trouble the kids give us."

"I'll see if I can make one of the champagne bottles go missing."

"That sounds wonderful."

The other man slapped a badge clipped to a blue lanyard on the table and rolled his eyes. "There you go. Sign here." He slid her passport back to her and placed a clipboard with a list of names on it in front of her, his finger indicating one of the blank boxes beside it. Jet signed with a flourish – she'd practiced all morning for just this eventuality – and scooped up her things and offered a parting smile to the friendly Russian. "I'll stop by when it's over if I'm not too tired."

"Good. My name's Anatoly."

"Nice to meet you. I'm Gabriela."

Jet walked along a hall to a set of service stairs and climbed them to the stadium pool deck, which was at least eighty-five meters long by thirty wide, with the pool in the center. The wedding would take place at the southern end, where a platform was being erected by scores of sweating workers. An older woman with a severe expression approached Jet and took in her badge with a glance, hands on her hips.

"I'm Madame Levant, the event director. What are you doing up here?" she asked in brusque French.

"I…I just checked in. I'm part of the daycare staff."

"Maybe they didn't tell you. That's going to be handled at the hotel, not here."

"Oh. I wasn't sure. I mean, how do the kids get there?"

"It isn't going to be all the children. Just a courtesy for the parents with large families who don't want to be disruptive. They'll be told to sign their children in at the hotel. You won't have to come here at all."

"Okay. It wasn't clear. But that makes it easy."

Her frown lines deepened. "Very good. Is there anything else?"

"I…is there a good doctor nearby? I think I might have gotten some bad food."

"My dear, I don't know what I look like, but I'm not an information booth. Ask someone at one of the service desks. I'm rather busy at the moment."

The woman spun on her heel and stalked off, and Jet barely kept from smiling. She'd established a precedent for her alibi that the woman might remember, and Jet might need to use the woman's authority with whoever was supervising the nursery when she put her plan into play.

Once back on the street, Jet hurried past the office where the leering Anatoly was stationed, and made straight for the hotel. A metal detector had been set up at the lobby entrance since she'd been gone, and she passed through under the watchful gaze of three muscular men in dark suits with the telltale bulges of handguns in shoulder holsters pressing against their jackets. When she was through, she made her way to the reception desk and asked about a doctor or a nearby pharmacy, and was directed to a store several blocks away. She thanked the clerk and took the elevator to her room, and then lay on the bed and closed her eyes.

Relaxation spread from her core, and soon she was asleep, the imperative to nap part of her training – there was no telling how the operation would go, and she instinctively snatched rest when she could in case she was forced to stay awake for an extended period if something went wrong.

When she awoke, she quickly rinsed off and then slipped into her work outfit of comfortable navy blue pants and a dark brown top. She checked her reflection in the mirror and, after reapplying her makeup for the right effect, slipped out of the room with her passport and wallet in her windbreaker pocket, along with the disassembled cell phone. She would return for her bag after the shooting, or Giancarlo would arrange to have it retrieved once she was safely away. If things went correctly, nobody would suspect her of being the killer, and the hotel would be the last place they would think of to search — at least, that was what the Mossad's big brains had concluded.

She checked the harbor again and noted a large yacht with a helicopter on the rear upper deck that matched the photo of the Russian's boat. So the target was on schedule; now the only thing that remained was to play out the next two hours, endure the role of nanny, and sneak into the office and blow the target's head off. The worst part sounded like dealing with other people's kids, but she would do what she had to for the mission.

Jet met her boss in the lobby — a ruddy-complexioned Frenchwoman named Giselle with an ample waistline and a nervous laugh — who walked her through her duties and introduced her to two other young women who would also be playing babysitter. Jet apologized when she begged off to go use the bathroom, and told Giselle about having gotten poisoned that morning. Giselle seemed sympathetic, and Jet felt sure that she'd put up little resistance when Jet had to disappear later, laid low by stomach flu.

The children began arriving an hour before the start of the ceremony, and Jet gritted her teeth as the area set aside for playing filled with toddlers. She made two more trips to the bathroom, each progressively longer, and at a quarter of seven apologized to Giselle for having to go yet again. By that point, the older woman was occupied with her duties, and she waved her assent to Jet without question, barely noticing her when she left.

Jet continued past the restrooms to the elevator and took it to her floor, where she proceeded to the fire stairs and ascended to the roof. To her relief the area was empty, and she rushed to the edge and lowered herself over it until she was hanging by her fingers. She took a deep breath and released her hold, and when she hit the office roof, tucked and rolled to diffuse the momentum of the drop. A twinge of pain lanced up her left leg, but Jet forced herself to her feet, and after confirming that nothing was torn or broken, ran in a crouch to the roof door, which was unlocked.

She found the office within moments and was inside in a blink, and moved to the wall cabinet where parts of the rifle were hidden. She pushed files out of the way until her fingers felt a full magazine, which she withdrew and set on the table. Next, she walked to a bookcase and felt along the top until she found the barrel, which she placed beside the magazine. In two more minutes she had all the parts laid out, and she quickly assembled the gun, taking her time, glad that Giancarlo had left the scope affixed to the firing mechanism so there would be no chance of it being knocked out of true during reassembly.

After chambering a round, Jet moved to the window and slid it to the side a few inches – not enough to draw attention, but sufficient to fire through. She steadied the rifle on the edge of the desk and peered through the scope at the wedding party, which now consisted of several hundred people standing around talking in anticipation of the commencement of the ceremony. Jet swept the crowd with the rifle, pausing at men who resembled the target, and then her eye was drawn to a long planter that ran the length of the waterfront side of the terrace, where Karev was standing, surrounded by four hard-looking men with crew cuts and no necks, dressed in ill-fitting suits. She settled the crosshairs on Karev's head, but he moved to greet someone out of her view, and the best she could do was to follow him with the scope, waiting until he took a seat or held still long enough for her to take the kill shot.

Somebody else approached him and shook hands, but he was moving too much, and she resigned herself to being patient, a quality she'd cultivated over years of similar assignments. She glanced down at her watch and saw that it was seven, so it wouldn't be much longer, even if the ceremony got off to a late start.

Jet squinted through the scope at the Russian and noted that much of the crowd was taking their seats. She drew measured breaths and her pulse slowed in anticipation of taking the shot, and she checked to confirm that the safety was off, her finger hovering over the trigger guard.

The light was going out of the sky as Karev moved with his entourage to a row of chairs near the front of the assembly, and after looking around, he took a seat. She settled the crosshairs on the back of his head, but then he moved out of view again when he leaned and twisted to shake hands with someone behind him.

*Steady. You've got time. Wait until everyone's seated so nobody steps in front of him and blocks the shot just as you're firing.*

The gathering was finally seated, and Jet was steadying her aim again when one of the bodyguards pushed down the aisle and handed Karev a phone. He held it to his ear, the head of the person seated behind him blocking a shot, and after a few moments of conversation, abruptly rose with his party and made for the stairs.

Jet cursed as she followed him with the scope – he was moving too fast to be sure of the shot.

He paused at the stairs, and Jet drew a bead on his chest.

A little boy ran up to him and he bent down to scoop him up, dropping from view for a moment. Jet swore again, this time out loud, as she settled the crosshairs on his neck, only to have the shot blocked by the boy's body as Karev kissed his cheek, set him down, and knelt once more to tousle his hair.

And then the Russian was descending the stairs with his men and disappeared from view.

Jet waited until he reappeared on the promenade, moving hurriedly, almost impossible to hit from her vantage point. When she was sure she couldn't tag him, she quickly dismantled the rifle, keeping the scope on the desk. She hid the various components where she'd found them, and then tracked the Russian's progress as he marched with his men toward where his tender bobbed with dozens of others, waiting to take him to his boat.

Whatever had happened, he was clearly going back to his yacht.

Which left Jet with few options, none of them good.

She considered calling Giancarlo, but dismissed the idea until she'd gotten clear of the building and confirmed there was nothing to be done. The Russian was still alive, and the mission aborted.

# Chapter 9

Jet burst from the rear exit of the office building and, seeing nobody on the narrow walkway that backed onto the arched supports for the road above, took off at a run toward the stadium. The streetlights that lined the waterfront had yet to turn on, and she was able to make good speed without drawing the attention of the security team. When she neared the stadium, she slowed to a brisk walk and continued past it without looking up at where the ceremony was now in progress.

Movement on the water caught her eye, and she stopped at the harbor's edge and looked out over the yachts. The Russian's boat was lit up like a Christmas tree, and she could see the crew raising the tender from the water, the whine of the crane faint across the marina.

Jet drew the cell from her pocket, inserted the battery, and speed-dialed Giancarlo's phone. He answered on the second ring. Jet didn't wait for him to speak.

"Something spooked him. He took off. He's on the boat."

"Shit."

"No kidding."

"Where are you?"

"Near the docks. I replaced everything where I found it."

"There was no way to make the shot?"

"Negative."

A pause. "What now?"

"I'll let you know as soon as I figure it out."

Jet hung up and watched as the big boat's crew freed the mooring lines from the bow and stern, and then with a low rumble from its engines, the huge craft pointed its nose at the harbor entrance. Her mind racing, she looked around and confirmed she was the only one watching the boat leave. Unaccustomed to failure, she mentally groped for something she could do, but came up blank.

The engine tone changed and the yacht's bow swung to the right and approached a lit dock near the harbor mouth. When Jet realized what it was doing, she sprinted down the waterfront, sticking to the shadows as she ran.

She closed the distance as the yacht tied off at the fuel dock, and slowed to a comfortable pace as the attendant dragged a heavy hose to the fuel ports and began pumping diesel into the huge tanks. The crew had obviously been unprepared for the hasty departure, and their lack of forethought might provide her the opportunity she needed. She studied the yacht as the bodyguards assembled on the second-level deck while two crew supervised the fueling, and the beginnings of an idea began to form.

Her gaze flitted to the helicopter and then back to the bodyguards. She didn't know what the range of a small helo like that might be, but it had to be a reasonable distance or it wouldn't have been of any practical use.

Which meant that if she could somehow make it onto the boat and execute the Russian, she had a viable means of escape.

She eyed the fuel dock but saw no way she could sneak past the crew, who were chatting with the attendant as the fuel pumped. Even if she could make it past the security gate and down onto the dock, the question was then how she could leap onto the yacht as it departed, without being seen.

Jet looked over at the tenders. She could steal a boat and follow the yacht until it was out of the harbor, and then hope to catch up to it while its engines spooled up to speed.

Her stomach sank at the thought. It wasn't bad, but it also wasn't foolproof, and there was a better than good chance that someone on the boat would spot her as she neared, especially given the quality of radar on a mega-yacht like the Russian's.

That didn't leave her many choices. The one that was her best shot was the one she liked the least.

Her rumination was cut short by the clank of the first fuel hatch closing. The attendant waited while one of the crew opened the second and inserted the nozzle, signaling the fueling was half over. Much as she didn't want to have to make an impulsive decision, time was running out, and her options were narrowing.

Jet looked in both directions, and seeing nobody nearby, swung her leg over the chain that ran the length of the walkway, and crept onto the rocks. She picked her way down to the water's edge and, after another glance at the ship, stepped into the water, which fortunately was relatively warm that time of year. She shivered as it reached her neck, and then she was fully immersed, the tang of petroleum on the surface making her retch as she swam toward the boat.

She pulled herself along with smooth, efficient strokes, taking care to avoid making any sound, only poking her head out of the water when she needed to breathe. Her clothes and boots acted as a drag, and it took her longer to near the massive hull than she'd thought. Jet was still fifteen yards away when the engines rumbled to life, signaling that her time was running out.

Jet reached the swim platform at the stern as the crew were stowing the dock lines. She hauled herself onto the teak surface just as the props engaged. The wash from the huge propellers nearly tore her off, but soon she lay dripping and breathing heavily as the yacht moved from the fuel dock and glided toward the harbor mouth.

Now that she'd accomplished the first part of her plan, she would need to find somewhere to hide, secure a weapon if she could, locate the target, and terminate him without being killed by his guards – all within a compressed timeframe while they were still close enough to land for her to escape from the yacht and make it to shore.

She mounted the steps from the swim platform and peered over the edge of the transom. The crew had finished with the lines, but several of the bodyguards were lingering in the main salon as the boat picked up speed. If they remained there much longer, it would preclude her from sneaking past them, and she couldn't stay out in the open on the platform once they were on the open sea.

Jet lowered herself back down the steps and eyed the stern. There was a large hatch for the watercraft garage, and beside it a watertight door. She tried the handle, and the door opened outward. The sound of the engines increased alarmingly from down a walkway to the engine room. She ducked in, pulled the door shut behind her, and found herself in total darkness; the light that had switched on automatically when she'd opened the door had shut off when she closed it. She groped along the wall until she found a switch, and the walkway lit up from a row of overhead fluorescent bulbs.

Jet made her way forward until she was between two engines, each the size of a car. The sound was deafening. She scanned the area in front of the motors, where a series of filters and pipes were mounted on the bulkhead wall, each neatly labeled.

She moved to the filters and regarded the assemblies. It would be child's play to shut off the fuel to the engines, which would leave the yacht dead in the water and cause pandemonium above. The problem being that the shutoff valves were obvious, and the second the crew found them closed, they'd know that there was an intruder on the boat, which would seriously restrict her ability to get to the Russian.

But if she could create a vacuum leak that was large enough to interrupt the fuel flow…

That would take longer to locate and wouldn't be immediate evidence a saboteur had made it aboard.

Her gaze followed the piping that led to the engines from the filters, and settled on the rows of injectors. If she could find a wrench and loosen a couple, the vacuum would be broken, and the engine would shut down.

That seemed the most viable solution. She reached for the tool cabinet that was mounted on the wall near the filters and was rummaging through it when the swim platform door opened, and the lights abruptly shut off.

# Chapter 10

*Tallinn, Estonia*

A pair of black Mercedes sedans pulled up to the wrought-iron gate that protected a palatial estate. Two guards with submachine guns dangling from shoulder straps approached from the gatehouse, and one of them slid the barrier a meter to the side while the other slipped through the gap and walked to the first car.

The driver's window slid down and a chauffeur in a black suit looked up at the guard.

"We're here to see your boss. Kalda," he said. "He's expecting us."

"Let's see some identification."

The driver passed the guard his driver's license and waited while the man fiddled with a portable radio and murmured into it. He stepped closer to the car as he lowered the two-way and handed the driver his ID.

"You can park by the main building. Someone will escort you to the meeting."

The driver nodded, and the gate swung open. The cars drove along a cobblestone drive that led to a trio of structures, one obviously a residence, with two long outbuildings on either side. A man was waiting on the porch of the home, his double-breasted suit impeccably cut. The lead Mercedes stopped in front and the driver killed the engine. Two men climbed from the back as the second car parked behind the lead vehicle, and another pair emerged from the rear.

The suited man stepped from the porch and indicated the outbuildings. "Gentlemen, this way. Oliver is expecting you."

Nobody spoke as the group walked to the first structure. Inside, their escort led them to a large conference room, where Oliver was waiting in his wheeled cart, entering commands on its screen. A young Thai woman in a blue silk sheath slit to her hip stood beside him, her face a picture of tranquility. Oliver looked up as the newcomers entered, and the fleshy folds of his face arranged themselves into something resembling a manatee's smile.

"Welcome to my humble digs," he said. "Have a seat. Can I get you anything? Anything at all? Malee here will attend to your wishes."

The newcomers sat at a polished conference table, upon which were arranged a collection of glass pitchers and bottles of vodka and rare single-malt scotch. Malee prepared their orders, and when everyone had drinks in hand, Oliver directed his trolley to the head of the table and motioned to her.

"A snack. Something light," he said with a wink.

She gave a slight bow and exited the room, and returned moments later with a jumbo bag of peanut M&Ms. He took the bag from her and crammed a fist the size of a boneless ham into the sack, and then gobbled a mouthful of candy before sighing contentedly.

"Thanks for the drinks," said Friedrich, the group's leader. "We'll get right to the point. The polls are still showing far too much public support for the project in spite of your efforts. That wasn't what we contracted for. So we're…concerned. And disappointed."

Oliver nodded and chomped on another handful of candy, his expression thoughtful. "I'm also following the polls. Approval has slipped from sixty-two percent to forty-five. I'd say that's significant, for the time we've been working on the project."

"Not good enough. Our think tank tells us that anything more than twenty percent would be disastrous. We can't exert sufficient pressure unless public opposition appears to be nearly unanimous."

"Yes, yes. I understand. In fact, even as we speak, I'm working on something that should put the final bullet in the project. We all know that significant money has been spread across the political spectrums in the target countries to build support, but that's also a potential weakness. Not everyone concerned with the project will be willing to spend tens of millions to see it through, and if we make it expensive enough to build consensus, I believe we'll be able to create the opposition you need by the time of the final vote."

"Our contract was clear about the timeline as well as the result. You assured us that you could achieve that result. Frankly, we now have doubts."

Oliver's eyes narrowed to fleshy slits. He'd been considered one of the top players in his field for half a decade and wasn't accustomed to being overtly challenged, especially on his own turf. He'd built his empire from nothing, starting out as a poor hacker in his teens, to a rich man in his own right, with his organization's tendrils extending around the globe. He made a visible effort to control his response to Friedrich's statement, and rather than exploding in a rage, as he was known to do, he elected to toss another half dozen M&Ms into his maw and chew them wordlessly.

He swallowed and stared Friedrich down. "If you're dissatisfied with our approach, you can feel free to cancel the contract whenever you like and we'll call it a day."

Friedrich took a gulp of his scotch and set the glass down. "We're not here to go to war, Oliver. We just want reassurance that you have a plan to get us where we need to—"

He was interrupted by a geeky man in his late twenties, who burst through the door and over to Oliver.

"What is it?" Oliver demanded.

"He's on the move. You wanted to be told the second he was."

Oliver addressed the gathered men. "I'm afraid I need to cut our chat short. I have a critical situation that's in play, and I have to deal with it personally. If you like, feel free to enjoy my hospitality in my absence. As I said, Malee and her companions can entertain you if you like, and I have a Michelin-rated chef on staff, if you'd like to eat. But I need to attend to this immediately. I'm sorry."

"This is most irregular, Oliver…"

"Yes, most everything in my line of work is." He stared the men down. "If I don't see you on your way out, it's always a pleasure. Hopefully over the next few days we'll see the next phase of my strategy play out, and you'll appreciate the intricacy of it. We're playing chess here, gentlemen, and I believe in always thinking several moves ahead."

Oliver backed the cart away from the table and wheeled to the door, leaving the four men staring at his enormous bulk barely squeezing through the doorway, the young man ahead of him moving down the hall at a rapid pace. Malee offered a professional smile and asked, in perfect German, whether they would like a freshener on their cocktails...or anything else?

Friedrich demurred, and the group rose to return to their cars. Once outside, one leaned into Friedrich and muttered in his ear, "I hope he knows what the hell he's doing. Fat tub of shit looks like a disaster waiting to happen."

"Looks can be deceiving. His reputation is more than deserved. My contacts in our intelligence service assure me that there's nobody more capable. They've even used him for delicate situations. That's where the lead came from. They wouldn't have steered us to him if they didn't think he could perform. We just need to let him know that we expect our results on time."

"Well, as one who's just met him, he doesn't present as a top player."

Friedrich stopped by his open car door and stepped out of earshot of the driver, who was holding it open. "They tried to recruit him when he was eighteen, but his criminal record proved to be a problem – he'd been arrested as a juvenile for hacking into several classified databases for kicks. Since then, he's built one of the biggest markets for clandestine goods and services, and practically owns what they call the dark web. That's made him impossibly wealthy."

"Then why is he bothering with a project like this?"

"He's got a chip on his shoulder. Needs to prove he's the best. That's what my contact told me, at any rate. It's not about the money; it's about the challenge. It's the same reason he's still active in some of the criminal activities he's associated with. He's still got the hacker's rebellion, even if he's now part of the establishment he hates by virtue of his wealth. That's why he was willing to do it. Not the fifty million dollars."

"You say it as though it was a trifle."

"To him it is. But it was the minimum to get his interest. He doesn't look at anything less."

The man looked unconvinced, but he gave a grudging shrug. "I'll defer to your knowledge of such things and pay whatever it takes. But we need him to perform."

Friedrich nodded and stepped toward the car. "On that we completely agree."

# Chapter 11

*Monte Carlo, Monaco*

Jet froze behind one of the big engines with a wrench in hand. The compartment was dark except from the dim glow of the power indicator lights on the equipment housings that were bolted to the walls. She remained in place for thirty seconds, and when no threat materialized through the stern door, she exhaled the breath she'd been holding and continued going through the toolbox. One of the crew had probably decided to check on the engine room and had assumed someone had left the lights on. That nobody had come in with guns blazing confirmed her assumption, and after finding the right adjustable wrench, she went to work on the port engine's injectors, wincing as diesel began spraying from the loosened sockets with every turn.

It wasn't long before the motor sputtered, coughed, and fell silent. Jet hurried to the starboard engine and loosened several of the injectors, and when the engine tone changed from a smooth roar to a stuttering clatter, she replaced the wrench in the toolbox and ran to the watertight door, calculating that she had no more than a minute or two before the crew appeared to identify the problem.

Jet eased the door open, her eyes now completely adjusted to the dark, and was up the transom steps in a flash. As she'd expected, nobody was in the first-level salon, the bodyguards likely having retired to their quarters below and the active crew on the upper decks, where the owner's party would be. She ran toward the forward stairwell that led down to the stateroom level in the hull, where she hoped to find a cubbyhole in which she could hide until she could secure a better weapon than the long-bladed screwdriver in her back pocket – a reasonable option in close quarters, but no match for the bodyguards' guns, even in her skilled hands.

Voices echoed from the upper decks, signaling that she didn't have long before the crew would be wise to her gambit. She took the steps to the lower level two at a time, noting a circular stairway by the galley that led upward. Heavy footsteps on the circular stairs transformed into legs and then the suited torso of one of the bodyguards as she ducked out of sight.

Jet crept along the lower-level passage. She stopped at a storage room and had just tried the knob when the door next to it swung open and a tall bodyguard stepped out, pulling on his suit jacket over a shoulder holster.

Surprise slowed him the critical quarter second it took for her to launch at him and drive the screwdriver up through the roof of his mouth and into his brain. Blood gushed from his nose, and his limbs went as slack as a puppet with the strings cut. He collapsed to the deck, twitching spasmodically. Jet didn't wait to watch the man's death throes, instead reaching down to fish a Beretta 9mm pistol from his shoulder holster. She checked to ensure a round was chambered and thumbed off the safety as she considered her next move.

The starboard engine had flamed out, leaving the ship rolling gently in the moderate swell. Alarms clamored from the helm as voices called out orders, and she waited, listening, before retracing her steps to the stairway and climbing to the salon level, where emergency lights recessed in the floor had come on when the engines had died.

Figures scurried on the rear deck and moved toward the transom access way, but nobody was paying any attention to the cavernous salon. She crept to the circular stairway and was almost to it when a voice called out from the rear of the salon in Russian.

"You! Stop or I shoot!"

Jet continued forward. The man yelled the warning again in heavily accented French, giving Jet a critical moment to decide on her play. She didn't know how many of the guards had entered the salon from the rear deck, but she opted for the unexpected.

"What the hell's wrong with you idiots!" she cried in Russian, and dropped to the thick carpet while whipping the Beretta toward the salon doors.

A gunshot rang out and a divot of gnarled walnut flew by her head from the port wall. She returned fire, but the gunman was too quick and ducked behind the salon wall, anticipating her shot. She loosed three more rounds and then leapt to her feet and sprinted for the circular stairway, only to find herself staring down the barrel of a gun when she was halfway to the next level.

The bodyguard's eyes were dark as lead, and she didn't have a chance to raise her pistol, the expression in them conveying that he was a nanosecond from putting a bullet in her skull. The corner of his mouth twitched at the unexpected sight of a soaked, bedraggled, blood-splattered woman who looked like she'd wrestled a bear, but his gun didn't waver.

"Drop the gun. No second chance. Do it or you're dead," he said in Russian, his face all angles and hard planes.

Trapped on a stairway between gunmen below and at least one above, Jet tossed the Beretta away with a small shrug.

"Come up the rest of the way. Nice and easy. No fast moves," he said, stepping back. She forced herself to mount the remaining steps and spotted two more guards, guns drawn and aimed at her. The first gunman's pistol slammed down on the side of her head and she slumped to the teak, unconscious.

A hard slap jarred Jet back to awareness. She slowly opened her eyes. She could feel warm blood tracing from her hairline down her left cheek, and it took several blinks to be able to focus on anything. When she could, she saw the familiar profile of the target she'd been sent to kill, staring out at the twinkling shore lights through one of the expansive tinted windows.

Four guards stood around where she was seated on a chair near an elaborate bar, her wrists bound behind her with what felt like nylon rope. She coughed, and a spike of agony shrieked through her skull.

The color drained from her face at the intensity of the pain, and she concentrated on taking deep, measured breaths while her brain recovered from the pummeling it had endured.

"Who are you?" one of the guards barked in Russian.

Jet pretended confusion, stalling for time. The big Russian took a step closer, and she was assaulted by the odors of cloyingly sweet cologne, stale cigarettes, and perspiration.

The man raised his fist to strike and growled at her again. "Last time. Who are you? Who sent you?"

Jet knew that anything she said would be useless, so she remained silent and relied on wide eyes and a puzzled expression to convey a helplessness she didn't have to fake. The man's mouth tightened in a thin line, and he was readying to hit her when Karev turned toward her, a crystal tumbler of vodka in his hand.

"You can tell us what we want to know, or we can drag it out of you. The choice is yours," he said in Russian. "I can guarantee that the latter will be most unpleasant; whereas if you tell us the truth, I'll see to it that you aren't harmed any further."

Jet stayed quiet, trying not to be obvious about testing the bindings on her wrists or bracing her boots against the deck in preparation to bolt from the chair. Even with her hands tied, she knew ten ways to kill the Russian before the guards could stop her. All she needed was an opening.

Karev seemed to sense her intent and toasted her with the half-full glass before tossing it back and swallowing with a grimace. He walked to the bar and poured himself another drink, and then regarded her like she was a science experiment.

"Who are you, and who sent you?" he asked in a measured tone, his expression reasonable.

She decided to try shaking her head and pretending she didn't speak Russian.

"I don't understand…" she managed in French.

"A lie," the first guard spat. "She understood just fine when she called out to us in the salon. Spoke like a Moscow prostitute."

"You see? Your lies won't do you any good. It's obvious that you're here to sabotage the ship and kill me," Karev said. "We found the guard's body downstairs, so there's no point denying it. But make no mistake – we will get answers. Are you working alone? What's the plan?" He took another long swallow of vodka and set the glass on the granite surface of the bar. "Most importantly, who sent you on this suicide mission?"

"Я тебя из ада достану и выебу до слепоты!!!" Jet snarled in Russian, opting to pretend to be native and using a familiar Russian insult. "I'll never tell you anything."

Karev laughed with genuine amusement. "Well! Aren't you the brave one. She speaks, and all she can manage are lies and vulgarities. Sad. I'd hoped for better." He looked around the second-level lounge and his lips twisted in an ugly smile. "I see you've decided that you want to do this the dramatic way. My men will be happy to oblige. By the time they're done with you, you'll beg for death, your body violated in ways you can't imagine. They're highly skilled, and judging by their mood, more than willing to show you their moves." He reached for his drink. "My crew found your amateurish sabotage job. We'll be back underway in minutes. Let that sink in. Nobody can help you. You'll never leave this ship. Your last hours can either be the worst you've ever experienced, or I can make it painless. The choice is yours."

Jet's jade eyes flashed and she held his stare. "I have nothing to say."

He sighed in resignation. "Right now you don't. But after my men take turns on you, and break most of the bones in your body, I suspect you'll be singing a different tune." He looked over at the guards and exhaled heavily. "Take her below. I have calls to make," Karev said, with a wave of his hand. "Enjoy your fate, whoever you are."

The guards approached her with malevolent grins. They were more alert than they'd appeared at the wedding, which was bad for her, but all she would need was a small opening and she could wreak havoc. Her stare never left Karev as the men hauled her to her feet, and she let her body go limp to make it as hard as possible for them to manhandle her down the stairs — a small thing, given her weight, but she needed every advantage she could manage, and if she could enrage them sufficiently, they might make a mistake.

Karev gave her an arrogant smirk and was preparing to say something when the side window exploded inward, sending a shower of flame and glass through the upper deck and blowing the guards and Jet off their feet.

# Chapter 12

Smoke filled the upper salon from the explosion, and Jet rolled away from her captors, only to hear staccato automatic rifle fire from around the yacht. Bullet holes punched through the superstructure and sent wood splintering everywhere, and one of the guards, who Jet could see was bleeding from his ears, screamed when a slug struck him in the stomach.

Jet looked around the ruins of the lounge and spotted Karev lying on his back on the far side, covered with shards of glass. She debated trying to get to him for the kill, but more automatic fire stitched through the broken windows, shredding the flooring, furniture, and the bodies of two more bodyguards. Screams of alarm from below cut through the gunfire, and warning yells boomed from the circular stairway and the rear deck.

Jet tried to make out where the gunfire was coming from, and her eyes widened at the sight of a white drone, its four propellers allowing it to hover near the superstructure as it rained a hail of bullets down on the rear deck. She struggled to her feet and ran to the far window, and then ducked as another explosion rocked the boat, this time from the pilothouse above.

She peered out the window and spied two more drones approaching – one with some sort of modified machine gun melded to its belly and the other carrying what Jet assumed was an explosive charge.

The drone with the explosive accelerated as it neared, and pistol fire from the rear deck targeted it as it sped toward the boat. It struck the stern platform, and the resulting blast sent a half dozen bodyguards and crew flying, the force of the explosion and shrapnel killing them instantly. She scanned the night sky and saw another four drones hovering nearby, methodically firing at the ship. Jet lowered herself to the floor and felt for a glass shard and, when she found one, wedged the glass into a crack in the flooring and sawed the rope tying her wrists, careful to avoid slashing her skin.

Pounding from the stairs interrupted her before she was free. She rolled away from the shard, struggled to her feet, and then sprinted for the rear doorway, now a gaping rent in the back of the boat. Shooting from the stairs urged her through the opening without time for hesitation, and then she'd thrown herself into the darkness, sailing through the air, arcing down to the inky water four stories below.

Jet hit the surface hard, her feet breaking the worst of the impact. She allowed herself to sink below the surface, kicking to get away from the boat. She didn't think that the surviving guards would waste their time plinking at her when they were under a full-scale attack, but she reasoned that a little distance couldn't hurt. Jet worked at her bindings as she kicked; the rope was tougher than it had appeared, and when it finally separated and she could use her arms again, she didn't break the surface until her lungs were burning like liquid fire.

Her head bobbed in the water as she watched the drones continued their onslaught, alternating between explosive kamikaze runs and strafing the superstructure with gunfire. The pristine white hull was now blackened by smoke, a hole near the waterline causing it to list as it took on water, and it looked like it had been through a war zone.

The captain finally managed to get the ship's engines started, and the big boat surged back toward Monte Carlo. Jet could make out at least nine drones in pursuit. Whatever water the ship was taking on hadn't slowed it badly enough to immobilize it, and it increased speed, trailing black smoke and flames.

One of the gun-equipped drones wobbled as it attempted to follow the ship and, after slowing, plunged into the sea forty meters from Jet. She swam toward it, keeping her eyes on its bobbing form, and reached it as the last of its battery power died, its four rotors spinning lazily as the life went out of them.

The drone was four feet square, obviously specially built, and Jet went to work on stripping the heavy gun and oversized magazine from it. When she finished, she tried swimming with it, but it was too bulky and barely floated, so was more hindrance than help. She flipped the device over and removed its hand-size control assembly, and then slipped it into the pocket of her pants before making for land only a few kilometers away.

Jet swam with efficient strokes, aware that the area would soon be swarming with helicopters and police boats. She didn't want to have to explain what she was doing in the middle of the Mediterranean at night. She hoped that the drone's control module might yield some clues as to who was behind the attack, but she would need to make it to shore in one piece and contact Giancarlo in order to do so. She ignored the stinging from her battered skull and, after a few minutes, estimated that she would be able to get to land within a half hour, worst case.

She was closing on a rocky spit of land when the thumping of the first helo's arrival reached her, and she reckoned that it would be sweeping the surface with a searchlight. Jet was far enough from the scene of the attack that she wasn't worried about being spotted, but she knew she wasn't in the clear yet; a soaking wet woman on the coast road at night, in a privileged neighborhood, would require an explanation, so she'd have to be careful to avoid any contact while she made her way to a phone. She'd memorized Giancarlo's number and had no question that she could reach him. When she did, she would request an immediate extraction.

Jet didn't know whether the Russian was dead or not, so she couldn't claim the mission a success, but from her last glimpse of him, he hadn't looked good. Jet figured the chances he'd survived the sustained assault were less than fifty percent – the spotter drones had obviously relayed a feed back to whoever was controlling them, and they must have placed Karev in the upper lounge, which had taken the lion's share of the damage.

Jet reached the shore and dragged herself onto the rocks, her mind racing. Karev hadn't seemed particularly surprised to find an assassin on his yacht, which told her that he knew he had enemies willing to kill him. It was obvious that someone had thrown considerable resources at attacking the ship, which meant there was another player on the game board that Jet hadn't been appraised of, possibly because the Mossad didn't know about them, or because the director had chosen to omit that important tidbit of information for his own reasons.

Whatever the case, she'd done everything she could to fulfill her mandate. If she'd failed, it hadn't been for lack of trying, although the bitterness of an aborted mission rose in her throat as she shrugged off her top and wrung the water out of it. She was sure she looked like a train wreck, but that was the least of her worries at this point – she only needed to appear reasonable enough not to arouse suspicion if anyone drove by, nothing more. Her next step was to find a phone, make contact with Giancarlo, get to a safe house and a secure line, and dump the whole mess back in the director's lap. Her part in the drama was finished.

Jet trudged up to the road. The waterfront villas on either side of the beach access were dark, no doubt owned by the incredibly rich who only spent a few days a year there. Once on pavement, she crossed to the far side and began her trek, which with any luck would put her back in Monte Carlo in less than an hour.

# Chapter 13

*Barcelona, Spain*

Bright lights illuminated the theater stage, where two podiums stood at opposite ends. A debate had been underway for twenty minutes and was due to wrap up in another ten due to television scheduling. It was being aired live, but the networks knew there was a limit to the public's attention span; even for a controversial proposal that had been hotly contested, viewers would only tune in for so long.

A dapper man with olive skin and thick black hair combed straight back off a receding brow was speaking in a polished tone.

"The arguments against the project going forward are all based on fear and speculation. This pipeline will create thousands of jobs, will eliminate much of Europe's dependence on Russian natural gas, and will lower costs for all concerned. There is no part of it that's bad. We've gone over the economic projections for Spain, and the results are conclusive: we need this pipeline, and we need it now!"

A portion of the audience applauded, but a chorus of boos accompanied the clapping. The moderator, who was off to the far side of the stage, cleared his throat and pointed to the other speaker at the far podium.

"For rebuttal to Minister Fernandez's statement, Candidate Gutierrez of the Green Party has one minute, and then we will hear closing arguments from both sides," he said. "Señor Gutierrez, the floor is yours."

Gutierrez, whose sparse tufts of hair and silver-framed spectacles gave him the appearance of an owl, nodded and began to speak. "As I said earlier, we've heard plenty about economic reasons for the pipeline – none of which are guaranteed, and which I believe I've shown are based on false assumptions. We've heard rosy projections and talk of job creation, but the reality is that the big winners in this, should the project be allowed to proceed, will be the multibillion-dollar corporations who hope to access the European market and who will spend whatever it takes, lie about anything they need to, in order to fatten their wallets. This is the reason our planet is polluted, our oceans clogged with plastic and poisoned by radiation…why technology hasn't afforded every human a better life. Because they want to protect the status quo, which is the raping of the globe for profit."

He stared around the theater.

"This is our chance to say no. No, we won't let billionaires further compromise our home. No, we won't let them buy votes so our government can act against our best interests. Of course Minister Fernandez thinks a pipeline would be a brilliant idea. I'm quite sure his cushy position with one of the sponsors is already ensured for whenever he leaves office. He is the face of corruption that's endemic to our system, and it's time to reject all of this – starting now!"

The theater's applause was louder than for Fernandez's segment, and the boos had converted to cheers. The moderator waited for the clapping to die down, and then smiled at the gathering and checked his notes.

"Very well. Time for closing arguments, gentlemen. You each have three minutes. Minister Fernandez, you won the coin toss to determine who goes first, so the floor is yours."

Fernandez glanced over at Gutierrez and shook his head. "Señor Gutierrez has had to resort to baseless personal insults and slanderous accusations to attempt to make his case. I maintain that he has failed to do so in spite of his desperate measures. It's telling that when backed into a corner by inconvenient facts, all he's got are appeals to vague notions of saving the planet and insults directed at me. So let's review some of these facts, shall we? Right now, we're wholly dependent on Russia for the natural gas that warms us all winter. If Russia decides to cut that off, we'll have to buy far more expensive product from the United States, in which case many will suffer financially, and some will freeze because they can't make ends meet. The pipeline would eliminate the monopoly.

"Another fact is that it would create a workforce to maintain it. A highly paid workforce. Do I need to remind anyone of the woeful employment numbers we've endured since the financial collapse? The pipeline would reverse that in many areas of the country. Construction companies would see tens of millions of euros for their part in building it, as well as for the pump relay stations. Another fact is that the price of natural gas would decline for everyone in this room. Competition would ensure it did."

Fernandez sighed before continuing. "There's literally no downside for the people of Spain. None. Everyone wins. Yet Candidate Gutierrez's party would rob you of that victory and ensure that the status quo continues – one of few jobs, high prices, and dependence on a country that could turn off the tap whenever it liked, effectively damaging our economy far more than could anything but a full-scale war. That's his alternative to progress and prosperity." He paused dramatically. "He *is* right about one thing: it's time to say no. No to fear, no to poverty, no to living on our knees for a foreign master. Don't allow fearmongering to cloud your judgment when it's time to vote on this referendum. Think of your children's futures, if nothing else. The current deluded policy of blocking progress at every turn must end if they're to have one. And the time to end it is now."

The moderator gestured to Gutierrez, who shook his head and glared at Fernandez before speaking.

"The news was filled with reports of the terrorist attack on a segment of the pipeline being built in Morocco. That is what Spain is inviting into its borders if we allow the project to proceed. Is that what the country wants? What's best for Spain? Lunatics willing to stop at nothing staging attacks and assassinating people? Please. Minister Fernandez spoke of the future. Is that what you want for ours? To be turned into Iraq or Syria? And for what? For a few pesetas of possible savings and an unknown number of jobs that might never materialize?"

He gripped the edges of the podium and leaned forward. "Let's be clear on what this referendum is about. It's about powerful pecuniary interests that have bet on the pipeline coming to fruition generating windfall profits at the country's expense. It's about an environmental hazard that dwarfs anything yet envisioned. It's about ruthless men doing what they have to in order to get their way. It's about convincing you that a corrupt administration wants what's best for you rather than what's in its own financial interests. Because that's what the argument boils down to: money. Note that the good minister never mentions the stakes for the supporters of the pipeline – the profits they'll generate, the advantages they'll gain. We're supposed to forget about all that and believe promises from a regime that's failed to deliver on any of the campaign platform that got them elected. I for one haven't forgotten. And neither should you. Don't give these criminals any more chances to abuse the country for their benefit and the benefit of their benefactors. Say no to corporate greed and recklessness. Vote no on the referendum."

The debate finished, the opposing speakers shook hands in the center of the stage to an ovation, and the cameras shut off as the theater cleared. Fernandez made his way through the backstage door to his waiting Mercedes AMG GT S coupe and slid behind the wheel. He smiled to himself as the powerful eight-cylinder engine roared to life, taking childlike pleasure in the rumble from the exhaust, loud as a drag racer.

As he pulled onto the C-32 expressway and accelerated into the fast lane, the car's massive horsepower pushed him back in the seat like he was piloting a fighter jet. He replayed the debate in his mind as he drove, wondering at his adversary's tenacity, if not the speciousness of his arguments. The real question was whether voters would be stupid enough to kill the project based on smoke and mirrors and disingenuous rhetoric. He liked to think that the public was smarter than that, but had been in government too long to really believe it.

And the media wasn't helping. Even outlets that had been positive on the project had begun questioning the wisdom, and those that had been against it to start with were now practically foaming at the mouth in their opposition. He'd never seen anything like it for an infrastructure project and suspected an unseen hand at work. There was no other explanation for the pervasive hostility. Contacts he'd plied successfully for years had no time to meet with him for lunch or take his phone calls. It was the strangest thing he'd ever experienced, and portended more ugliness in the weeks leading up to the vote.

He glanced at his watch, an expensive Panerai his wife had gotten him for his fiftieth birthday, and glanced in his rearview mirror before signaling to get over in advance of his rapidly approaching exit. The car suddenly surged forward, and the speedometer accelerated into the triple digits as the big engine redlined. Fernandez stomped on the brake pedal, but it had little effect, and the digital readout climbed from 120 to 130 to 140.

He reached for the transmission shifter to take the car out of gear, but lost control as he swerved to avoid a car in front of him. A scream tore from his lips when the AMG crashed through a guardrail and launched from the embankment, pinwheeling as it took flight. It seemed to hang in the air, suspended by an invisible force, and then slammed into an overpass pillar and exploded in a ball of flame.

# Chapter 14

*Monte Carlo, Monaco*

Jet sat at a long table in the safe house with a plate of food in front of her and a tablet computer. She chewed the stew without interest, merely replacing calories she'd burned swimming, and scanned the news for reports on the yacht attack. So far the local outlets had described the onslaught as a regrettable mechanical problem that had resulted in the yacht being partially destroyed by fire, which spoke to the amount of clout the Russian's group had. That not only the police but the media could be bought off and convinced to advance a false narrative didn't surprise her, but that Karev's people would bother did.

Giancarlo had taken the drone control module to a technician an hour earlier, after she'd delivered her report to headquarters on a secure phone. The director had clearly been unhappy with the outcome, even if he hadn't said so. The one redeeming aspect was that she'd had the presence of mind to secure the module, which they were now working on to determine who'd built it and who'd been operating it. A tall order, she knew from her computer background, but she was sure that the director had capable assets nearby in Europe who could make short work of it.

"So to summarize, you don't know if the target's alive or not, you don't know why his boat was hit or who is responsible for the attack, and your identity was compromised – you were seen by the target and his entourage," the director had said when she'd concluded her report. "Did I miss anything?"

"My identity wasn't compromised. I didn't have any ID with me. I took action after he unexpectedly left the ceremony, which deprived me of the shot. Most would have walked away at that point, but I went the extra mile to get him. Unfortunately that didn't work. But my cover isn't blown. As to knowing whether he's alive or not, he was obviously injured in the first blast. I would think that you could check the local hospitals and the morgue."

"That occurred to me," he snapped. "And the attack?"

"It came out of nowhere, but whoever's behind it is well funded and up to date on technology. I've never seen anything like those drones. They have to be custom. They aren't American manufacture, nor ours. I would recognize either. And they're too big for hobbyists. They were carrying substantial payloads. That's why I brought in the module. It's the best shot you've got to identify the origin."

"I'm not criticizing the actions you took. It's just…frustrating. We appreciate your going the extra distance to try to fulfill the sanction."

The line had gone dead, and Giancarlo's phone had rung three minutes later. He'd departed almost immediately with the module, leaving her to her thoughts. Her first action had been to disinfect and stitch her scalp where the gun butt had lacerated it, which she did using the medical kit from Giancarlo's car. It had bled a lot, as head wounds tended to do, but she'd gotten three stitches in place and her hair hid the damage, so she could travel without issue.

Giancarlo had assured her that one of his operatives was working the hotel as a maid and would retrieve her things the following day, once the wedding party and security had departed. Which left her cooling her heels, wondering how soon she could be on a plane and back to her family, the mission one of the only ones she'd ever carried out that hadn't been an eventual success.

Her ambivalence about that surprised her, but only a little. She'd long ago abandoned any pretense of caring about the Mossad's machinations or what the organization thought about her. She'd proven herself more than anyone, and if she'd been sent into an unwinnable battle, she wasn't going to beat herself up over it. Something had triggered the Russian's abrupt departure from the wedding, and she hadn't had a clear shot she could have taken. None of that was her fault, and it didn't speak to her skills or commitment.

She was confident the director would still provide her family with the promised protection either way, so this was merely a bad day to her, nothing more.

At least that was what she told herself. Jet wasn't going to allow her mind to obsess over what had gone wrong or to second-guess what moves she could have made differently. None of that would change anything, so there was no point.

Hannah's and Matt's faces flittered through her thoughts, and she felt a strong urge to call and talk to them in spite of the hour. Another impulse she wouldn't allow to grow, and couldn't act upon. Not while in the field, and until she was pulled out of Monaco, she was still in play, like it or not.

Jet finished her meal and carried the dish to the sink, and then yawned and stretched, her strained muscles reminding her of her earlier exertion. She checked the time on the tablet, yawned again, and then padded to the couch and lay down to rest. Within moments she was asleep, her breathing even, her face as calm as a mountain lake at dawn.

What seemed like moments later, she jolted awake, roused by someone closing the front door. Daylight streamed through the curtains, and she was up in an instant, immediately alert. Giancarlo strode into the room, looking haggard and sleep deprived.

"The director needs you to call as soon as possible," he said.

Jet sat up. She didn't bother to ask why. Giancarlo walked to the stairs, his steps heavy. "I'm going to get some sleep. You know how the phone works."

She waited until he disappeared upstairs, and walked over to the secure handset on the dining table. Jet pressed redial, and the line rang once before being answered by voicemail. She waited for the prompt, and when it instructed her to leave a message, instead entered a three-digit code and waited as the line rang again.

The director answered, his voice gruff. "We have information on the drone. Very interesting."

Jet didn't say anything. She'd been hoping he was going to tell her when she could leave, but his tone didn't sound promising.

"We've isolated its manufacture to Estonia," he continued. "A company we have some data on from unrelated prior reports. It's suspected of furnishing devices, money, and know-how to terrorists."

She frowned. "I don't understand. Why would terrorists want to kill the Russian?"

"That isn't our theory. Rather, it's that the Estonian company might be involved in some way we haven't pieced together yet."

"Murder for hire?" she asked.

"Unknown. But there's a further wrinkle. We just learned that the malware that's been planted on our infrastructure computers may not be Russian after all. Now the experts believe it might be Estonian. One of the reports we got about the Estonian company is that they do mercenary work for an exclusive list of clients. That gives them the necessary know-how to stage a wet op."

"So Karev was working with Estonians, who subsequently tried to kill him? That doesn't make any sense."

"I'm not saying that's the case. Another possibility is that he was framed – set up by the Estonians so we would do the job for them. We know the CIA can spoof any nationality of hacker they want. There's no reason to believe that a private group of sufficient sophistication couldn't do the same."

"I was trying to terminate an innocent man? I thought you said the intel was bulletproof."

"I didn't say he was innocent. Nobody at his level of power is. The question isn't whether he's guilty, but rather of what."

"That isn't what I signed up for."

"Look, it's entirely possible that he was involved with the Estonians and they decided to take him out. Maybe so they didn't have to split the ransom. Anything's possible. But right now we don't know enough to be dangerous about the Estonians and the Russian, and if we don't pay up, someone's going to shut down our infrastructure."

Jet paused. "Why are you telling me this?" she asked suspiciously.

"We need you to infiltrate the company. Little is known about the man who runs it, who's something of a shut-in. He's supposed to be a computer genius, but he's rarely seen. If we can get you into the company, we're hoping that you can verify whether our worst fears are justified. We don't have much time, and you're already in play. With your background in technology and fieldwork, you're somewhat unique."

"That's your plan? Fly me to Estonia and hope that somehow I can find my way in? And then what? Start asking around about blackmail, or developing computer viruses, or whether anyone's missing twenty killer drones?"

"Of course not. We're putting together a brief for you. Your friend there will have your things back from the hotel by noon, and your cover's still intact. You can use the Spanish ID for what we have in mind."

"Which is?"

"There's a good chance you can walk right into the company. They're hiring."

Jet snorted derisively. "Who comes up with this stuff? I'm supposed to show up and apply for a job, out of all the hackers in Europe? Tell me what part of this makes any sense to you. Because I'm not seeing it."

Steel crept into the director's voice. "There's a method to my madness. They're looking for a specific kind of employee. A fluent Spanish speaker with advanced computer skills for translating and Spanish programming. You fit the bill perfectly."

"Except that I have no background in my official persona, remember? I'm a nanny."

"We're modifying that as we speak. By the time you hit the ground, you'll have eight years of experience that will stand up to scrutiny, working for companies in France, Spain, and Belgium. I'll shoot you the details before your flight."

"Which assumes that I'm willing to extend my absence from my family and go on this goose chase."

"You understand the time pressure and the stakes. I'm afraid this isn't something you can walk away from. I don't have any plan B. You're it."

"What would you do if I weren't available?"

The director sighed. "The reason we're taking such good care of your family is so you're always available. So there's no reason to try to answer a hypothetical. Besides, I knew that once I explained the timing and the fact that you already have a perfect cover story, you'd agree. We don't have the leeway to try to get someone else prepared, not that we have anyone who would fit the bill as well as you."

She understood why he'd brought up Hannah and Matt. Leverage. Subtle as a wrecking ball.

"Lucky me."

"There's a late afternoon flight out of Nice through Helsinki that will get you to Tallinn by nightfall."

"Great. What do they speak there?"

"Estonian, mostly, but some Russian from the Soviet era. You'll figure it out. I'll ensure a full background is included in the file."

"I'm going to need a couple of secure phones. Mine got lost on my swim."

"Done."

"And the usual. Money. A weapon."

"The latter might be a problem. We don't really have anyone in Estonia besides a few low-level watchers."

"Fly someone in who can act as a case officer, then. Don't hang me out to dry."

"I'll see who's available."

"What about the Russian? Any word on whether he made it?"

"Not yet. We're monitoring the hospital traffic. There was no mention of him at the morgue. Nor any of his staff. We suspect they might have thrown them overboard wrapped in chains before they made it into the harbor."

"Makes sense if they wanted to keep it quiet. The question is why."

"We're hoping you can help find out."

Jet disconnected and considered what she was being asked to do. It didn't sound especially difficult, but she had the uncomfortable impression that the director was making this up as he went along, which didn't bode well for her odds. The information was obviously changing in real time, but if that was the case, she should have never been deployed to execute Karev. Now it sounded at least possible that he had nothing to do with the extortion attempt, and the Mossad was being played for fools, setting up his murder based on false information.

Nothing about the situation was appealing, but the director's message that she couldn't reject his request had come through loud and clear. She made a mental note to have a meeting with him when this operation was over, to reestablish her right to refuse anything she didn't feel comfortable with. The last couple of missions he'd crossed the line and ordered her to take action she didn't want to, and she couldn't allow him to continue or it was just a matter of time until he got her killed.

She walked over to the tablet and checked the time. Seven thirty a.m. With nothing to do until Giancarlo awoke and coordinated getting her gear, there was no reason not to get more sleep and allow her body to rejuvenate after the prior night's battering. She returned to the couch and lay down, and as before was out within moments, the only sound in the room her soft breathing and the quiet whirring of the overhead fan's orbit.

# Chapter 15

*Tallinn, Estonia*

Jet sat across from a matronly woman with a pie face who was reading her résumé with the intensity of a scholar studying a lost gospel. Jet had arrived late the night before and had checked into a hotel near the employment agency that was handling the screening for the suspect company. Her case officer had met her down the street from the hotel, introduced himself, and handed her a satchel with phones and money. She'd concealed the bruising beneath her hairline with makeup, and between that and her hair brushed artfully, the injury was undetectable, although the stitches still throbbed with every pulse.

The woman, the employment agency office manager who'd introduced herself as Magda, looked up from the résumé and cleared her throat.

"Very impressive," Magda said in Russian. Jet had modified the CV to indicate she spoke some Russian, for ease of communication, in addition to Spanish, French, and English, which seemed reasonable for a translator interested in languages. "And why are you available for work here?"

"I love the country. It has one of the highest literacy rates in Europe, and it's becoming a real hub for technology." Jet smiled. "And a large number of eligible men."

Magda returned the smile and winked. "Ah, yes. Their reputations precede them, I think. It is a good place to live if you can stand the winters, which last about eight months of the year."

Jet laughed politely. "It isn't too cold now."

"This is one of the two good months. But you're correct about opportunities of all sorts here. Many companies are relocating or opening offices due to the favorable business climate and the labor pool, which is overheated in the technology sector. You're very fortunate you have the skills my clients are looking for. It should be an easy placement."

"That's good to hear. I need something as soon as possible."

"You're available to start immediately?"

"Absolutely. Today, if possible." Jet lowered her eyes. "Money's been tight since I left Antwerp."

"Hmm. And why did you leave that position?"

"Our division was phased out. Offshored to someplace like India." Jet shrugged. "It's not uncommon these days, although the quality of the work can leave much to be desired."

"I see it all the time. Fortunately, not here. But if the Belgians don't want you, we certainly do."

"Great. I was particularly interested in the ad you ran online for a Spanish translator with programming skills. It looked perfect."

"Yes, it will be a good fit. All of the documents you would be working from would be in English, which you're proficient in, correct?"

"That's right. I can read and write at college level."

"Excellent. And your list of programming languages is impressive."

"I enjoy coding." Which was true, if an incomplete explanation.

"Well then, let me make a call and shoot your résumé to their human resources person. If they give you a thumbs-up, we can take a ride over to their offices. They're on the edge of town – a big parcel." Magda hesitated. "The only thing I must caution you about is the owner. He's...he's unusual, even by tech world standards. Doesn't like to mingle or attend functions. He's somewhat of a legend in his field, but he's eccentric, which I suppose he can afford to be given how successful he's been."

"That doesn't sound too bad," Jet said doubtfully, not wanting to seem too eager given the warning.

"Well, he can be difficult to deal with at times. He's somewhat moody, and he tends to make snap judgments. That said, he's also incredibly generous with his staff, as you'll see if they authorize me to make an offer."

"Can you give me an idea of the range?"

"Nearly a third more than your last job, with a lower cost of living. If they decide they want you, they'll want to keep you happy. Nobody wants to lose a valuable resource to a competitor, and the poaching among rivals can be heated."

"I'm not looking to bounce around. I'd like to stay put, if that's possible."

"Certainly. Now, to the issue of work permits. We can arrange for a temporary, dated today, if you start with them, and in sixty days the company can get you a permanent one, assuming you're willing to sign a two-year contract. They sponsor you and take care of everything."

"That sounds great."

Magda's fingers flew over the keyboard in front of her, and she quickly scanned the two-page résumé and sent it off to the company, Oleco Industries. When she was done, she sat back and eyed Jet. "Where are you staying?"

"I got a room at the Brandenburg hotel. It isn't too bad, but if things work out, I'll need to get an apartment, or at least a room with someone until I can find something more permanent."

Magda made a face. "I know the place. You're being kind. It's pretty run-down, more of a boardinghouse favored by a lot of budget travelers from Russia."

"It'll do for a short while."

"I have a number of contacts. If the company decides to hire you, I can find you something more reasonable. And between you and me, if they don't want you, I can place you with three other firms before the day's over." Magda had already checked Jet's references that morning before she'd arrived, having received her bogus résumé the prior night, so there was little barrier other than Oleco's response time. "Can I offer you some tea or coffee while we wait? They're usually very proactive, so it shouldn't be too long. They're anxious to fill the position."

"Tea, please."

Magda depressed a button on her desk intercom and a severe blonde with legs to her chin entered. Magda spoke in rapid-fire Estonian, and the woman nodded and left. Magda studied Jet for a moment and then sat forward.

"No family? Children?"

Jet shook her head. "No. I never met the right match." She'd had her background altered to reflect a single, unattached woman since the job was no longer a nanny.

"Well, I certainly think your odds are good of finding someone suitable here. You're a lovely young lady. I'm sure you'll have suitors lined up within no time."

Jet did her best to pretend to blush. "That would be wonderful."

"Yes. It seems so easy when you're young, I remember. But you start moving toward thirty, and your options get fewer."

"All the good ones are married," Jet said with conviction. "Or they have something wrong with them. Or they only want one thing."

"It seems nothing has changed since I was your age. But you'll find that our men tend to be honorable, as long as they aren't drinkers. That's a problem here. Same with Finland next door. Probably has to do with too little sun and cold weather much of the year. There's not much else to do."

"I don't drink."

"That's a plus. Although maybe not for the ones who only want one thing."

They both laughed, and Jet tried to conceal her impatience. She despised small talk, and the woman was chatty. She'd hoped to do the interview and be shown out until the company contacted Magda, but luck wasn't on her side, so she had to stay in character and feign agreeableness. Inwardly, she'd have rather fought a knife fight, but she put on a good show and prattled on about imaginary dating hurdles and the paucity of decent males in Belgium and Spain.

Magda's line rang an hour later, and she spoke for two minutes before hanging up and beaming at Jet.

"Well, today's your lucky day. They want to see you as soon as you can get there," she said.

"That's great!"

"Yes, it is. But I had a feeling they'd move quickly. One of the owner's quirks is that he prefers hiring female staff."

"Why?"

Magda shrugged and looked away. "It's just a preference. He told me once that women tend to be more loyal if you treat them well, whereas males are always scheming to go off and take what they've learned to compete. Whatever the case, it's fortunate for you."

"I'll say."

Magda rose and motioned to Jet. "I'll give you a ride over to the offices. They're not obvious if you don't know your way around."

"Thanks."

The drive took almost twenty minutes. The facilities were on the outskirts of the capital city, surrounded by lush trees. Security guards allowed them onto the grounds, and after parking, Magda led Jet to one of the buildings, where a woman in her thirties in black slacks and a matching suit jacket over a white blouse greeted them with a professional smile that never warmed her eyes.

"Magda, nice to see you again. This is our new applicant?" she asked in Russian, extending her hand.

Jet took it and shook, the woman's fingers cool and dry. "Yes. Gabriela Mendez. Nice to meet you."

"Katye Hellat."

"I think you'll find Ms. Mendez is exactly what you were looking for, Katye," Magda assured her.

"I certainly hope so," Katye replied, and guided them into the lobby, where a pert secretary smiled at them from behind a reception desk. "This way, Gabriela. Magda, you can wait out here. Riina can get you refreshments."

Magda took a seat on a contemporary black sofa, and Jet followed Katye to a corner office, where Katye spent ten minutes grilling her about her background and skills before standing and escorting her to meet the owner of the company.

Katye rapped on the door, and a voice boomed in reply, "Come in."

She twisted the handle and Jet followed her into a lavish suite, where one of the fattest men Jet had ever seen was sitting in a custom cart, eyeing her from behind circular mirrored sunglasses. Jet swallowed, pretending to be nervous, and Katye pointed to one of three chairs in front of the man's desk.

"I'll leave the two of you to chat. Oliver, this is Gabriela, who I think will be a good fit for the Spanish translator job. Gabriela, Oliver Kalda."

Jet took the indicated seat, and Oliver grunted as he wheeled his chair forward. She placed her résumé on the desk, and he took it with sausage fingers and scanned it in under fifteen seconds before placing it back on the table and licking his lips.

"A pleasure to meet you, Gabriela," he said in Russian. "What brings a woman of your obvious…talents…to Tallinn?"

"Opportunity and a change of scenery," she said.

"This is quite different than Brussels or Madrid, no?"

"Yes, but in a good way, I think."

"Your Russian is better than mine," Oliver said, switching to English.

"Oh, I don't think so. Mine sounds more academic to my ear. You sound almost like a native," she said, also in English.

"I get a lot of practice," he replied in Spanish. "Russian and English are mandatory if you are going to do serious business here."

"Which fortunately I speak and read well enough to be proficient in, although my English is far better than my Russian," she said in Spanish.

"With a face like that, you'll be a pleasure to have around," Oliver said in German.

Jet blinked in confusion, pretending not to understand.

"And that ass. I could spend a week on that," he continued in German.

"I'm sorry," Jet said in Spanish. "I don't speak…is that German or Dutch?"

He shook his head. "No, it is I who must apologize. I thought your résumé said you spoke German, too," he said in English, smiling broadly.

"Ah, no. French, not German," Jet corrected.

"My mistake."

Oliver filled her in on her prospective duties, and after a few more questions, he tapped his cart screen and Katye materialized at the door.

"Yes?" she asked, eyebrows raised.

"She's perfect. Sign her up," Oliver said in Russian, and then eyed Jet again. "That is, assuming you want the job."

"Of course! I'd be delighted! When would you like me to start?"

"Today, if possible," Oliver said in English. "We tend to put in long hours, so we'll be in the office until well after dark. How many hours you put in is up to you, but our corporate culture is one of achievement, which is rewarded with bonuses in addition to your salary package." He grinned, and Jet decided the effect was distinctively creepy. "We work hard and play just as hard. I suspect you'll enjoy it here."

"I hope so. Thank you, Mr. Kalda," Jet said.

"Please. Oliver. My pleasure. I'm sure I'll see you around," he answered, and then, just as suddenly as the interview had begun, it was over, and he was engrossed in something on his screen, Jet and Katye dead to him.

"I'll tell Magda," Katye said to her at the office door. "After we get your paperwork taken care of, I'll introduce you to the translation team. Welcome aboard, Gabriela. I hope our confidence in you is justified."

"I won't let you down."

Katye smiled, and they walked together back to her office. Jet replayed the interview on the way – Oliver's supposed slip into German to catch her off guard, the offensive language designed to elicit a reaction if she understood what he was saying. It was slick, she had to admit, but her training and field experience had taught her not to make stupid mistakes, and showing any signs that she understood a language she supposedly didn't speak would have been disastrous.

As it was, she'd passed the test, although her feeling that Oliver was a first-class sleaze had been reinforced by the exchange. She suspected it was just a matter of time before the man made an advance, but she wasn't worried. She would only be there for a few days, tops, given the urgency of the cyber-attack threat, and she'd be able to avoid any solicitations for that long.

Of course, if that failed, she could always throat-punch him and watch him strangle on his own fat like a bulldog.

A not entirely unappealing idea, she reasoned. Outwardly she gave no hint of her dark thoughts other than the hint of a smile that made her look friendly and approachable to her new co-workers.

# Chapter 16

*Saint-Tropez, France*

Waves crashed against the rocky shore at Pointe de la Rabiou. Offshore, a forty-meter sailing yacht with a deep blue hull tacked back and forth, leaned over hard by a spirited wind. The rumble of the ferry from the Quai Jean Jaurès echoed across the water as its engines spooled up for the high-speed cruise to Cannes.

The sun was setting as two unmarked white vans pulled to a stop in the drive of a faux-Tuscan villa off the Impasse du Cap. Six men descended from each vehicle, all wearing dark suits, their hair clipped tight against their heads. Two of them rolled a gurney from the second van, and the wheels clattered on the cobblestones. The lead figure, his temples silver and his body less muscled than the rest, approached the entrance, his expression determined.

The door swung wide and the group entered, leaving one man outside, scanning the private road from behind wraparound sunglasses in spite of the waning light. Inside, the newcomers followed the man who'd admitted them through the house to the master bedroom, where a pair of bodyguards with AK-47s framed the doorway.

The lead figure nodded to the guards, who stepped aside. He knocked on the door and a voice called out in Russian. "Come in."

The group entered to find Nicolai Karev sitting up in bed, a cast on one arm and an IV in the other, his head bandaged, and his face burned on one side. A monitor displaying his vital signs stood by the nightstand. A short man sitting at the bedside, a physician's bag at his feet, looked up at the group as they entered.

Karev waved a hand at the newcomers. "One moment, Sergei," he said in Russian, and then returned to his discussion in French. "Anyway, once we were outside the harbor, we managed to get the helicopter going, and my men flew me out of there. Fortunately, a good friend of mine owns this home, and he was more than happy to let us use it while we're waiting for the bad news on the boat."

"That's an incredible story. You're lucky to be alive."

Karev grinned and then grimaced at the pain it caused his charred cheek. "I have the best doctor in France. How could I not be?"

The doctor smiled, collected his bag, and rose. "Remember to take the pain pills every four hours. I'll be by tomorrow to check on your condition."

Sergei frowned. "No, you won't."

"I beg your pardon?"

"Change of plans. Write down what a new doctor needs to be aware of."

The doctor looked to Karev, who managed a shrug. The doctor moved to a Louis XVI table and scribbled on a prescription pad, and then tore the sheet off and handed it to one of the men. "That should be sufficient, I'd think," he said.

Sergei nodded once, and the doctor got the hint. "Well, I'll be going, then," he said.

"Not a word about this to anyone or there will be consequences," Sergei warned. "Understood?"

The doctor blanched, but grunted assent. "Of course. Completely confidential."

"See to it."

When the doctor had left, escorted to the front door by two more guards, Karev eyed Sergei with disapproval. "Why so brusque, Sergei?"

"We're getting you out of here. Now. We need to move."

"Why? We're completely safe here. Nobody knows–"

"You and the guards have been using your phones. That places you here. We both know what the group that attacked you is capable of. Might as well have sent up a signal flare."

Karev's expression grew dour. "Damn. You really think–"

"With all due respect, my job isn't to guess, it's to see to it that you're safe. Right now you're compromised. It's just a matter of time until they come for you." Sergei turned to his men. "Prepare everything. I want to be out of here in five minutes."

"I must be slower than usual from the drugs, or I would have thought of the phones. Although getting a position from the phone company's a long shot, you're right. It was foolish." Karev paused. "Where are we going?"

"I've arranged for a penthouse in Nice. It will be easier to defend than a home. Only one private elevator for the penthouse, which occupies the entire floor."

"Then I can keep my doctor! Nice isn't that far."

Sergei shook his head. "Better one of our own. I have a qualified man on a plane from Moscow. He'll be in Nice by the time we get there." He looked around the room. "Who have you spoken to by phone since you arrived?"

"Besides you? Nobody. I mean, my wife, to let her know I'm alive and not to worry. And my daughter. That's it. I was out of it most of yesterday and last night."

"They'll have been monitoring your family's lines. Did you tell your wife or Tanya where you were?"

"No. Just that I was safe, and not to believe what they read in the papers."

"I already took care of that. No mention of the attack," Sergei said. "But that's the least of our worries. We can assume your wife and daughter are being monitored, so the enemy knows you're still alive." He glanced at the blipping monitor that was tracing Karev's heartbeat across the screen. "Do you have anything here other than the medical equipment?"

"No. All my things are still on the boat."

"I don't want to chance sending anyone to the boat. They'll be watching it."

Karev sighed. "The painkillers have made me foggy. It's good one of us is thinking clearly."

"At least you weren't too badly injured."

"We lost ten men. It could have been worse."

"It always could."

Karev's eyes locked on Sergei's. "If it's who we think, I want him. Scorched earth."

Sergei's mood visibly darkened. "We can worry about that once we've mounted a good defense." He fished a small two-way radio from his pocket and spoke into it, and then straightened. "Everything's ready. We'll keep the IV hooked up, but disconnect the monitor for the ride."

"That's fine. I think it was overkill, anyway. If I die en route, you'll know it without the machine."

"How does the face feel?"

"Like hell. But the doctor says it will heal well. Shouldn't scar."

"That's fortunate."

Sergei watched without comment as his men lifted their boss from the bed and set him on the gurney, and then placed a Kevlar vest over his chest before attaching the IV bag to the gurney stand. Another rolled the vital signs monitor to the door and waited there for Sergei's go-ahead.

He turned to Karev. "The vest is merely a precaution."

Karev nodded. "I should have had you in Monaco instead of leaving you in Moscow."

Sergei smiled for the first time. "Seeing how the others fared, I'd say you did me a favor."

Karev's frown deepened. "There was a woman on board before we were attacked. An assassin."

Sergei scowled to match Karev's expression. "Tell me about it in the van."

# Chapter 17

*Tel Aviv, Israel*

The director looked up from his work pile as two of his staff entered his office and sat at the small conference table. He stubbed out his cigarette, coughed twice, walked over to them, and took a seat.

"Well?" he asked. "What have you got? Adam?"

Adam, a man in his thirties with wiry hair and stylish tortoiseshell glasses, motioned to his companion. "Reuven can summarize."

The director stared at them both, his demeanor glum, his skin an unhealthy shade of gray. "Do I need to issue an invitation or say a password? Speak."

Reuven shifted in his seat. "As you know, we've been studying the malware used in the prison escape," he began.

The director cut him off. "Don't waste my time with what I already know. What do you have for me?"

"I'm afraid it's bad news. Our tech experts have found a signature in the malware that identifies it. We've run checks of other critical infrastructure systems throughout the country, and it looks like eighty percent of the servers are infected."

"Eighty percent? How is that possible?"

"We're working through how it happened, but what's important is that the malware is on the vast majority of the systems that control just about everything, from traffic lights to power grids, communication networks, internet providers, and airports."

The director extracted a pack of cigarettes from his shirt pocket and tapped one free. He looked around the office, rose and went to retrieve the ashtray from his desk, lit the cigarette, and returned to the table, trailing smoke like a sullen dragon.

"So we change the critical systems," he said.

Adam and Reuven exchanged a look. "We're afraid that isn't realistic," Adam said. "The cost would be exorbitant. And it would take far too long. Many of the servers have to be ordered or are special builds, and we can't guarantee there isn't some sort of dead man's switch that once a control system is taken off-line, its absence doesn't trigger the rest to execute. It wouldn't be outside the realm of possibility, given the sophistication of the breach."

"What about our nukes?" the director asked in a low voice.

"Not a hazard. They're air-gapped and running on twenty-year-old technology."

He grunted and puffed on the cigarette. "What's the net result of what you're telling me?"

"The disruption would be catastrophic if the malware is triggered. Especially with hostile forces in Lebanon, Gaza, and Syria waiting for an opportunity they can exploit. With the country effectively immobilized, we wouldn't be able to mount nearly the defense we would need to. That eighty percent number also applies to military systems. It would be chaos for days, or weeks, depending on which servers we're talking. We would be uniquely vulnerable." Reuven paused. "The flight of capital from the country would be something it would take years to recover from, assuming we did at all. If we're so vulnerable that some hostile amateur can take down every meaningful system, nobody in their right mind is going to want to have operations here, much less live here. And we all know what that would mean to the economy."

Adam nodded. "Part of the problem is that we can't know what the malware is programmed to do. In the case of the prison, it cut the power and overrode the security backups designed to keep prisoners from escaping. But we're just guessing at what it might do to, say, a power plant or the railway network or traffic systems."

"What's the worst case?" the director asked.

Reuven frowned. "Let's take a power plant as an example. It might not cut off power like at the prison. Instead, it might cause generators to over-rev and explode or burn out. Or with the railway, imagine trains shunted onto the same tracks, headed at each other and unable to communicate. Or the airports with erroneous air traffic control information. Hospitals without power, or with all of their computer records fried. Every prison in the country open, with the convicts running amok in the neighboring areas. Traffic being given green lights in both directions. Police and firefighters unable to communicate or operating based on bad information. There's literally no end to what the malware might do. But we have to assume it can and will do everything I just described…and worse."

"Look at what our Stuxnet attack on the Iranians achieved. It basically destroyed a fifth of their centrifuges by targeting the programmable logic controllers and the software. Now imagine that multiplied by a thousand or by ten thousand," Adam said.

"You're not painting a very pretty picture," the director observed. "Or giving me any options. It's obvious that the Palestinians would be emboldened, as would our enemies, and that the financial consequences would be devastating. But I still don't understand why you can't just remove the malware now that you've identified it. Or write some code that blocks it from executing. I'm not a tech guru, but there has to be a way."

"Because it appears that it may have burrowed into the firmware. Which means the only way to eradicate it is to junk the hardware. Which is why I said it would be insanely expensive and impractical."

"How expensive?"

Adam sat back, eyes glued to the ceiling. "Possibly more than the ransom. But it's the damage pulling all the systems simultaneously would cause to the infrastructure that's the real cost – not that four billion euros isn't significant. And frankly I'm not sure doing so is even possible. We're talking thousands and thousands of servers. It would be like a neutron bomb went off. The result would paralyze the country." Adam frowned. "My hunch is that the engineers who developed the malware considered the possibility and have a fail-safe built in."

"What about somehow disabling the internet until we can change out the software and hardware?"

"We could shut down the entire country, I suppose, but changing out systems would take weeks or months, and most of our infrastructure relies on the internet to communicate with other elements. The end result could be nearly as devastating as anything the malware did. Worse, as I said before, if the malware can't communicate with the command and control servers, it could trigger an automatic action across all the nodes. We have to assume that was built in. This is an incredibly sophisticated little bug we're talking, and obviously a lot of thought went into designing it. Pulling the systems off-line or shutting them down had to be considered by the engineers, and you can bet they have a nasty surprised baked in if we try."

"If they're using the internet to communicate with these command and control servers, why can't we filter for them on the infected systems, and when they do, monitor the traffic, locate them, and block them?"

Reuven ran his fingers through his hair. "That's one of the things we're looking at. The problem is that we believe they're using the dark net – the Tor system, which hides the end servers from us. There are ways around that, but it will take days or weeks to be sure we've located them all, assuming we ever do."

The director's expression darkened. "Then what's your recommendation? Seems like you've shot down everything I can think of. You two are the big brains that understand this stuff. Give me something to work with."

"I think the safest course is to monitor the internet for traffic from the known infected sites, as you suggested, and see if we can penetrate the Tor system and triangulate the command and control servers. The risk being that if we're able to block them, there still might be a countdown trigger, where if communications don't occur on a scheduled basis for whatever reason, the malware automatically activates." Reuven glanced at Adam and then back to the director. "The safest course is to pay the ransom and hope that the threat goes away. That they honor their word."

The director's mouth tightened and he shook his head. "We don't negotiate with terrorists. Ever. We won't start now. That's not an option. You need to find a way around this, or a way to neutralize the threat. We can't have our country brought to its knees by extortion. It's unacceptable."

"All we're saying is that, unpleasant as it is, they may have painted us into a corner there's no way out of."

The director stood, his expression hard as flint. "Gentlemen, the thing about a cornered rat is that there's always a way out if it's desperate enough. Always. The rat will do anything, try anything, fight harder than you could ever imagine, and if necessary, die trying. If we've been cornered, then we need to ensure whoever thought that was a bright idea pays an astronomical price for doing so, or the country is finished. Which means your teams need to do whatever it takes, work around the clock, commandeer any resources necessary." He thought for a moment. "I'll bring the Americans in on this. There's no alternative."

"Are you sure that's—"

"You've left me no choice. Now go. Leave me to consider how to proceed from here. I understand the implications you've laid out. I'll need to brief the cabinet and the prime minister and tell them that we're working on a solution. Which means I can't lie, so you need to be pursuing one. Understand?"

Reuven and Adam pushed their chairs back from the table and stood. "Yes, sir," they said in unison.

The director didn't have to watch them leave to know the dark look that passed between them on the way out.

He sank behind his desk and stared vacantly at the reports in front of him, felt for his cigarettes, and then swore out loud before reaching for the phone to make the first in a series of calls he'd been dreading ever since he'd first been notified of the threat.

# Chapter 18

*Tallinn, Estonia*

Jet hurried out of the meager hotel bathroom to answer her ringing cell phone. She stood naked, dripping on the linoleum floor, and stabbed the phone to life.

"Yes?"

"We've made progress," the director said. "We believe that the company you're working for is either responsible for, or is a part of, the ransom plot."

"I don't understand. What does that have to do with attacking the Russian?"

"It's possible he was involved as well, and they had a falling-out. I have it on good authority that criminals routinely do that."

Jet considered the director's words. "What do you want me to do?"

"Keep your eyes open. I need more information before I come to any conclusions. I'll be meeting with our best and brightest all day. In the meantime, memorialize anything you can with your phone camera, but don't get caught."

"If I am, they'll have the evidence on the camera. Not smart."

"The newer devices we've developed are unhackable. They store their data in a section of memory that self-erases if anyone unauthorized tries to retrieve it. As you know, yours is password protected, but there's an additional layer of security beneath that operating system. Three wrong tries on either password and the memory is wiped, and there's no way to recover it." The director paused. "We're running out of time, so expect something more kinetic from our end shortly."

"I assumed you didn't send me for sightseeing."

"Safe guess."

Jet's first full day at work began with a tour of the facilities by her supervisor, a woman about her age named Piia, who was chatty and openly friendly with Jet and, from what she could tell, all of her subordinates, who consisted of seven other young women with specialties in other languages. Piia's English was better than Jet was claiming her Russian to be, which she explained was due to studying in London for half her education, so they stuck to that language for the orientation.

"All of the translation and programming takes place in this building," she said. "It's larger than it looks. There are four underground levels, including a cafeteria and a rec room for breaks."

"That's got to be odd, working underground. What was the logic to building it that way?" Jet asked.

"Not that weird. Oliver's installed natural light bulbs that adjust the amount of UV for the seasons, which is better than what we get above ground. You've never done a winter here, but believe me, you won't be missing anything by staying below. As to why, it's natural insulation. It gets below freezing here four to six months of the year, but the design serves almost as a wine cellar, where it's sixty-four degrees year-round without the heaters or air conditioners on, depending on the season. So it's way less expensive to heat or cool from that temperature than to try to bring minus ten up to sixty-nine."

"That makes sense."

"Most of us are cubicle rats, anyway, so it's not like we're used to offices with windows. That's mostly for upper management." She paused. "What do you think of Oliver?"

Jet shrugged. "He seems okay, I guess. A little eccentric. Why?"

"He's a genius. They say his IQ is close to two hundred. But he can be moody, and…his social graces aren't the greatest."

"I didn't notice," Jet lied.

"He's basically harmless, but it's still probably best if you stay out of his way. He's really generous, but he's got a temper, and you don't want to be in his sights if he's angry." She looked around. "And if he says or does anything inappropriate, best to come to me with it."

"Like...what?"

"Like I said. His social skills aren't the best. Sometimes...look, he obviously likes attractive women. That's why three-quarters of the staff is female and young. But he doesn't always indicate interest appropriately. It's probably a personality disorder of some kind. I don't mind, because I've never had any problems. I'm just saying, be aware that he's different, and try not to draw his attention."

Jet swallowed hard and nodded, as though the description and apology for sexual harassment made perfect sense. Oliver was just a grabby teddy bear, and think nothing of it. Jet didn't point out the obvious problems with the facile reasoning – that wasn't her battle to fight. But it was certainly consistent with his offensive interjection when he thought she couldn't understand him.

A thought occurred to her. "Doesn't he have a girlfriend or something?"

Piia rolled her eyes. "I think that's part of the issue. This only started when he broke up with Anna. They'd been together for five years, and then they had a big blowout and broke up."

"What was she like?"

"I didn't know her that well. She worked alongside Oliver on some of the special projects. But she seemed nice. Big girl, always smiling. A gamer, loved cosplay, as does Oliver."

"Cosplay?"

"Yeah. It's big in some circles. Costume play. It's a role-playing thing where people pretend to be characters from comics or video games or anime. They dress up. It's really big in geek circles in places like Japan, and it's gone kind of viral in some of the hacker undergrounds. Anna's favorite character was Charlotte – from some video game she loved."

Jet nodded, as though grown-ups dressing up in costumes and pretending to be fictional characters was as normal as brushing your teeth. "Who did Oliver pretend to be?"

"Nobody knows. We used to say that it was the company's biggest secret." Piia paused. "I thought he and Anna were made for each other, and it completely surprised everyone when she took off. Oliver made a statement to the team that she'd decided to pursue other opportunities, and that was that. But the rumor is she dumped him." Piia stopped at an elevator and pressed the down button. "Between you and me, it had to be hard living here twenty-four seven. I'd have gone nuts. Oliver never leaves the compound except to go to his place in Helsinki. Even then, he has a helicopter pick him up on the grounds."

"He lives here?"

"Oh. Sorry. I forget that new people don't know all the dirt. Yes, that big house is his home, not just a historical residence. They lived there together. I've only been inside a few times, but it's insanely high tech. It's a couple of hundred years old from the outside, but on the inside it could be a gaming suite in Denmark or London. If you can think of a contemporary technology, he's had it installed. Smart house with computer-controlled everything, the whole place wired with high-speed fiber, a home theater that's better than anything commercial, massive screens in every room…it cost a fortune, but then again, he has endless supplies of money, so why not?"

"Wow. Sounds amazing. But back to the girlfriend. Is she still in Tallinn? That has to be weird, having gone out with the richest guy in the country, and then suddenly you're on your own, right?"

The elevator arrived and they stepped in. Piia selected the bottom floor, and the polished stainless steel doors slid closed with a whisper and they descended almost imperceptibly.

"I don't know where she went. I heard Amsterdam, but that could just be gossip. I honestly didn't pay that much attention. I'm not here to write a memoir, you know? Just do my job, collect my pay, and try to have as much fun as possible while doing it." She looked Jet up and down. "Which is my advice for you too. Keep your eye on the ball, don't get distracted by scuttlebutt, and bank your checks. Pretty soon you'll be set up. For all his quirks, Oliver is one of the best guys I've ever heard of to work for."

*Other than being a predator and a deviate,* Jet thought.

The door opened and Piia showed her the gaming lounge, the dining area, and the cafeteria, which was as modern as any she'd seen. The walls weren't the industrial gray concrete she'd expected; rather, whole sections were screens made from LEDs, with lifelike renditions of forests, and blue sky glowing with realistic effect.

"That's pretty cool," Jet remarked.

"Yeah. I told you it was better than upstairs. Because of our location, the winter months are really dark out, so this is actually a big improvement."

The next two floors were huge cubicle farms, with at least a hundred workers per floor. For whatever reason, the translation division was on the main level, but with the faux-window walls even in the work areas, the overall impression was anything but oppressive.

Outside, Jet indicated the other building. "What's that?"

"Special projects. It's off-limits to anyone unauthorized. Oliver's got a whole suite in there, which is where he tends to stay most of the time, in addition to his office in this building that he uses for meetings. Other than that, nobody really knows what's in there. The special projects staff keep to themselves."

"You mean they're standoffish?"

"More than that. They have their own facilities. We never see them. They have a different entrance to the grounds."

"Wow. That's…unusual."

"Not really. A lot of what the company does is security work, and I hear it handles top secret stuff for the government, too. So it would make sense to compartmentalize everything. If that group has to have clearances, you wouldn't want them chatting with people who don't in case they let something slip, right?"

"I never thought of it that way. I guess it makes sense."

Piia glanced at her watch. "I have a couple of things I need to do. Meet you back in our area in ten? I'll show you what we're working on so you can get up to speed."

"Perfect."

Piia walked back inside, and Jet slipped her small cell phone from her pocket and took a few surreptitious photos before returning to the building and making for the elevator. She took it to the bottom floor and wandered through the rec areas to the cafeteria, pretending to be interested in the menu, but with her phone hidden in one hand, silently recording video of the surroundings as she went.

She repeated the maneuver on the next floors, her badge sufficient to keep anyone from questioning her, at least until the final floor, where a supervisor approached Jet and asked her what she was doing.

"Looking for a bathroom. I'm new," Jet said.

The woman eyed her badge and indicated a pair of doors in the middle of the cubicle area. "There's one on your floor too. We tend to stay on our levels unless we're downstairs."

Appropriately chastened, Jet mumbled an apology, and said she'd use one on the main floor now that she knew where they were. She walked back to the elevator, the woman's eyes following her all the way there.

Piia was waiting for her upstairs, and Jet hurried to her cubicle and prepared for a long day of tedium, translating technical documents into Spanish. When she was sure nobody was watching her, she did a quick check of her system and was relieved to find there were no keyloggers or other spyware monitoring her use, and the file-sharing operating system was an off-the-shelf brand whose security backdoors she was conversant with.

At lunch she mingled with her co-workers in the lounge and suffered through their banter while trying to extract as much gossip as she could without being obvious. After half an hour she concluded that she might as well have been talking to a wall, and it was almost a relief to sit back at her workstation and begin her covert job of probing the company intranet for weaknesses. She alternated her translating and burrowing deeper into the system files until she found what she'd been hoping for. Jet made a mental note of how to retrieve the data when she needed it, and then hunkered down to complete her assigned tasks, which were so mundane she wanted to kill herself by the end of the shift.

The sky was darkening from turquoise to violet when she exited the building with a stream of other workers. Her mind was numb from the tedium of rote translation as she made her way with the group to the main gate. A pair of uniformed security guards approached her when she was halfway there, and she stopped.

"What is it?" she asked.

One of them looked at her badge while the other stood by his side, his expression wooden. "We were reviewing the security tapes and we saw that you have a phone," he said in Russian. "They're not allowed on the grounds. Sorry."

"Oh. Nobody told me. I'm new. This is my first day. It won't happen again."

The guard held out his hand. "I'm afraid I'll have to confiscate it. The rules are the rules. The boss is very sensitive to data security. If you fill out a voucher, you'll be reimbursed for the cost of the phone."

She frowned. "But all my contacts are in there."

"Yeah, that can be a pain, but we need the phone. If you want, you can write down all your numbers. We can accompany you to your work area."

Jet mulled over how to handle the situation. It would look strange if she just handed it over, but she'd lied – she didn't have any numbers she hadn't memorized. She opted for rolling her eyes, exhaling in annoyance, and retrieving the phone from her pocket and handing it to him.

"I'll stop in tomorrow for the voucher. That's brand new. You're lucky I still have my old one with all the contacts."

"They should have told you about the rule. Who's your manager?"

Jet glanced at the gate. "Maybe they did. It was a lot to take in. Look, I'm sorry. You have the phone. I don't want to get into trouble, okay? I must have forgotten. Give me a break…please?"

She tried her most contrite smile, and her eyes flashed green in the gloaming. The guards looked at each other, and the one who had done all the talking held out a conciliatory hand. "Just this once. But don't bring a cell onto the premises again or it'll be written up. We've got our job to do, too. We're taking a chance letting you off the hook."

Her smile broadened. "I won't forget. Promise. And I really appreciate it."

"Okay, Gabriela," he said, eyes darting to her name tag. "My name's Indrek. If you stop by the security office tomorrow, we can get a voucher issued."

"I'll look for you," she said, and turned to continue her walk to the gate. She tossed them another smile over her shoulder, swinging her hips a little more than usual for their benefit, angry at her carelessness for having been picked up by surveillance cameras so well concealed she hadn't spotted them. She wondered whether the entire facility was monitored, including the workstations, and decided that it was unlikely, as that would introduce a security risk of its own if the workers were doing proprietary tasks – it was probably the corridors and the elevators and possibly the rec level.

More likely was that the supervisor who'd stopped her had called in her presence on her floor and had spotted the telltale bulge of the phone in her back pocket, small as it was.

Either way, it was a careless blunder on Jet's part, and she couldn't allow herself any more of those. Just because there was no obvious menace didn't mean danger wasn't waiting around a corner. She'd let down her guard and gotten off light. There was no assurance that would happen again.

Once back at the hotel, she checked the hairs she'd left across drawers and the closet door. Nobody had opened the drawers, but the closet hair was missing.

It was possible that the maid had brushed against it and dislodged it, but unlikely – Jet had placed it high above eye level. She opened the door and examined the cheap in-room safe. The hair she'd affixed across the door joint was still in place. She removed it and entered her four-digit code. Her spare phone, money, and passports were still there, but it troubled her that someone had opened the closet.

Jet powered the cell on and dialed the director's line to give him a report, and by the time she hung up with him, she was sure that tomorrow would be one of the longest days of her life.

# Chapter 19

Jet had just arrived for work and was walking to her building when a helicopter neared and set down on the far side of the field. Oliver's distinctive form in his cart appeared from the special projects building and made its way along a paved path to the landing area, where a ramp extended from an Airbus Helicopters H155. He wheeled aboard the aircraft, the crew retracted the ramp, and then the helo was airborne and soaring overhead.

When Jet entered the building, the rich smell of coffee filled the ground-floor cubicle maze, and Jet availed herself of a cup so she wouldn't stand out. She debated going to security to fill out her voucher and decided to do so at lunch rather than taking out time from her workday. She wanted to play the part of a model employee, nose to the grindstone, and didn't want to do anything that could draw suspicion to her after the prior afternoon's indiscretions.

The decision turned out to be a good one, because Piia stopped by to check on her a few minutes after she'd gotten settled. She asked how she was faring, and Jet assured her that she was comfortable with the work and plowing through it, and would stay late to make the deadline she'd been handed with the bundle of documents. If Piia had been notified by security of Jet's apprehension with the phone, she didn't mention it, and Jet believed that the guards had kept their word and cut her some slack.

The day crawled by, with Jet avoiding any attempts to go further into the company's file system, confining her efforts to the minutiae of translations. The security guard hadn't been in the office when she'd submitted the voucher, but the woman on duty took her claim and filed it with a look filled with disapproval.

The other workers began packing up at six p.m., and Jet stayed until Piia stopped in again and asked her how much longer she was going to be.

"Oh, probably another hour or so," Jet replied. "I need to stay immersed or it'll take twice as long to do tomorrow. Sorry. It's going slower than I'd hoped."

"Well, I've got an appointment this evening or I'd stay to give you moral support. I appreciate your dedication."

"No problem. I thought I'd be able to get everything finished by the end of the day."

"Don't be too hard on yourself. You're new. We figure it will take a week or two to get adjusted."

The building was still two hours later when Jet logged out of her translation screen and brought up the master file directory. She toggled to the backdoor and tried a series of commands the Mossad technology experts had given her, and the second one worked – she was in. She typed in a few more commands and quickly found the security backdoor that they'd told her existed on this rev of the software as well as a number of the company's routers, and entered the menu tree for the master security system. It was common for the security software to have a simulation mode used while construction was still underway that would spoof a restart and full check of the system, and the tech geek had assured her that she could easily program in a loop that would reboot the check when it ended, ensuring that she'd have as much time as she needed for her errand.

Her fingers flew over the keys, and ten minutes later she'd crafted a simple command series that would keep the system in simulation check mode until she canceled it, or someone figured out the problem. Given the ease with which she'd tricked the guards the prior evening, she wasn't worried – the likelihood that anyone who'd been part of the original construction installation was on duty at night was a calculated risk she felt safe taking. Whoever was there would probably take a while to detect there even was an issue, and then would have to contact someone else to get instructions, which meant either a trip to the compound, remote diagnostics, or even better, phone troubleshooting, none of which would happen quickly.

Jet didn't know how long it would take to locate the files she was after, but if she didn't find them within twenty minutes, she'd bail. Any more than that and she'd be too exposed, and if she was caught, there would be no talking her way out of it like with the phone. She did a final check of her handiwork, and when she was sure she hadn't missed anything, initiated the shutdown sequence and quickly retreated from the root directory before powering down her system and making her way to the bathroom.

Once inside the ladies' room, she brushed past the stalls to a window at the end. She pulled it open and peered out into the darkness, and when she was sure nobody was nearby, heaved herself up and through it. Jet landed on the grass by the back of the building and crept along the base until she reached the end. After another glance around, she eyed the special projects building, which was cloaked in darkness.

A schematic in the system files had told her that Oliver's suite was on the ground floor and occupied the far corner of the structure, complete with a pair of picture windows from which he could survey his domain. She darted between the buildings and moved to one of the three entrances, all deserted now that the workday was over.

There was always a chance that the staff in that building were night owls, but she had no choice but to risk it. The director had made clear that time wasn't their friend, and had made her new objective her top priority, whatever the cost.

The door lever turned, the fingerprint-scanning lock having been disabled by her software patch, and she pushed the steel slab open a foot and peeked into the empty lobby. The main floor offices were dark, the corridors dimly lit with after-hours lighting. She squeezed through the gap and worked her way along the hall to the fat man's suite.

That door had also been unlocked by her software, and she slipped inside, waiting until her eyes adjusted to move to his computer. A glance at the ceiling showed the motion detectors and infrared that she'd suspected an advanced system would have, and she offered a silent prayer that her patch was working as intended, because otherwise an army of security guards would be closing on her in moments, once they knew the sanctum sanctorum had been breached.

Oliver's system password was a major obstacle, but she had a number of possibilities she intended to try before giving up. Worst case, she'd remove the hard disk and take it with her, which was inelegant and would take days to decrypt, but she didn't have a lot of options. There had been no way to install a keylogger, and she hadn't found a master password in the security files, so had to use her intuition.

She inserted a thumb drive into one of the ports and let the program she'd written early that morning run through all the possibles she'd been able to come up with. It tried Oliver's date of birth, birthplace, first pet, old addresses, and variations of his name with no success. Jet hadn't expected much, as those were too easy, but she had to try. He didn't have any children, so it next moved to his parents' names and birth dates in all possible variations, again without any joy. She glanced at the cheap watch she'd been given with the paperwork by her handler and saw that she'd already burned four valuable minutes she didn't have.

Eventually the program ran out of options, and she was no closer to her goal than when she'd arrived. Her brow wrinkled as she considered other choices, and she was about to abandon the stealth way and remove the hard disk when an idea occurred to her. She typed in Anna and pressed Enter.

Nothing but the now-familiar incorrect password message.

She continued tapping in variations on capitalization and eventually gave up and eyed the server case before giving one last try – Anna's name and Oliver's combined, like teen lovers might carve into a tree.

The menu blinked and she was in.

She allowed herself a small smile. The obese misogynist had a romantic streak, which would be his undoing. The poetic justice was ironic, but she pushed the thought aside and focused on scanning his files for anything that looked suspect, copying whole subdirectory contents to the USB drive. When it was full, she swapped it out with another and continued to download until everything that might contain data on drones or secret projects was stored on her dongles.

Jet pocketed the devices and was stepping away from the computer when a folder she'd overlooked in the upper left-hand corner of the display caught her eye, labeled simply "Vids." She selected it and opened it, and found a dozen video files identified with names that meant nothing to her. She double-clicked on the first, and a media player opened on the desktop and blinked to life.

Thirty seconds into the footage she shut it down, sickened, and withdrew the dongle that still had space on it from her pocket, reinserted it into his system, and copied the entire folder. Apparently Oliver wasn't just a creep and an eccentric, but he was also a pedophile, favoring forbidden videos of girls barely older than Hannah in depraved acts with old men.

A sound from the hall stopped her, and she removed the dongle and pocketed it before creeping to the door and listening. Footfalls from the hall approached and flashlight beams played along the far wall, signaling that her luck had run out.

She only had seconds before the guards turned the corner, so she bolted in the opposite direction, staying low so the cubicles in the center of the immense space hid her progress. She made it to the end of one of the rows and paused at the sound of male voices from the direction of Oliver's suite. Was it possible that she might go undetected? She'd left no evidence of her presence, but she didn't dare hope she'd get away free.

The flashlight beams moved along the cubicles, signaling that her gambit hadn't worked, and she continued along the next leg of offices, a map of the layout in mind. If she could get to one of the exits…

She nearly ran headlong into a uniformed security guard with a pistol in hand, coming from the opposite direction. Her instincts took over, and a sharp blow to his arm numbed his forearm. He screamed and dropped the gun. She followed through and drove her foot into the man's abdomen, doubling him over with an explosive exhalation. Another kick finished him, and he fell back against the wall, unconscious. Jet scooped up his pistol and checked to ensure a round was chambered, and then took off at a run for the nearest exit, all pretense of subtlety abandoned.

"Hey!" a voice yelled behind her in Russian, but she didn't turn, and rounded another corner, putting the guards out of sight, if only for a moment. The restroom signs appeared on her left and she ducked into the men's room, tore to the window that was the twin of the ladies' room, and pushed it open.

Jet was through the window in an instant and running flat out across the grass when shots barked from behind her. Judging by the sound, they were out of range, but she increased her speed and didn't slow until she reached the perimeter wall. She twisted to look back and saw three guards hoofing it with guns drawn, but far enough from her that she could take evasive action.

Jet slid the pistol into her pants and ran toward a tall tree near the wall, allowing her momentum to carry her three meters up the trunk. She pushed off with her right leg and closed the gap to the wall, and her fingers locked onto the top as her feet scrabbled at the rough surface below. She gritted her teeth and heaved upward, and she was over the top and dropping to the far side when two more gunshots rang out.

She recovered from a hard landing and sprinted toward a scattering of homes a hundred meters away. When she reached them, she eyed the sad collection of cars parked in front, and selected a Fiat sedan that looked older than she was. A blow from the pistol butt shattered the passenger-side window and she was in, feeling for the wires below the steering wheel. She pulled the ignition wire tips free of the switch and started the engine, ignoring a shout from the house as she slid behind the wheel.

A glance at the gas gauge showed less than a quarter tank. She jammed the manual transmission into gear and tromped on the accelerator, sending the little car skidding along the street away from the company compound.

Jet eyed the rearview mirror and spotted a pair of SUVs roaring out of the gates and headed straight at the homes, so her feint hadn't lost them. Now she was in a junker vehicle long past its prime, up against the new high-horsepower motors bearing down on her. She didn't have time to regret not having a phone to pull up a map of the area, and instead worked through the gears, keeping her headlights off, slowing with her emergency brake at intersections in order to avoid triggering the tail lights.

Headlights bounced along behind her, and she turned onto a smaller street, the pavement of which was riddled with potholes. The Fiat's tires protested the maneuver and the axles creaked as it bounced along the road. She made a hard left onto another street and floored the gas again, downshifting to get the most power out of the lawnmower-sized engine. The motor whined into the redline and she swerved around a car in her lane, deaf to the honk that greeted her from an oncoming vehicle she almost hit head-on.

Jet checked the mirrors as she continued toward town, and when she didn't see any SUVs giving chase, eventually slowed and switched on the lights. Having been spotted, now she was in a race to make it back to the hotel before security checked the logs to see who had still been on the grounds, figured out it was her, and called the police with her information.

That was the optimistic spin. If she was right about the company being involved in the murder attempt on the Russian, the police were likely the least of her problems. The company might decide to eliminate the middleman and go after her themselves, in which case the clock was ticking even faster. She had to assume the worst and coaxed the skittish little car to higher speed as she wended along the road, using the lights from the downtown high-rises as a rough guide to her location.

Once in metropolitan traffic, she resigned herself to driving normally, and snuck a glance at the gun she'd liberated. It was a Russian Makarov PM, 9mm, serviceable if older, a weapon Jet was more than familiar with. She would have gladly traded it for her passport and cell phone, but at least she had a weapon. It was small comfort, but after the chase and near miss, she'd take what she could get, although she needed to jettison the car as soon as possible and find her way to the hotel on foot – the owner would have reported it as stolen by now, which meant every minute on the road increased her chances of being pulled over. Not something she relished while in possession of a stolen gun and a couple of USB drives with possible top secret material on them.

The image of an old lecher's tumescent member and the horrified expression on the little girl's face popped unbidden into her mind, and she pushed it away with a frown. She didn't have the luxury of thinking through what it all meant. For now, she had to get her gear and move, because the noose was tightening, and she could feel its coil on her throat.

She turned into an alley near where she believed the hotel to be and stopped the car by a dumpster, leaving it running for the next thief's convenience. A pair of vagrants sitting in a doorway drinking from a bottle watched her step from the vehicle, and then she was gone, jogging in the opposite direction, the Makarov butt hard against her lower back as her boots beat a rapid tattoo on the pavement.

# Chapter 20

*Ibiza, Spain*

Music pulsed from towering speaker columns that framed a neon-wrapped DJ booth as lights strobed across the dancing crowd. Cheering celebrants waved glow sticks in the night air and tanned skin glistened with perspiration, the girls beautiful and the boys handsome in the way of the children of the rich everywhere on earth.

The DJ, a skinny man with a shaved head and most of his visible body inked with tattoos, bobbed his head with the hypnotic beat, seemingly lost in a trance of his own making.

A trio of stunning women in gold hot pants and matching halter tops undulated by the booth. Their faces were painted with phosphorescent colors, one with the features of a cat, another with the signs of the zodiac, the third with occult symbols. All had ribbed abs and four percent body fat and showed no signs of tiring even after two hours straight of energetic dancing. The males watching them had faces dusted with fashionable two days' growths of beard, their features angular and lean and bronzed by the sun.

Near the stage, a statuesque blonde wearing a kind of modified toga that left little to the imagination leaned into another equally stunning brunette and kissed her on the mouth. The pair embraced among the dancers, bodies melding together as their lips devoured each other, and then the blonde pulled away, her eyes sparkling, and high-fived her companion. Nearby, a pair of swarthy young men, clad in Versace shirts, white linen slacks, and Gucci loafers, watched the girls with hungry eyes, gold chains around their necks and Cartier watches dangling languorously from their wrists.

Four bulky men stood near the blonde with hands folded in front of them, watching the show without reaction. All had earbuds and wore tropical-weight jackets in spite of the heat, and their eyes roamed over the crowd without rest.

"I wanna get high," the blonde yelled to her friend.

"You *are* high, Tanya!" her companion shouted back. They both laughed delightedly, and Tanya glanced over at their young admirers.

"I mean on something else."

"Like what?"

"I don't know. But I want to."

"Let's grab a drink. I'm parched."

The two girls pushed through the throng to a long onyx bar, where shirtless bartenders flexed and preened while preparing cocktails. Tanya threw an annoyed look at the nearest as he shook a martini shaker and poured two glasses full for another party down the bar, and then waved at him to get his attention, already impatient. The young man held up a finger to signal he'd be there in a moment, and said something to a doe-eyed girl with jet black hair parted in the middle.

Tanya turned to her friend. "What an asshole. He's ignoring us."

"He's finishing up. Working the tip. Give him a second."

"I don't have a second. I want a drink."

The bartender ambled over and offered a winning grin. "What'll it be?"

"What kind of vodka do you have?" Tanya asked in accented English.

The man recited his selection, and Tanya frowned. "Don't you have anything good?"

"Customers like the Stoli and the Grey Goose."

She made a face and then relented. "Two Stoli cosmos. Well iced, with a lemon twist. Not too heavy on the sweet."

"You got it."

He made the drinks quickly, pouring theatrically before placing the glasses before them with a flourish. Tanya signaled to the bodyguards, and one of them stepped forward and pawed a wad of euros from his pocket to pay while the girls spun to watch the dancers.

The two young men who'd been eyeing them sauntered over, and the taller of the pair smiled. "Cooling off?" he asked in English.

Tanya looked them up and down and decided she liked what she saw. "Yeah. It's baking on the floor."

"It's usually not that hot this time of year. Way cooler on the water. It's gorgeous down at the marina."

"You have a boat here?"

He nodded. "We come for a month every year. Best parties in Europe."

Tanya tossed back half her drink. "I don't know. I'm bored. So's my friend."

"What's your name?"

"Tanya. This is Liv."

"I'm Mansour, and this is Amir. We're cousins."

"What kind of boat do you have?" Liv asked.

"A big one. Feadship. It's our family's. One of them, anyway."

"Cool. And they let you take it?"

"They have others. Why not?" Amir said with a grin.

"Where are you from? Your accent's awesome," Mansour said.

"Moscow," Tanya said.

"Oh, wow. You like it here?"

"Like I said. We're bored. We want to party, but everyone's been a drag so far."

"You should come down to the boat. We've been partying for days. Got anything you can imagine."

Tanya raised an eyebrow. "Really? We've got good imaginations."

"You name it, we've got it," Mansour said with a wink. "Our car's outside. You want to lose this dump, or stick around and get more bored?"

Tanya and Liv exchanged a glance. "This had better be good. You have any X?"

"Of course. I said anything, didn't I?"

Tanya finished her drink and took Liv's hand. "Then you're on."

Amir and Mansour escorted them through the crowd, the bodyguards in tow. When they reached the valet area, Mansour tossed the man a twenty-euro note and a tag. The valet scurried off, and another took the bodyguards' tag with a five and a disappointed look. "You want to ride down with us?" Mansour asked. "We can bring you back whenever you want."

A red Ferrari California convertible growled up the lane and stopped in front of them. Tanya smiled and nudged Liv.

"Sure."

"You want the front or the back?" Amir asked. "I'll hop in back with whoever doesn't want shotgun."

Liv shrugged and giggled. "There isn't much room back there."

"We'll manage. It's not that far."

Amir leaned the passenger seat forward and Liv climbed in back, scissoring her long legs beneath her on the seat. Amir rounded the hood and wedged himself beside her, and then Mansour was behind the wheel with Tanya next to him.

One of the bodyguards approached her and grumbled in Russian. She snapped at him, threw Mansour a smile, and put her hand on his. "We going to sit here all night? I told you we're bored."

Mansour put the car in gear and roared away as the bodyguards scrambled into a brown sedan. They slammed their doors and the driver accelerated away with a screech of rubber, the Ferrari's lights already down at the base of the drive.

Mansour swung onto the winding road and raised a cell phone to his ear as he drove. He spoke a few words and then slid it back into his pocket. "Calling the boat to let the crew know we're coming with guests."

"How long have you been here?"

"Couple of weeks. We've been bouncing back and forth between Mallorca. There was a killer party there last weekend at my dad's buddy's house on the water. It was epic." He goosed the gas and the sleek car leapt forward. "But not as epic as tonight's going to be."

"We'll see about that, Mansour," Tanya said, her tone teasing.

"Speed up," the bodyguard in the passenger seat growled at the driver.

"I am," he snapped, eyes glued to the Ferrari in front of them.

"They're pulling away."

"Thing's a rocket, and the kid's driving like he's nuts."

"Catch up to them. Now."

The driver downshifted and floored the accelerator, and then braked hard when a lorry lurched from a side road and cut him off. He palmed the accelerator as the car drifted sideways, and the truck's brake lights flashed and the big vehicle stopped in the middle of the two-lane road, blocking them.

"Idiots," the driver said, and rolled down his window to wave at the truck. "Get this heap off the road."

Two men emerged from beneath a tarp over the truck bed. The bodyguards were reaching for their guns when the men's suppressed H&K MP5 submachine guns shredded the windshield and spackled the interior of the car with blood and brains. They approached, firing bursts, and changed magazines as they neared, continuing to pepper the interior until they'd reached the vehicle and confirmed the bodyguards were dead.

One of the shooters knocked what remained of the windshield from the frame with his gun and then handed it to his partner. He opened the driver's door and heaved the dead man from behind the wheel. The other gunman called out, and two more men ran from the truck and hauled the driver into the back.

A minute later the lorry drove off, tailed by the car full of dead guards, driven by the first gunman. The only evidence that anything had transpired was a scattering of broken glass in the road and a smear of the driver's coagulating blood.

The lorry made the next turn onto a rutted gravel road that led down to the water, and five minutes later, the vehicle was at the bottom of the Mediterranean in fifty feet of depth, where with any luck at all it wouldn't be discovered for days.

The gunmen returned to the lorry, climbed into the back, and passed cigarettes and a bottle of rum around, their job for the night finished, the only thing remaining a ride to a waiting boat that would run them to the mainland, where they'd disappear without a trace after collecting their pay. None of them had any idea who the men in the car were, nor did they care. They were professionals, well paid to dispose of trouble for their clientele, and all they had to know was that the men had needed killing and the price had been right.

"That went well. Wish they were all like that, huh?" one asked, drawing thick smoke deep into his lungs.

"Didn't even get off a shot. Shame. Almost too easy."

The first shrugged. "No such thing. They wanted it done without any drama. Customer's always right."

The second laughed and took a long pull on the bottle before handing it back.

"Long as their money's green, that is."

"Always."

# Chapter 21

*Helsinki, Finland*

The windows of a hulking mansion on a waterfront estate in the Soukanranta suburb of Helsinki glowed amber against a backdrop of dense trees. Two Mercedes sedans were parked in the long driveway, and four men in windbreakers and dark pants stood at the four corners of the house, hands in their pockets as they stared out at the surroundings.

Inside, Oliver had his cart wedged against a twelve-person dining table, a napkin tied around his neck, fork in one hand and knife in the other, and a partially carved pheasant, bronzed and gleaming with a honey glaze, on a silver platter in front of him. A bottle of 1982 Cheval Blanc sat beside it, the Riedel goblet near his right hand a third full of the opaque nectar.

Jowls quivering, his jaws worked with the steady relentlessness of a machine as he masticated a huge bite of roast bird. Tiny pinpoints of sweat collected on his brow from his efforts. He was reading from his cart's screen, his eyes racing over the technical jargon displayed there, forehead creased.

A young woman clad in white slacks and jacket stood off to one side, attentively waiting for him to request something more, a pitcher of ice water with lemon peels floating in it by her side. If he noticed her, he gave no indication, engrossed in the document and his meal.

A telephone rang from deep in the house, and another servant appeared moments later with a handset.

"Sir, sorry to disturb you. It's your office. They say it's urgent."

Oliver scowled and looked at the wedge of pheasant he'd

skewered with his fork in preparation to take another bite. He set the fork and knife down and held out a meaty hand for the phone. The woman scurried over and handed it to him, and then departed on crepe soles.

"This had better be good," he grumbled.

"We've had a break-in," said Lars, his second-in-command.

"What? Where?"

"We think it's possible they were after your office."

"Did they get in?"

"Unknown at present."

"How is that possible? A mouse couldn't fart without triggering a half dozen alarms."

"It appears she bypassed the security system and neutralized it."

Oliver looked over at the young woman. "Go. I'll call if I need anything," he said in Finnish.

"Of course, sir," she said, and slipped away.

Oliver returned his attention to the call. "You said 'she.' Then you know who's responsible?"

"Yes, and no. She escaped. Hurt one of the guards pretty badly."

"One woman was able to evade the most expensive security in Estonia? Explain how that happened."

"We're still trying to piece it together. It appears she was able to get off the grounds before the team took action."

"Who was in charge?"

"Kelinsky."

"You say one of the guards was hurt?"

"Yes. Broken ribs. Probable concussion." A pause. "She got his gun away from him."

"This must be a joke. Tell me it's a joke."

"We believe she was a professional."

"Again – who is she? How did she get onto the grounds?"

"A recent hire. You met her yesterday. Gabriela Mendez. A translator."

Oliver drew a deep breath. "Her? This makes no sense. She's no pro. There must be some sort of mistake."

"I pulled the security logs. Apparently she was caught with a cell phone yesterday, but the guards didn't write up an official report. We're going through her computer logs right now to see what she accessed, but we have to assume that it's not good."

Oliver thought for several beats. "Kelinsky's responsible for security. This is a disaster. I'm…I'm very disappointed. See to it that he's dealt with appropriately."

"Perhaps we should wait until the police–"

"Have you involved them?"

"We had to. Some of the men fired shots."

"Shit."

"It gets worse. We tried to access her phone, and the memory module self-destructed. It's military-grade countermeasures. So we can assume a state actor."

"Not necessarily. Those can be had on the dark web."

"Everything points to a state."

Oliver took a sip of wine, which left a purple mustache above his lips. "No state would send in a mere girl by herself to attempt to breach our operation. I suspect the Russian."

"It's possible. But we consider it unlikely."

"Leave the thinking to me. What I want to know is why she wasn't screened properly. We should have picked this up before she was hired – that tells me that the agency, and our people, didn't do their job, either." Oliver glared at the pheasant like it had insulted him. "As to Kelinsky, perhaps his passing can serve a higher purpose, since he's failed the one I've overpaid him for."

"What are you thinking?"

"Are the police there yet?"

"No. But they're on their way."

"Has Kelinsky spoken to them? Who called it in?"

"One of the others."

Oliver tapped his fork on the table absentmindedly. "First things first. We'll need to do a complete system scan and see what, if anything, was compromised. Confirm that Kelinsky didn't speak to anyone after the shots were fired. If not, his death should be blamed on the girl. That will turn up the heat on her and ensure she can't get out of Tallinn without being apprehended. She probably thinks she got away clean. We can use the official channels to grab her, and then we'll deal with her from there."

"So…he was shot while she was escaping?"

"Or his throat was slit before she made it into the building. I think I like that better. Leave his body where it will be found later. But be quick about it, so forensics timing lines up."

"Will do."

"I'm going to remain here for the time being. Might be best to avoid having to answer any questions. The record shows I was nowhere around?"

"It does."

"Good. Now, what steps have you taken to locate her? She can't have gotten far."

"We have a team on it. Our best."

"Considering what's transpired, that doesn't mean a lot."

"The guards were taken by surprise. There was no precedent for this. It won't happen again."

"Perfect," Oliver said, his tone scathing. "Then we'll be safe from rogue translators breaking into our most classified areas in the future. That's very reassuring."

"I'll go attend to Kelinsky."

"Do that. And keep me informed. I want this resolved quickly. There's too much at stake for any more missteps."

# Chapter 22

*Tallinn, Estonia*

Jet crept along the deserted streets until she arrived at her hotel. A marine layer covered the port city and blocked any glimmer from the moon and stars, so the only illumination was that which seeped through windows or from ancient rusting streetlamps. She stood at the corner, peering around it at the front of the building, and studied the vehicles parked along the sidewalks, checking for signs of observation – windows open a few inches, cigarette butts amassed on the pavement, windshields fogged over, telltale exhaust drifting from a running engine.

Seeing nothing, Jet walked unhurriedly to the hotel, antennae quivering as she tried to detect any watchers. She reached the front door and glanced around the street and, when she was sure that she was unobserved, ducked through the entrance. The night clerk looked up from his magazine with blurry red alcoholic eyes and muttered a half-hearted greeting before returning to his reading, leaving her to choose between a Soviet-era elevator or the stairs.

She skirted the elevator and took the steps two at a time, pausing to listen at each landing. Her room was on the fourth floor of the six-story building, and the climb took her less than a minute. When she reached her level, Jet hesitated at the fire door and pressed her ear against the slab and, when she heard nothing in the hall on the far side, pushed it open on rusty hinges.

Jet made her way to her room, one of eight on the floor that faced the street. She was feeling for her keys when a sound from outside drew her to the hallway window. Two SUVs had pulled up outside the hotel. She watched as armed men spilled from the doors, and was already in motion, sprinting for the fire door again, her lead too slim to dare to retrieve her things.

Jet was through the door and mounting the steps to the top level in a blink, and reached the sixth floor just as she heard boots coming up from the lobby level. She looked around and spotted the iron rungs of a ladder leading to a trapdoor above, and pulled herself up as the footsteps grew louder.

She pushed the door open and heaved herself up and out onto the roof, and then lowered the hatch back into place, wishing there was some obvious way to block it but seeing no means to do so.

The building to her right was a story higher than the hotel, so she ran to the opposite side. That structure was only four stories tall. She debated jumping, but dismissed the impulse in favor of running at the higher building and scrambling up the face, fumbling for handholds in the poorly joined brickwork. She'd just made it to the roof and was pulling herself over the lip when the hotel roof hatch behind her slammed open with a clang. Voices emanated from the opening, but she didn't stop to listen, instead tearing for the new building's roof door and twisting the handle.

*Locked.*

Jet ran to the far side and saw that the next building was another six-story structure. She lowered her legs over the edge and slid down until she was gripping the lip with her hands. She dropped one story to the tar-paper roof and rolled, and then bolted for that edifice's roof door, which also turned out to be dead bolted from inside.

She ran to the side of the building that faced an alley and looked over.

A metal fire escape led from the top floor to the level above the alley. Jet lay stomach down on the roof and slid her legs over the lip, and repeated her lowering maneuver until she was hanging from the roof by her fingers. She released the rim and hit the fire escape with a boom, the sound as loud as a cannon in the quiet of the street.

Jet ignored the pain in her ankles and descended to the next level and then the next, the hammering of her feet on the iron steps echoing off the façades. She was nearly to the alley when the first shots rang out from the adjacent roof, the sound muffled from suppressors but still loud as firecrackers. A few rounds winged off the fire escape, but none came close, and she continued to the level above the alley and dropped from the platform, rolling when she landed before leaping up and running flat out to the next street.

If the goons were on a comm channel, she could expect company by the time she made it to the end of the block, so she whipped the pistol from the small of her back and flicked the safety off. The shooting had stopped now that she was out of range, and she poured on the steam, driving herself as hard as she could, the twinges from her ankles little more than an annoyance.

Jet stopped at the corner of the last building in the row and listened for approaching engines. When she didn't hear any, she crossed the street and cut down the dark sidewalk, moving as fast as she could while sticking to the shadows. She was already to the next intersection and moving across it when headlights swung onto the street she'd just traversed, her slim lead now wider due to the ineptness of her pursuers.

Five minutes later she was as many blocks away, on an avenue with a string of nightclubs and bars that stretched for half a kilometer. She entered the second one she came to, its lit sign worse for wear with a few bulbs burned out, and headed to a long bar, where a handful of men sat nursing drinks.

"Is there a phone here?" she asked the bartender in Russian, who inclined his head toward the rear of the lounge. She walked to the back and found an ancient pay phone between two bathroom doors, and breathed through her nose as she felt for coins in her pocket.

Her control officer, Simon, answered immediately, and Jet spoke in rapid-fire Hebrew, her voice low.

"There's a problem. I was able to get off the grounds, but it got messy, and now I've got a hit team hunting me. They were at my hotel, so my passport and phone are compromised. I need an extraction, and quick."

Simon grunted. "There's another wrinkle. We've been monitoring the police channels for chatter, and an APB went out on you a little while ago – murder. So airports are out."

"Murder? I didn't hit the guard hard enough for it to be lethal."

"Gunshot. Reports describe you as armed and dangerous. Where are you?"

"In a dive bar. I don't have much money, and no ID besides my company badge."

"Ditch it. They have your Gabriela name. That's blown."

"Then what?"

"Bars stay open late. Call me in an hour. Let me see what HQ can put together."

"I'm dead meat come morning. They have my photo from the company and my passport. As soon as it's light out, game over."

"Which is why I said call in an hour."

Jet replaced the handset and walked into the women's room, her nose wrinkling at the stench. She counted her money and saw that she had the equivalent of a hundred and twenty euros – more than enough to nurse a beer, but not enough to do anything more meaningful, especially with the police looking for her.

She splashed water on her face and washed the grime off her hands and, after blotting herself dry, returned to the bar and ordered a beer and a bottle of mineral water. She paid and carried the drinks to one of the little tables that dotted the floor, and drank greedily from the water before taking a sip of the beer, which was there for show. A few of the male patrons appraised her, and one of the younger approached with a swagger and an oily smile that probably worked wonders with the local girls. He flashed a mouth of crooked teeth and said something in Estonian, which Jet ignored, giving him her best thousand-yard stare. His smile faded several degrees, and he tried again in Russian.

"Looking for some company?"

"I'm waiting for my boyfriend," she replied.

"I wouldn't leave you alone in a dump like this if I was your boyfriend."

"Which you aren't," she said, her tone unfriendly.

"Hey. I'm just trying to be–"

She cut him off. "Look, I'm sure you're a nice guy, but I want you to leave me alone. I'm trying to think, and you're not helping. I'm not interested in what you're selling, so you're wasting both our time."

The man frowned and his eyes hardened, and when he turned to return to the bar, he muttered something distinctly hostile sounding in Estonian. She supposed she could have been nicer, but she'd had enough drama for one night and didn't need the local wolves circling and adding to her woes.

Jet sipped her beer while occasionally checking the time, and after fending off another clumsy solicitation by an even younger man who was clearly a couple of drinks away from passing out, she retreated to the pay phone and called Simon again.

"We've got a way to get you out of Tallinn," he said.

"When?"

"As soon as you can make it down to the commercial marina. There's a captain who can take you across to Finland, no questions asked."

"Have you used him before?"

"No. But he comes recommended."

"By who?"

A pause. "A local smuggler. He uses the boat to ferry drugs to Finland. Heroin from Russia."

She fought to keep her voice down. "You set me up with a drug dealer?"

"I had an hour to find someone who could do the impossible for a murder suspect on the run. It's not like we have a huge network in Estonia. You're lucky we found anyone."

"Funny. I don't feel lucky." She paused. "And now I have to try to cross town in the middle of the night with the cops looking for me."

"I have a car. I can pick you up if you want. Give me the address."

She told him the street and bar name, and he signed off after saying he would be there in twenty minutes. Jet spent the next fifteen in the bathroom, not wanting to deal with the inebriates in the lounge, and when she emerged, she walked straight to the entrance without looking at the men she'd spurned.

The sidewalk was largely empty except for a few stragglers gathered in clumps to smoke and a homeless man, who was shuffling along, begging for change. Jet removed her last coins from her pocket and dropped them into his outstretched hand, and he mumbled a thanks in Estonian before moving on, trailing the pungent odor of unwashed clothes and dried urine.

An ancient Lada sedan rolled up, and Simon glanced through the windshield. She slid into the passenger seat, and he drove around the corner and parked. "Get in the trunk," he said.

Jet nodded, the move not unexpected. The police were looking for a woman. A single man driving a beater wouldn't trigger their radar, but a couple out at the late hour might.

"Night just keeps getting better and better," she said, and handed him the USB drives. "See to it those make it to the director tonight."

They stepped from the car and he opened the trunk, which was barely large enough for her to fit in with her knees to her chest. When the trunk lid closed, she was plunged into darkness, made worse once Simon pulled away and the shoddy suspension transmitted every rut and bump through the metal floor and into her hip, spine, and throbbing head.

Ten minutes into the drive, a siren whooped from behind the car, and Simon slowed and then stopped. Jet freed the pistol from her waistband and held it at the ready as a cop questioned him only a few feet from where she lay trapped. After an eternity of back and forth, the engine started and they were moving again, Jet still with the gun in her hand, any relief she'd felt at being picked up gone at the very real prospect of having to shoot her way out of a traffic stop.

Eventually the car rolled to a halt again, engine running. Simon appeared moments later and popped the trunk, his gaze roaming over the surroundings as she unfolded herself and stood on unsteady legs. The sharp tang of salt air burned Jet's nostrils as she returned the pistol to the small of her back, and Simon's eyes finally settled on her.

"Boat you're looking for is the *Arkady*. Captain's name is Jaagup. Said he's halfway down the last dock."

She stretched, ignoring the protests from her legs. "Get the data to HQ as soon as you can."

"Will do." He sniffed at the combination of rotting seaweed and dead fish wafting from the dock area. "Nice night for a sail. My counterpart will meet you in Helsinki. You're to call him when you arrive. Name's Moishe." He rattled off a number.

Jet repeated it and then moved toward the water at a trot. She disappeared into the light fog hanging over the waterfront, to where a sad collection of fishing scows bobbed and strained at their lines in the dark, the area silent except for the rustling of feathers from a few seabirds perched atop pilings and the clump of her footsteps on the slippery dock.

# Chapter 23

*Nice, France*

It was a few hours before dawn when Sergei knocked on Karev's bedroom door and pushed it open without waiting for a response. The security chief switched on the lights and Karev jolted awake. He blinked groggily and stared daggers through Sergei.

"What is it?" he barked.

"We need to move again. Something's happened."

Karev waited for Sergei to continue. Sergei approached the bed and spoke in a quiet voice. "Tanya's been kidnapped."

"What?"

"As you know, she was in Ibiza. Her security detail went dark six hours ago. When we couldn't raise them after an hour of trying, I had one of the men fly there to assess the situation in person. The report isn't good. He says the whole group's vanished, Tanya included. All of their things are still at the hotel, but nobody's seen them since they left an event they were attending – some kind of rave or concert. What we know is that she parked her car with the valet. It's still there, and the party's going strong. The valets said that she and her friend Liv were last seen with a couple of young men in a red Ferrari. The security detail followed them in their own car…and that's the last anyone saw of them."

"How can four armed men and their vehicle disappear? They have phones. They would have sent out some sort of distress call if they were under attack."

"That's the protocol. But it obviously wasn't followed."

"What about the girls' cells? Pay off the police and have them track them."

"We already did that. They're not showing up. So they either destroyed the phones or removed the batteries."

"And the guards?"

"Same story."

Karev thought for a second. "Who owns the Ferrari?"

"Checking. Likely a rental on that small an island. But if this is a kidnapping, they'll have used a fake passport and driver's license. Probably paid in cash. You know the drill."

Karev's stare darkened. "This has to be that fat prick."

Sergei shook his head. "Not necessarily."

"Come on. Who else would dare? And the timing…"

"I believe it's him. But my point is, we can't be sure."

"You should have foreseen this."

"I instructed the men not to allow the girls to go anywhere, but Tanya refused to cooperate."

"You should have forced her!"

"You know her. She's nineteen and headstrong. Short of cuffing her, they couldn't do anything."

"I would have approved it." Karev glowered at Sergei. "Has he contacted us?"

"Not yet. But he will. Assuming it's him."

"It is." Karev paused to think. "This is beyond personal. He's taken a business disagreement and crossed a host of lines."

"I'd say destroying your boat and killing your men qualifies," Sergei said.

"You know there are at least a dozen people who want me dead. But how many would be foolhardy enough to risk the blowback from kidnapping Tanya? None of them are suicidal. That leaves the one man who has nobody and believes himself to be untouchable. It's him. I know it."

"I'm not disagreeing. I'm simply saying that until he contacts us, we can't assume we know anything but that Tanya is missing."

"She's never disappeared like this. She knows better."

"I have the local police searching for her in an unofficial capacity. We don't need the media involved."

"Send as many men as you require. Tear the island apart."

Sergei's voice softened. "We'll do the best we can, but it's unlikely we'll get anywhere. They knew what they were doing if they were able to take down the security detail. That tells me they did their homework. Those men were all ex-Spetsnaz."

"Then where does that leave us?"

"Waiting for them to contact you."

Karev scowled. "Him. There is no them. You may not be certain, but I am. The use of drones, the timing of the attack, and now Tanya…" Karev shook his head. "I want him to pay. I don't care what it costs. He's a dead man. And if he's harmed a hair on her head…there's no punishment too harsh, no torture too sustained. I'll make it take weeks."

"We'll do everything we can, but the first thing we need to do is to move you to a more secure location. Which means back to Russia. You're too exposed here."

Karev glared at Sergei. "Listen to me. The man tried to kill me, and now he's taken my daughter. I want you to bring the full weight of the Russian state to bear. Call in whatever favors you need to. He won't get away with this."

Sergei nodded. "I'll contact everyone and alert them to the situation. But they won't be willing to take action unless we have hard evidence he's behind the attack and the kidnapping. A hunch won't do it. No disrespect intended."

Karev's glare intensified. "Just do it."

"I will. Right now, we need to get to the airport. I've chartered a jet to take us home."

"I don't turn tail and run, Sergei."

"Nobody's asking you to. But I'm responsible for keeping you alive, and I can't do my job in an uncontrolled environment. Nice is too unfamiliar. I don't want to hand your enemies an advantage. You need to trust me on this."

"I want my daughter back."

"And I'll move heaven and earth to do it," Sergei assured him. "But for now, I've got vehicles waiting downstairs. We can discuss this on the plane."

Sergei's men helped Karev into a wheelchair with an IV stand, and two of them flanked the oligarch in the elevator while Sergei stood behind them. At the parking garage level, they pushed the chair to a silver van and loaded him into the back. A white SUV sat with its engine idling a few meters away, with four more of Sergei's gunmen behind tinted glass, watching the garage entrance, submachine guns at the ready. A BMW 7 Series waited beside it with another of Sergei's men behind the wheel.

Sergei's cell rang, and he stared at the screen in puzzlement for a second before answering. He listened for five seconds and then walked to where Karev waited and handed him the phone.

"I have your daughter," a robotic, synthesized voice said.

"You're a dead man," Karev spat.

"Let's not waste time. She'll be fine as long as you keep your mouth shut. Open it, and she's dead."

"How do I know she isn't already?"

"That isn't how I roll. You of all people should know that by now."

"You tried to kill me."

"We had a deal. You reneged. That was…inconvenient, although I was able to recover. But in my world, there are either allies or enemies. When you failed to perform as promised, you became my enemy. You're privy to sensitive information. I can't afford to have that in my enemy's possession."

"You didn't deliver. I was forced to take matters into my own hands at great expense. You didn't earn your money. As to your other scheme, I told you I want no part of it. You're insane."

"You know too much. Since you survived, I needed leverage. Your daughter has had to pay that price. Keep your mouth shut and you'll get the little slut back in one piece. If not, I'll deliver her in boxes."

The line went dead. Karev stared at the handset like it was a live scorpion, and then handed it to Sergei, who removed the battery and threw it across the garage.

"This phone isn't listed anywhere. The only place he could have gotten it was from Tanya. So at least we know she's alive."

"I knew it was him," Karev hissed. "He's completely mad. All of this is to ensure our silence."

"We need to move. If he was able to triangulate my phone, we could be hit at any moment."

The men rolled the Russian into the van and locked his wheels before strapping the contrivance to eyelets in the ribbing. When Karev was secure, Sergei slid the side door closed, marched to the BMW, and climbed into the passenger seat.

The big sedan led the way out of the garage, and the van and SUV followed as it sped down the street toward the airport highway. There was no traffic in the predawn, but the convoy proceeded cautiously, wanting to avoid a confrontation with any overzealous police working the graveyard shift. The vehicles kept to the speed limit and were approaching the airport private terminal entrance when a delivery van skidded to a stop ahead of them, blocking the access road. Two more vans pulled from a side street and boxed them in from behind.

The gunmen in the SUV leapt out and moved to defend Karev's vehicle, but a hail of rounds from the vans cut them down as they fired at the attackers. Karev's driver and bodyguards threw open the van doors and fired, using them as cover, and the attackers concentrated their fire on them as Sergei's driver floored the accelerator and the big BMW skidded off the road, around the blocking van, and sped toward the airport.

Six black-clad figures with balaclavas concealing their faces closed on Karev's van as the gunmen in the chase vehicles laid down covering fire. The skirmish was over in moments as the Russians died, picked off by shooters with night vision scopes, who dispatched them with surgical precision.

The masked gunmen approached Karev's van at a run and, after confirming that the guards were dead, swung the side door open and regarded Karev. He swore at them in Russian and swung at them with his cast, but two of them restrained him while a third emptied the contents of a syringe into his IV line.

Karev continued to curse, but his voice grew thick, and then his chin dropped to his chest. The gunmen lifted the wheelchair from the bed and rushed it to the box van in front, and had Karev stowed in the rear in no more than thirty seconds.

The vehicles turned around and raced away from the Russian's convoy, leaving six men dead and three wounded sprawled on the asphalt in the faint predawn glow. By the time their lights had vanished in the darkness, the last of the wounded had expired, their blood black on the pavement, fingers clenched like claws as they'd fought for their last breaths.

# Chapter 24

*Helsinki, Finland*

Oliver sat at his bedroom table, tapping the cart's screen, a glass of juice and a snack on a tray beside him. A soft rapping sound from the doorway startled him, and he stopped what he was doing.

"Yes?"

The door opened and Lars stepped in. Oliver waved a greeting and returned to his screen. "So you made it."

"As soon as I could. Nothing more I can do in Tallinn right now." He hesitated. "She managed to evade our team at the hotel. They got off some shots, but nothing."

"This is like some kind of nightmare," Oliver growled. "When did I start hiring incompetents?"

"We both know they're the best. They were just a little too late. But not to worry. The police are scouring the city for her. She can't move without being seen. It's just a matter of time."

"You say that with such assurance. I'm afraid I can't share your optimism. She's managed to penetrate our defenses, break into a secure building, escape a score of guards, and slip past our top wet team."

"The police are erecting roadblocks. The trains and airport are being watched. Her photograph is being circulated. Her passport and money were at the hotel. There's no way she can leave the country."

"You assume she can't get new documents. If this is what it's beginning to look like, I wouldn't be so sure. And you know the border with Russia is porous in places. If she's working for the Russian…"

"Have you given any thought to the daughter?"

Oliver laughed. "Why should I? She's serving her purpose. There's no way Karev will move against me as long as we have her. And soon it won't matter what he does. He managed to cheat fate once, but he won't again. As soon as he shows his face, he's a dead man."

"I don't like how he just vanished from the Nice condo."

"We had to expect him to eventually wise up. Or at least his security people to start doing a better job. This is a temporary setback."

"And the other matter?"

Oliver tapped the screen again and stared at it for a few moments before answering. "Everything is going according to plan. By this time tomorrow, all of the nodes will have downloaded the software. At that point, there's nothing they can do but pay us."

"You know they won't."

Oliver sighed. "I know they won't want to. But once we demonstrate exactly how destructive our little worm is, they'll acquiesce."

"If the prison didn't do it…"

"That was nothing compared to what's coming next. They'll be begging to hand us the money by the time we're done." He checked the time in the corner of the screen. "We need to move. I was waiting for your arrival. I don't feel comfortable here. It's too easy to track my helicopter's flight logs."

"I arranged a charter plane, as you requested. No passenger manifest. Paid in cash."

"Then let's get to the airport." He looked around the room. "I'll miss this, but we do what we must. I've already put it up for sale. It'll be listed next week."

"A shame. I've always liked the place," Lars said.

"There's no choice. Once the software triggers, I'm going underground for at least five years. I can operate the company remotely from anywhere. But it'll be too hot to stay anywhere I could be located."

Lars nodded. He didn't understand his master, but he was paid well, so didn't need to. The man was already worth several billion dollars; another four billion from the Israelis wouldn't change anything for him. Yet he was risking everything for the most audacious heist in history.

Which was the only part that made any sense. Oliver was obsessed with being the best at anything he tried, so it only followed that if he was going to turn to blackmail, he was going to do it on an epic scale.

Lars suspected that there was something else at play behind his motivations to target Israel, but they never discussed it. Oliver had always done as he pleased, and nothing Lars could say would dissuade him from finishing out this hand.

Of course, Lars also would benefit from the ploy – he would be the public face of the company once Oliver was out of the picture, and would be paid a king's ransom to sell off the various pieces of the organization to suitors eager for the accumulated know-how and book of business. Because Oliver shunned publicity, the company wasn't widely associated with being his creature, and Lars had for years handled the few interviews and puff pieces fed to the media. As far as most were concerned, Oleco Industries was just another tech company piloted by faceless engineers and administrators, which was indeed true of the legitimate arm.

The special projects section would simply shut down, the sound stage dismantled, the staff scattered to the four winds, its dealings on the dark web and all evidence of its criminal activities sanitized.

Oliver swallowed the rest of his juice and set the plate of pastries on his cart tray, and then backed away from the desk using the joystick in the armrest.

"I'm all packed. Bag is downstairs," he said.

"Then let's do this," Lars agreed, and walked to the bedroom door. "I'll see you at the entrance."

Oliver had a special elevator that just fit his cart. All guests took the stairs. It was another idiosyncrasy that he couldn't tolerate close proximity to others, and the thought of anyone being in his elevator with him made his skin crawl. He wheeled himself along the marbled hall to the gleaming steel door, which opened when it sensed his cart nearing, and he smiled in satisfaction at how perfectly the technology worked.

"Soon," he whispered to himself. "Soon."

# Chapter 25

*Tallinn, Estonia*

The *Arkady* turned out to be an old fishing trawler with copper seams of rust trailing down the hull into the water. Jet approached, eyeing it skeptically, and stopped at the sight of a glowing ember moving along the back deck. She squinted to make out whether there was more than one man on the boat, and when she saw only one figure in the dark, she called out softly.

"Jaagup?"

"That's right," he replied in Russian. "You must be my passenger. Hop on and I'll start the engine so we can get underway."

Jet stepped over the gunwale onto the crusty deck, the vessel's rank mix of diesel fuel and fish guts as noxious as tear gas. Jaagup didn't move to help her aboard, instead tossing the hand-rolled cigarette stub over the side and heading to the pilothouse.

The motor sputtered to life on the first try. Jet watched Jaagup examine the cluster of instruments and then move to the bow to cast off the mooring line. It splashed in the inky water, and he repeated the process on the stern line before returning to the helm and putting the boat in gear.

Jet joined him in the pilothouse, where the stench wasn't as powerful, and eyed the controls dubiously. "This thing's seaworthy?"

"Sure. Don't let the exterior fool you. The mechanical and electrical are first class. See? The radar's new, and the autopilot will take us straight to the Finnish dock using the GPS coordinates. Only complication is the weather could be better. Seas could be pretty rough on the crossing. You get seasick?" he asked.

"No."

"That's good. It's not the North Sea, but it can still get snotty."

"Your bilge pumps work well, I hope?"

He dipped his head and offered her a yellowed grin. "Even have a few life preservers around here somewhere."

The boat steamed out of the harbor, and the wind-driven swells picked up almost immediately. "How long will it take to get to Helsinki?" she asked.

"Maybe five hours. Depends on the prevailing winds and the sea conditions."

"What is it – seventy-five kilometers?"

"About that."

She regarded the back deck. "So speed isn't one of this thing's attributes."

"I'm rarely in a hurry. Attracts too much attention if an old rust bucket like this was cruising along at twenty knots."

"Will it actually do that?"

"Hypothetically. We'll be doing around ten."

"I could swim faster," she grumbled.

"You're welcome to try. But the hypothermia would get you in a few minutes." He felt in his peacoat for a packet of tobacco and, after engaging the autopilot, tapped out a slug onto a cigarette paper and rolled another smoke. "You can go below if you're cold. I've got blankets, and it's warmer out of the wind. The bunks are serviceable, and the galley's fairly well stocked."

Jet considered the situation and headed to the companionway that led to the cabins. The wooden ladder was worn from decades of use, but the galley and staterooms were surprisingly clean. She made herself a cup of hot tea, ignoring the hull's increasing pitching, and sat at the chart table while the single engine droned monotonously. She yawned and considered napping, but decided to keep an eye on Jaagup instead – something about him gave her the creeps, and she trusted her instincts. It could have been because she knew he was a drug smuggler, but she preferred staying in the pilothouse to trusting a mercenary who willingly transported poison for profit.

She was halfway up the ladder when she heard him speaking

softly. A few seconds went by and the radio squawked, the volume turned low, and another voice answered. Both were speaking Russian, so she understood the gist of the discussion, which confirmed her impression of the good captain: he'd just told whoever he was talking to that he'd relay their coordinates in a moment.

Jet's arrival in the pilothouse startled Jaagup, and he set the radio mic back in place with a furtive look. Jet faced him with her hands on her hips.

"Who were you talking to?" she demanded.

"Navy. Wanted to log my run," he said.

"Why were you speaking Russian instead of Estonian?"

His response took a moment too long as he thought of a believable answer. "It's the language the armed forces uses on hailing channels."

She nodded as though she believed him. "How fast will this thing actually go?"

"I've had her up to seventeen knots, but not in seas like this."

"Show me."

"You won't like it."

The Makarov appeared in her right hand, and she trained the weapon on him. "I'm not going to ask you twice."

Jaagup's expression darkened. "What the hell do you think you're doing?"

"I heard you giving our position to someone. I don't think it was the navy. Now firewall the throttle or I'll do it myself; in which case I don't need you, do I?"

He was faster than he appeared, and after thrusting the throttle forward, he used the sudden surge to spin and level a kick at her chest with one of his heavy boots. She'd been expecting a move and he missed, but not her parry, which was a kick of her own to his hip.

Jaagup threw himself at her with a howl of pain, and she fired once. The round caught him in the chest, but he kept coming and knocked the barrel aside. The bear hug he enveloped her in threatened to smother her, and she squeezed the trigger again. This time the shot punched into his stomach, and he screamed in agony as he released her and slid to the deck. She stepped away, pistol leveled at him, and gripped a handle as the boat pounded against the steep face of an oncoming wave.

She watched Jaagup struggle for breath as he bled out, and when he exhaled a final rasping groan, she turned to the helm. The speed gauge read fourteen knots, and she pushed the throttle even further forward, hoping to eke another few revs out of the craft. The engine was nearing the redline as the speedo climbed to sixteen, and she studied the radar for any blips that were approaching her.

The unit was set to twelve kilometers, and she increased the range to twenty-four and peered at the glowing screen. She didn't see anything suspect, so maybe she'd nipped the captain's betrayal before he could impart anything meaningful. Nevertheless, she kept the boat bashing into the waves, the engine laboring alarmingly for another hour, and only when she didn't see any signs of pursuit did she back off to a more comfortable speed.

Jet went through the dead man's pockets and removed a cell phone and his wallet, along with a fat wad of euros – whether Mossad money or whatever he'd been paid to sell her out, she didn't care. She suspected that there was a fast boat with gunmen aboard somewhere at one of the pleasure craft marinas that lined the Tallinn shore; but without a decent fix on her coordinates, in the dead of night in storm conditions she'd be almost impossible to catch, especially with at least a dozen other bogies on the screen, mostly fishing boats who'd braved the conditions to ply their trade.

She switched off the running lights, eyes glued to the radar so the boat didn't collide with anything, and the hours passed slowly, the pounding uncomfortable but bearable at the reduced speed. Somewhere around the halfway point she pushed Jaagup's corpse into the prop wash, consigning his remains to the sea so she wouldn't have to explain a dead man riddled with bullets, and washed down the bloody deck of the pilothouse with a saltwater hose from the fishing platform.

Once the body was gone and the deck clean, she switched the running lights back on and glanced at the autopilot, which told her she had an hour and forty-seven minutes to go until she arrived at the Helsinki dock. Her experience with the captain convinced her to err on the side of caution, so when she entered the commercial marina near Uspenski Cathedral, she continued past the waypoint set in the GPS and instead ran the boat aground several hundred meters beyond the dock that had been set as their destination, where there were only rocks. She leapt from the bow as steel shrieked in tortured protest, and was running in the darkness before any watchers would have a chance to react.

Jet didn't stop until she was well concealed behind a parked delivery truck, and after surveying the area, she moved stealthily to where she guessed Moishe would be waiting for their arrival – hopefully in a car, given the weather. She easily spotted the likely vehicle, its exhaust giving it away in the frigid air, but she took her time and did a sweep of the lot before sneaking up on it from behind.

The man behind the wheel jumped in surprise when she rapped on the passenger window, and he stiffened at the sight of her gun. He recovered quickly and unlocked her door and, when she swung it open, nodded in frosty greeting.

"Gabriela, I presume. Didn't see you come in."

She slid into the seat and pulled the door closed. "Your captain double-crossed us, so it didn't seem like a good idea to stick to the script."

He eyed the pistol. "I'm assuming you took care of it."

She set the gun in her lap. "I did. Let's get out of here. Never know how much he told them before I caught on."

"I have a safe house nearby. An apartment. It's clean."

"As long as it's got heat and a shower, it sounds perfect."

# Chapter 26

*Nice, France*

Karev inhaled deeply as he slowly regained consciousness. He moaned involuntarily and stirred, and fought to make sense out of a chaotic collage of memories – explosions, shooting, his security team being cut down like summer grass. His eyes fluttered open and he blinked away a dryness that seemed to extend from his corneas all the way down his throat, and forced himself to focus. Blurred images swam into view, and he could make out a lamp on a circular table. A man was seated beside it, texting on his phone.

Karev tried to clear his throat and speak. "What–"

The word was a croak that sounded alien to him. The man glanced at the Russian, stood, and moved out of sight. Karev tried to turn his head to follow him, but the muscles in his neck refused to obey, and all he could do was stare at the lamp like he was paralyzed.

Eventually he could move more than just his eyes, and sensation returned to his limbs with the prickly stinging of appendages to which circulation had suddenly returned. The sensation was reassuring but uncomfortable, and he remembered being injected with something just before he'd faded out. Whatever it was had done a number on him, to the point where trying to swallow required a monumental effort, and willing his fingers to move took every ounce of concentration he could muster.

A figure moved between the lamp and his position, and he tried to speak again.

"What...where...am...I?"

"Nicolai Karev, you've been a naughty boy. You're lucky that we're patient," the figure said in Russian.

"What…is this?"

"You're in good hands. We've taken you into custody, of a sort, for plotting crimes against our country."

"You killed my men."

"We had no alternative. But note that we spared your life."

"Why?"

"So that you can tell us what we need to know."

Karev closed his eyes. "None of this makes any sense. My daughter…"

"We don't care about your daughter. But if you ever want to see her again, you're going to have to cooperate with us. As you can see, we're serious."

"I don't understand what you want."

"We know about your partner."

Karev's head began to pound. "I don't have a partner."

"You know who we mean. Oliver Kalda."

Karev's eyes widened. "Him? He tried to kill me. And he kidnapped my daughter. He has her."

The man's face leaned into Karev's field of vision. He was middle-aged, with several days of beard coloring his jaw, his face largely unremarkable except for the intensity of his gaze. "What are you talking about?"

"First of all, Kalda isn't my partner. Second, he kidnapped my daughter after his attempt to murder me failed. What are you failing to understand?"

The man's expression hardened. "We know he's working with you. Lies will do you no good."

"Wrong. He was working *for* me. He's a hacker. But he kept increasing his rates while failing to deliver as promised, so I stopped paying him. That's when he tried to kill me. That's the entirety of our relationship. And now he has my daughter." Karev paused. "Whatever you believe you know is completely wrong."

"You say he was working for you. On what?"

"What do you care?" Karev snapped.

"You're in no position to ask questions."

Karev barely controlled his anger. "There's a natural gas pipeline proposal to bring supplies from Nigeria to Europe. It would greatly damage some of my interests. I hired him to mold public opinion against it. Whoever you are, it has nothing to do with you."

The man frowned. "Why did he kidnap your daughter? Just to get you to pay?"

Karev thought quickly and, when he answered, chose his words carefully. "To keep me from talking about something else he's involved in. The man's a braggart. He let slip that he was…he's far more dangerous than I thought when I hired him. Obviously. I've got a ruined yacht to show for it, and my daughter…you need to release me. I've done nothing to you."

"Tell me about this other thing he's involved in."

Karev's mouth tightened into a slit. "No. He made clear it would mean my daughter's life if I breathed a word of it."

"It sounds like that's what we're interested in."

"You can do whatever you like to me, but if it's a choice between my life or my daughter's, there's nothing to discuss."

The man left Karev to ruminate on the impasse. When he returned, Karev felt like his faculties had fully recovered, and he was sharp as ever, the after-effects of the drug having left his system. He turned his head to face the interrogator, who was accompanied by another, older man. The interrogator stepped aside, and the other man spoke.

"I understand Oliver Kalda kidnapped your daughter."

"That's right. From Ibiza."

"Tell me about your relationship with him. Why he did this."

"I already told him," Karev said, indicating the interrogator.

"Humor me."

Karev repeated the account and finished with his warning that he wasn't going to say anything more. "You need to release me so I can get her back. At that point I'll gladly tell you everything you want to know."

"I'm afraid that's not possible."

"You're holding me illegally."

"I prefer to call it extrajudicially. But no reason to split hairs. Mr. Karev, my country is facing a monumental threat, which we believe you have material information about. We can either do this the civilized way or the...unpleasant way."

"Do you have children?" Karev asked.

"That isn't the question."

"If you did, you'd understand that if it is a choice between sacrificing your child's life or your own, you'll choose your own. Hard to explain to someone without kids."

"There's obviously no guarantee that your daughter's still alive, much less that he'll release her if you do as he wishes."

"I have unlimited resources. I'll find her in short order. If you're who I believe you are, you'll know where to find me once I do. I'm high profile. It's not like I'm hard to locate."

"I don't doubt that you'll do everything you can to find her, but my problem is that there is no way my superiors will release you. That said, perhaps there's a solution that will get us both what we want."

Karev waited for the man's proposal. When it came, he fought to keep from showing any emotion, and nodded slowly.

"That could work. But if it fails, it will be on your head."

"Our operatives aren't prone to failure. As your security team discovered. You say she was taken in Ibiza? Tell me everything you know. Time's wasting."

# Chapter 27

*Helsinki, Finland*

Jet sat on the edge of the bed in the safe house with yet another new encrypted cell phone clamped to her ear. She'd gotten three hours of sleep before Moishe had roused her with the news that the director wanted to speak to her – that an advance team had scouted out what they had believed was Oliver's Finland mansion, only to find it deserted.

The director sounded more fatigued than Jet did.

"That's where we are," he said, finishing his account. "We cut a deal with the Russian to find his daughter and spring her in return for all the information he has on Kalda."

"Which may be nothing," Jet pointed out. "He could be playing us."

"Our people don't get that impression. Which brings me to my proposal. We're at a dead end now that Kalda's disappeared. His helicopter is still on the pad at the airport, but there's no trace of him. But if we can find the daughter, we have a chance of finding him. The Russian wants blood, and he says he knows where to find Kalda. But not until the daughter's safe."

"You want me to go to Ibiza? You're more than aware that sort of…investigation…isn't my specialty."

"We have nothing for you to do in Finland. The station chief is having a passport prepared so you can travel. It should be ready in a few hours. This is all part of the same operation, which is to neutralize the cyber threat. It's still existential, which means that you're still on the board."

"You could always let me go home."

"I need my best people on this. You're closer to Spain than we are, you speak the language, you're up to speed on the players, and you don't require hand-holding. You're our best shot."

Jet took a moment before she responded. "We need to have a candid discussion when this is over. I feel like a ping-pong ball, and you're making it pretty clear you're ignoring my veto power."

"I don't have a choice. This will be the end of the country if we don't stop him. That will affect all of us. Even you."

"Do you have anyone on Ibiza to run logistics?"

"No, but one of our Madrid hub knows the island well. He'll fly in as your advance team and secure you the usual items."

"Was Karev able to give you any leads to follow, or am I going in blind?"

"We know the concert venue where she was grabbed. We're working on something associated with that, and by the time you touch down this evening, we hope to have it."

"You realize there's a good chance that I won't be able to locate her, or that she's already been removed from the island, right?"

"Yes. But all journeys start with the first step. And this is all we've got."

"Anything more on the malware?"

"We've got our top people working on it."

Jet could tell by his tone that he was irritated at being questioned by an operative, but she felt that she needed to reestablish her autonomy. He was now using her like she was one of his assets, which she wasn't. She was a free agent, a troubleshooter and a specialized talent, and she was getting fed up at being ferried around Europe without any clear plan in mind.

"I'm going back to sleep until the passport is ready," she said. "Have you got any solution for the photos of me that the Estonians are circulating?"

"I'd advise you to modify your hair and makeup, but beyond that, the furor should die down soon enough. Although they're claiming you shot the shift supervisor, not that you delivered a lethal blow."

"I never fired a shot."

"Immaterial. This is a local matter, and unless you have some plans I'm unaware of to vacation in Tallinn, you're in no jeopardy."

"Then it hasn't gone out to Interpol?"

"No. Obviously their thinking is that you won't be able to cross a border without your passport, so you're trapped in Estonia. No point circulating it and potentially embarrassing themselves with how labile their border is."

"The new passport will be Spanish as well?"

"That seems best. Someone will come over and take a photo later today as the last step. Modify your appearance accordingly – the last one had you in your mid-thirties. This one will put you in your late twenties."

"Let's hope I can pull that off on no sleep after being chased halfway to the Arctic Circle."

"I have nothing but faith in you."

The line went dead, and Jet thumbed the phone off. The only reason she hadn't put up more of a fight was because she could put herself in the Russian's place and imagine how she'd feel if someone snatched Hannah. Even if she'd been chartered with executing him days before, it was impossible for her not to empathize with him. She yawned, checked the time, and made a mental note to wake up in two more hours. The catnap would refresh her, and hopefully some judiciously applied makeup and a different hairstyle would trick the camera into believing she was younger than she'd been in years – and that she'd felt in what seemed like a lifetime.

## Chapter 28

*Ibiza, Spain*

The sun was setting by the time Jet landed at Ibiza airport, after a short hop on a commuter flight from Madrid and the three-hour trek from Helsinki. She'd had no issues passing through document control, her likeness as twenty-six-year-old Lupe Castro so different from the matronly Gabriela Mendez she'd been only a day before that she was almost unrecognizable, which was the point.

She took a taxi to a popular waterfront restaurant, paid the driver, and looked for a green Fiat coupe in the parking lot. She spied it near a grove of trees at the farthest point from the entrance and plodded over with her new carry-on containing a change of clothes and a rudimentary makeup and hygiene kit.

A tall, good-looking man with black hair and an easy smile got out of the car as she neared and held his arms out for an embrace. Jet obliged for anyone who might have been watching, and whispered to him as she hugged him.

"Were you able to get everything?"

"Yes. We can talk about it on the way to the hotel."

"Is the place decent?"

"It'll do. Low profile. Noisy from all the partying kids, but not too bad considering the season." He tried his smile again. "I'm Dov."

"Lupe."

He pointed to a nylon backpack on the tiny rear seat. "There's a compact 9mm and two magazines in that bag along with a stiletto and a few other odds and ends." He started the engine. "Where shall we start?"

"Hotel. And there's no *we* – there's just me. I'll need you to work the phones and computers."

"That's fine. Have you ever been to Ibiza?"

"No."

"I have, many times, so I know my way around. I can show you where she was last seen."

Jet turned to him. "Don't take this the wrong way, but I work alone in the field. I can find what I need with a nav program. I want to drop my stuff off and get started. I'm expecting some intel from headquarters."

"I have the latest. There was some footage from the rave the girls were attending. Somebody outside on a cell phone when they took off in the Ferrari. Our people are running the faces through a facial-recognition program in case the kidnappers are in a database, which is a safe bet if this is a straight money deal."

"Any idea when they'll have a result?"

"As soon as possible."

She gave him a dirty look. "Can you be any more nonspecific?"

"Those were their exact words. But I got the impression by some time this evening."

"Once I'm checked in, I'll swing by the venue. Is it a club where there's activity every night?"

"More of an outdoor concert area, but yes, this time of year they have a nightly theme party, so there will be people there. Although I'm not sure what good that will do."

She gave a humorless smile. "Which is why I want you on a desk while I'm in the field."

That quieted Dov, and they drove the rest of the way without speaking. Jet inventoried the weapons while he navigated to the hotel, which was an older four-story with a faded façade located well off the beach. When they pulled to the curb, groups of scantily clad youths were congregating near the entrance and on several of the balconies, drinking beer and mingling. Dance music thumped from one of the rooms. Jet got out of the car and walked to the office with her bags, and the clerk signed her in without so much as a glance at her passport.

Dov had told her that he was in the room next door, and after she stowed her few things, she slipped the gun into her waistband, pocketed one of the magazines, snatched her phone off the table, and knocked on the connecting door. Dov opened an instant later, and she checked the time.

"What's your number?" she asked.

He gave her a Madrid cell number. "I'll send whatever we get from HQ to your phone as soon as we get it. And I'll call if we get a match on the kidnappers."

"Fair enough. I'll need the car."

He tossed her the keys. "Good luck."

"I'm not expecting much. But we have to give it our best shot."

The venue was on a hill overlooking the harbor, and she took her time on the winding road, the window down, the balmy breeze a welcome relief after the Tallinn and Helsinki nights. She was pulling into the venue when her phone chirped.

"Yes?"

"We got a hit on one of the kidnappers. He's a mercenary. Algerian. Former French Foreign Legion. Name's Alain Granger. Twenty-seven. Freelancing for three years. Involved in wet work in Chad, the Congo, and Libya. A real charmer."

Her phone pinged and she checked the screen. A photo of a handsome young man with olive skin stared back at her.

"Have them scan flight and ferry records," she instructed. "See if he's still on the island."

"Already put in the request."

"Anything else?"

"We're also pulling some favors with the local police."

"Jesus. No. Just…no. That's the fastest way to put professionals on alert."

"Wasn't my call. Apparently there are a few officers who've been helpful before. All they're doing is pulling hotel and villa records to see if he's registered anywhere."

"Waste of time." A professional would have used a fake ID when committing a crime. Even a lower-level merc would be able to come up with that. Half the storefronts in Marseille could gin up a respectable identity card in an hour for the right price.

"Just keeping you informed," Dov said.

"Call me if anything material comes up. I'm at the…place."

She terminated the discussion and swung into a parking space. The lot was half empty, no doubt due to the relatively early hour. Jet knew from her time in Spain that clubs would often stay open until dawn, and that few would go out before midnight – and often, that was just when dinner was starting.

Jet entered the venue, which was really just a field enclosed by a wall with two bars at one end and a stage with a DJ booth and lighting scaffolding above it, and looked for anything that might help her – CCTV cameras being the most obvious. Unfortunately the owners hadn't deemed it necessary to install any except over the cash registers to monitor those handling the money, and after a sweep of the area, she retraced her steps outside.

Jet smiled at the valets. "You guys remember a red Ferrari here from a few nights ago? Convertible?"

One of the young men rolled his eyes. "Sure. A Mondial. Piece of crap rental a couple of poseurs were driving. Why are so many people interested in it?"

"Oh. Did someone else ask?"

"Yeah. Some big guy, looked like his face had been rearranged with a hammer. Few nights ago."

"Probably insurance," Jet deflected. "Have you seen the pair who were driving it since then?"

The valets shook their heads. "There are a lot of places in Ibiza. You could hit three a night and never repeat for a couple of weeks."

She decided to change her approach. "Who rents Ferraris on the island?"

"Lola's Exotics. Downtown, by the marina."

"Think they'd still be open?"

One of the valets checked the time. "Maybe. I've seen people in there late a few times. But can't say for sure."

Jet returned to the Fiat and called Dov to tell him about Lola. "Can you see if someone can hack into their network? Should be a piece of cake for our techs."

"I'll relay the request."

Her next stop was the car rental office, which was dark. She looked through the iron gate at ten exotic vehicles and spotted the red Mondial near the back, next to a canary yellow Porsche 911 Turbo S and a lime green Lamborghini Huracán. Her phone rang and she answered as she walked back to the Fiat.

"Car was rented by Mansour Gharbi," Dov said. "Probably a fake name. But we're still running it against the hotel and villa database in case they got lazy."

"They might have. Probably figured Karev's people wouldn't involve the police. If so, they might have used only one layer of fakes."

"Which the Russians would eventually piece together as well."

"It would take civilians a week, minimum." A thought occurred to her. "Also have them look at room and villa rentals that started a day or two before the kidnapping. They'd have arrived early to set up the sting. It happened on a Thursday, so have them look at Tuesday through Thursday – those wouldn't be huge travel days. Also have them check on boat registries in the harbor. Could be they stayed on one."

"Good catch. I'm on it." Dov hesitated. "There's no record on the ferry or airline passenger manifests of Alain Granger arriving or leaving the island."

"Run Mansour Gharbi and see if anything comes up."

Jet walked to the water and looked out at the marinas. The ones on her left were for smaller private craft and were packed to capacity with sailboats and motor yachts. To the right was yet another harbor, this one occupied by larger mega-yachts. A pair of ferries were tethered to a pier at the base of a hill covered with white and khaki private homes, the rise topped by an ancient cathedral built from beige stone, its tower the highest visible point against a backdrop of twinkling stars.

She returned to the car and drove back toward the venue. As she ground through the gears, a thought popped into her mind, and she called Dov.

"Have HQ check the cell towers around the concert. We know from the time stamp on the video when they took off. See if anyone was making calls right around then."

"That could take some time."

"So better get started."

Jet pulled over and regarded the cell tower that had given her the idea. It was a long shot, but so was everything involved in finding the daughter. She closed her eyes and tried to imagine how things had gone down that night – according to the Russian, the bodyguards had suddenly gone dark, as had their phones. How had the kidnappers accomplished that?

Her first thought was an ambush, which would have had to have happened on the road she was on. Her phone trilled, interrupting her thought, and she held it to her ear.

"We may have something," Dov said.

"May?"

"They ran the list of rentals, as you requested. No Mansour Gharbi, but we cross-referenced against our list of known bad guys, and a name popped up: Sahid Bouzidi. A Libyan arms dealer. Rented a villa on the other side of the island on Wednesday for a week."

"I don't know. Ibiza's like Monte Carlo or Cannes. You can probably throw a rock and hit ten scumbags."

"It's the timing. Also, remember that Alain was involved in wet work in Libya. Could be coincidence. Or could be that Bouzidi was involved, and he reached out to him for this op as well."

Jet nodded to herself. The reasoning wasn't terrible. "Anything on the cell tower?"

"No. I'll let you know when I hear."

"You have an address for the villa?"

"Sending to your phone."

She entered the location into her nav program, which informed her that it was located up the coast, near Punta Arabi, on the water. According to the map it was only twelve kilometers, but nearly an hour due to the condition of the roads.

Absent any other leads, it seemed worth following up on, so she put the car in gear and pulled back onto the road, her thoughts filled with speculation about a kidnapped girl who might not even still be alive.

# Chapter 29

Jet parked around a bend from the villa and approached it on foot, the darkness near total on the unlit road. As she drew closer, she could make out a few guards with machine guns inside the gates. That was promising, although not definitive – it was entirely possible that an arms merchant required serious security, although on Ibiza it seemed unlikely. She'd switched her phone to vibrate, and when it tremored in her pocket, she withdrew it quickly, eyes locked on the villa.

"Yes?"

"Mansour Gharbi arrived via air on Wednesday. There's no record of him leaving. So it's likely he's still on the island." Dov paused expectantly. "Your cell tower idea hit pay dirt. There were three calls within five minutes of the Ferrari driving off. Two of the numbers are dark, but the third's still on the island. It's showing as inside the villa."

She nodded, her hunch confirmed. "The place has a security detail. Well armed."

"You don't see that often here. This isn't Moscow or Beirut."

"That was my thinking."

Jet studied the layout from behind a tree. The villa faced the ocean, but if the shoreline was anything like the rest of the island, there was a better than fifty percent chance it was sheer rock instead of sand, making an entry from the water difficult, if not impossible.

"Can you pull up satellite on the area?" she asked.

"Sure. But it won't be current."

"Doesn't matter. I want to know whether it fronts onto beach or rock."

"Right. Give me a minute." The line went quiet, and then he was back. "Looks like rock. High bluffs maybe ten meters above sea level."

"That's what I was afraid of."

"You might be able to make it, although it would be a hell of a climb. Depends. Hard to make out from the satellite."

"Sounds like a last resort. Figures they'd choose a defensible location." She exhaled in frustration. "I'll call if I need anything else."

"Roger that."

Jet considered the adjacent homes, both of which were dark. Maybe she could get onto the grounds and scale one of the perimeter walls? The guards were watching the road, so they wouldn't be expecting a threat from a neighbor.

She was debating the practicality when a taxi rounded the bend. It slowed as it drove past her and stopped at the villa gate. The rear doors opened and three scantily clad young women climbed out, giggling as they toddled on impossibly high heels to the gate. She strained to hear what they said to the guards, and caught only snatches – they were here for the party.

The women looked like prostitutes to Jet, which gave her an idea.

Jet looked down at her clothes – black pants and a navy blue shirt – and frowned. *That won't work.*

She made her way along the road and, when the villa was out of sight, crossed to the ocean side and skulked along in the gloom, staying pressed against the rows of privacy hedges that shielded the homes from traffic. When she reached one of the neighboring houses, she peered through the gate, saw that there were no lights on inside, and hoisted herself over the ironwork in a few seconds.

Jet darted to the house and stopped at the first window. She studied the wooden frame and stopped when she spotted a small silver tab: an alarm contact. She would have been surprised if an expensive home hadn't been wired, but she thought it likely that the owners hadn't bothered with the second floor. To confirm her hunch, she shimmied up the drain pipe at the corner of the house and swung onto the cantera ledge of the closest second-story window.

Which also had a silver tab.

The trip back to the ground took only a few moments, and when she was back on terra firma, she considered her options. She could drive back into town; but no stores would be open, and she hadn't packed any clothes that would be suitable for a hooker. While all she'd really need would be something suitably skimpy, she'd burn too much time on a round trip and would likely come up empty. That left breaking into homes until she found something that would work.

Jet skirted the house until she found the electrical junction box. Her stiletto blade sprang into place with a snick, and she pried at the edges until the box popped open, revealing a host of contact points. She knew from her training that the alarm would be on its own breaker, and quickly found the likeliest connection. It never ceased to amaze her that installers all over the world used the same techniques, given how simple it was to disable an expensive system, but she was grateful for it. She quickly disconnected the power, thankful for the knife's rubberized handle.

She did the same with two other possible connections and then closed the box and went to find the telephone line, which took five minutes. She didn't bother with disconnecting it, but simply sliced through it with the knife so it wouldn't alert the police on the off chance that the home had a battery backup for the alarm power.

If it was an audible alarm and it had a backup, of course, she'd be screwed, but there was no way around it, so she had to take the risk.

Jet moved to a window on the side of the house furthest from the villa and tried it to confirm that it was locked. Sometimes housekeepers would forget to button up a vacation home, so it was worth a try, but she had no luck. Jet removed the pistol from her waistband and shattered the pane closest to the locking mechanism, cringing at the sound, which was louder than she'd expected. When sirens didn't wail from the home, she reached through, unlocked the window, and was inside the house in a flash.

There was enough light in the home to make it to the second-floor bedrooms, and she illuminated the light on her phone and rifled through a chest of drawers in the master until she found a pair of shorts that looked like they could fit. She pulled off her pants and slid the shorts on, and frowned – they were too long and loose for her purposes.

Jet tried the closet next, but the owners leaned toward modest clothing, and the women's outfits were what she'd have chosen if she were in her sixties. There was nothing she could see on the men's side of the rack she could modify, so breaking in had so far been a waste of energy. She scowled at the garments and was turning to try one of the guest bedrooms when something caught her eye.

A pair of black spandex bike shorts.

Jet lifted them from the hanger and tried them on, and smiled. They fit like a glove. She took them off and slit the stitching that held a saddle pad in place, and after removing it, donned them again and moved to the next bedroom.

A chest stood next to the closet door. She slid open the top drawer and spied a colorful halter top and several bikinis. She tried on the top, which barely fit, but she didn't mind the discomfort if it exaggerated her charms. After inspecting the effect in the bathroom mirror, Jet returned to the bedroom, rummaged through the closet, and found a pair of sandals that were close enough to her size to work. She removed her boots and slid them on, and then made for the stairs, keenly aware that time was slipping away.

Jet exited through the back door and stashed her clothes and weapons by the gate, reluctant to go into a potentially lethal situation unarmed, but seeing no alternative. Her outfit was deliberately skintight and left no room for anything more substantial than a sewing needle, so she'd have to wing it with whatever she could find. Not that she was that worried – she knew twenty ways to kill a man even without a weapon.

Back on the street, she padded to the Fiat and drove to the nearby coast town of Santa Eulària des Riu, where she parked by one of the beach hotels and walked to its taxi stand. The drivers looked her over with knowing grins, and Jet sat in the back seat of the first in line and waited for the man to get behind the wheel.

She gave him the villa address, wondering if she was making a mistake. The drive went by quickly, and soon the car was rolling up to the villa gate. She removed her wad of money from between her breasts, paid the driver, and then stepped from the car and walked to where the guards were standing.

"So? Am I late? Where's the party?" she asked with a wink.

The guards eyed her, and one of them pulled the gate open. "Your friends are already here."

She cocked a hip and pushed out her chest. "They're not my friends. More like competitors," she said. "Although not really."

The guards laughed and stepped aside and watched her the entire way as she sashayed toward the enormous villa, her walk rivaling anything in a high-end strip club. When she disappeared into the villa, the first turned to his companion. "Some guys have all the luck, you know?"

The other man rubbed his index finger against his thumb and chuckled. "Luck has nothing to do with it, you cheap bastard."

# CHAPTER 30

Jet pushed through the front door and passed through an elegantly decorated foyer to a cavernous living room large enough to park a commercial airliner. The other girls were seated on a massive leather sectional, and one was leaning forward to snort a line of powder off the glass coffee table. The women looked up as she entered, but Jet was more interested in the three men seated beside them.

She immediately recognized Alain Granger from his photo, but her face revealed nothing. He was leaning close to one of the prostitutes, his hand on her leg, his face flushed from drugs and alcohol. He glanced up at Jet in confusion, and the woman he was groping frowned.

"Who're you?" she demanded.

"I could ask the same question," Jet said.

Alain looked to an older man with a partially bald pate encircled with dark ringlets, seated in a chair by the pocket doors. "I thought we only ordered three?"

The man shrugged and smirked at Jet. "You want to throw this one back? Might want to think twice. She looks like she could work you over good."

"If you don't like what you see, I can leave," Jet said to nobody in particular.

Alain and the older man exchanged a glance, and Alain shook his head. "No, no. The more the merrier. Come sit by me. You want a drink? Or some Colombian marching powder?"

Jet glanced at a half-empty bottle of Mumm's Cordon Rouge. "Maybe some of that. I love champagne. Is it French?"

The third man, who looked about Alain's age, reached for the bottle and splashed some in a flute before handing it to her. "French as a poodle," he declared, and the girls tittered at his wit.

"Thanks," Jet said, and took a tiny sip.

"What's your name?" Alain asked.

"Tiffany," Jet replied.

The girl beside Alain rolled her eyes. "Oh, brother."

"Well, Tiffany, this is Chloe, and this is Candy, and this," he said with an exaggerated gesture, "is Lola. I'm Alain, and this is my good friend Sahid and his nephew, Safik."

"I've never seen you around," Candy said to Jet.

"I just got here a few days ago." She shrugged. "High season."

"Where from?" Alain asked.

"Barcelona. It's too hot there this time of year. Ibiza's way nicer."

"I love Barcelona," Alain said.

"Yeah. The clubs are the bomb. And the food's amazing," Jet agreed.

"You want a little of this?" Alain asked, indicating the cocaine piled on the tabletop.

"Maybe later. I don't like to spoil the champagne."

"Sensible. I like that," Sahid said. Safik rose and walked to the stereo, and turned up the volume on a Euro pop tune.

"Why don't you girls dance for us?" he said a little too loudly.

The women looked at each other, stood obediently, and moved to the open terrace, where the Mediterranean stretched to the horizon, interrupted only by a jagged crag of island less than a kilometer away. Jet remained seated beside Alain and took another sip of champagne as the women began dancing with each other, their expressions frozen in mock ecstasy while the men watched.

She shifted closer to Alain and smiled when he put his hand on her bare leg. "You want me to dance, too?" she asked, and shifted her hand into his lap. "Or stay here with you?"

He laughed. "This is better, no?"

"I think so."

He leaned forward and cut off another line of coke, and inhaled it through a gold tube before sitting back and staring at the ceiling with glazed eyes. "Whooh," he exclaimed. "Sure you don't want some? It's amazing."

Sahid stood and carried his drink out to the girls. He began dancing with them, his hairy arms extended at shoulder height, his plump hips wiggling in time to the music, reminding Jet of nothing so much as a walrus. Jet rubbed Alain's thigh and felt his interest grow.

"So what are we celebrating tonight?" she asked.

"A nice payday. For you as well."

"Wonderful. What's on the menu? Any more going to join us?"

"No. Just me and my friends. And you and yours."

"Sounds perfect." She offered him another white smile, her emerald eyes glinting in the light from the chandelier, and touched a tribal tattoo on one of his bare arms. "I like that. Tattoos are hot."

Alain grinned in what Jet imagined he thought was a charming manner, and might have been to the village girls whose vision of glamour came straight from the television. "I have more."

Her hand returned to his crotch. "You'll have to show me."

He began to unbuckle his belt, and she kissed him quickly. "Not here."

"Why not? Maybe my friends would like to watch."

She leaned over to the champagne, pulled it out of the ice bucket, popped a cube in her mouth, and lifted the bucket as she rose. "First I want you all to myself. If you feel like sharing after, that's up to you."

He inspected her shorts and his eyes drifted along her caramel skin to her face. "Sounds reasonable," he said, and took her free hand as he stood. "This way."

He led her to the stairs, and Sahid called to him, "Where are you going, my friend?"

"Business to attend to!"

Sahid and his nephew laughed knowingly. "Don't take too long. The night's young."

Alain eyed Jet. "I don't know. This might take a while."

They ascended to the second floor, and Alain pushed a door open and flicked on the light as he guided Jet inside. She giggled and locked it behind them, and then turned and swung the ice bucket, striking Alain across the bridge of his nose. His scream of agony was cut off by a strike to his throat, and he collapsed to the marble floor, blood streaming down his face.

Jet was already in motion as he went down, and kicked him hard in the abdomen, knocking the wind out of him. She followed through with another kick to the groin, and he doubled up into a fetal position, momentarily stunned. She set the bucket down, pulled his belt free and wrapped it around her fist, and punched him in the side of the head with the buckle, knocking him senseless.

When he came to, he was lying on the bed, his hands tied behind him, eyes tearing. Jet stood beside him, the chrome blade of a letter opener in her hand.

"Make a sound and I'll take an eye out," she said. "And it would be a waste – your friends won't hear you over the music."

He glared at her. "Who are you?"

"Your worst nightmare, Alain. But let's stay on point. I'll ask questions. You answer them or I'll butcher you like a hog. Understand?"

"What do you want? Money?"

"I want answers. Let's start with where the girls are."

He looked confused. "I…they're downstairs. Are you crazy?"

"Not the whores. The ones you kidnapped."

Realization washed over his face. "Oh, God…"

"You have one chance to tell me the truth. If you don't, I'm going to stuff a washrag in your mouth and go to work on you. I know you're a tough guy, Foreign Legion and all, but believe me that you've never experienced anything like what I'll put you through."

"I don't know what you're talking about."

"That was your one chance, and you lied," she said, and struck him in the temple with the letter opener's hilt. His eyes rolled in his head and she wedged the washrag into his mouth, watching as he slowly turned blue, unable to breathe through his ruined nose. When traces of cyanosis had discolored his lips, she jerked the rag free, tearing the skin around his mouth in the process. He gulped air like a beached fish while she stood by impassively, and when he'd stopped gasping, she spoke in a whisper.

"Next time I go straight for the family jewels. You'll be singing soprano for the rest of your life. Now where are the girls?"

"I…I don't know. Not here. We took them to a beach. A boat picked them up. That's all I know."

"What boat? Whose?"

"Nobody told me. They just gave me a contact to call, and when we had them, we did. The contact told us where to take them, and then we were out of it." He licked away blood. "It was just a job. We didn't hurt them."

"This is just a job, too. What phone did you use to call this contact?"

His eyes darted to the side. "Mine."

"Where is it?"

"Charging. In the bathroom."

"What's the name of the contact?"

"He said it was Kirill. Ukrainian. I never laid eyes on him. I swear. He's probably long gone by now. Has to be." His eyes held hers. "Did her father send you?"

"Take a deep breath. Rag's going back in," she said, the letter opener hovering over his pupil. He sucked in a lungful of air, and she jammed the washcloth into his mouth and walked to the bathroom.

The phone was blinking green. She unplugged the charger, thumbed through the menu to the call log, and scanned the numbers. There were only four calls the night of the kidnapping – two to a single number, and one outbound to a different number, with an inbound call from the same number twenty minutes later.

She carried the phone to where Alain was squirming and flushing again, and removed the rag. His exhalation was hoarse, and he breathed heavily three times.

"Which of these numbers is it?" she asked, holding the phone up to his face so he could see them.

His fist caught her in the side of the ribs, and she dropped the letter opener and phone in surprise. His other hand grabbed for her hair, but she blocked it with her elbow and rabbit-punched him in the eye. He grunted in pain but swung for her again as he struggled to get off the bed, and the blow glanced off her shoulder. He was nearly on his feet when she opted to end it and jammed the heel of her hand into his nose, driving the cartilage into his cranium. She followed through with a strike to his larynx with the side of her hand, and the blow crushed his throat as he fell backward, already dying from the trauma to his brain.

Jet removed her cell from the waist of her shorts and called Dov. "I'm going to give you two numbers. Run a trace on both. I need to know who owns them, and if possible, where they are now." She read them off Alain's phone. "I could use that yesterday."

"Done. Anything else?"

"Alain had an accident. There might be problems with the local police."

"We can run interference for a while, but there are limits."

"It's possible they won't report it. Seems like the two who were with Alain might have been in on it, or at least knew what he was up to."

"Can you make it look like an accident?"

Jet glanced at the dead man. "Maybe. I'll advise when I'm clear."

She hung up and blotted the congealing blood off the marble floor. Two minutes later it was clean, and she'd rinsed the rag free of crimson. The bed was a different story – he'd bled onto the bedspread. She dragged him off the bed and removed the cover, and then piled it into the closet. The sheets beneath it were white, no trace of blood.

Jet removed his clothes and tossed them onto a chair, and then hauled his inert form to the sliding door that led to the balcony. She removed her top and set it on the floor and reached for the door handle. She opened it, and music blared from the terrace below. After listening for a moment, she dragged the dead man onto the railing so he was doubled over it, legs hanging on the sea side.

Jet took a deep breath and heaved with all her might, thankful for the hours she'd invested in pull-ups and upper-body workouts. His body flipped over the railing and fell out toward the rocks, barely missing the edge of the terrace directly under it.

She screamed in terror as he dropped, and leaned over the railing to see his body strike the jagged boulders beyond the terrace, one arm covering her breasts. Sahid appeared at the terrace edge, half naked, and looked up at where she stood, a look of horror on her face. Two of the prostitutes joined him, and he yelled to Jet over the music.

"What happened?"

"He…he was acting crazy," Jet stammered. "Said he could walk on the balcony railing like it was a tightrope from his military training. Then he slipped…" She pointed at his corpse twisted on the rocks. "Oh, God…"

Sahid bellowed for the bodyguards as Jet held her hand to her mouth and backed away from the balcony, her performance adequate, if not award-winning. She snatched up her top and slipped it on, and then tore down the stairs to the terrace, her phone in her waistband again.

"Oh, my God…oh, my God…" she repeated in simulated shock as she stared at Alain's ruined form. Sahid was pointing and barking instructions to the guards, who'd set down their weapons and were scrambling down the rocks to retrieve the dead man. The other girls were dumbstruck, and the nephew was sitting in an overstuffed chair, his face a blank, a bottle of expensive scotch in his hand.

"Screw this. I'm getting out of here," Candy said. "I don't need to spend all night with the cops."

"Me too," Lola echoed.

"It's…Jesus," Jet agreed.

"Get rid of the drugs," Sahid snapped to Safik. "Now."

"What about our money?" Lola said.

Sahid pulled some euros from his pocket and handed them to her. "You were never here, understand? You didn't see anything."

"Sure…" Candy agreed, eyeing the money in her friend's hand. "Whatever you say."

"What the hell was he thinking?" Safik murmured from his seat. "Showing off for some whore? He must have been stoned out of his mind."

Jet didn't wait to hear more and followed the others out the door as the guards dragged Alain's remains to the terrace. Once outside, the girls ran for the gate, and Candy turned to Jet when she arrived. "We're not splitting the money with you."

"I don't care," Jet spat. "I just want to go home."

Lola fished a phone from her micro-purse and called a taxi. Jet glared at the women and shouldered past them. "I'd rather walk."

"Suit yourself, princess," Candy snarled. "Bet you wish you'd never shown up."

Jet ignored the hookers and took off down the road. When she was out of sight, she waited behind one of the hedges until the taxi drove past her position, and circled back to the neighboring house to change and collect her things. The arms dealer seemed more concerned with avoiding narcotics charges than calling the police, so perhaps he and the guards would dispose of the body and the news would never hit the wire.

She scaled the wall and pulled on her clothes, and was pocketing her gun and knife when her phone vibrated.

Dov's voice sounded tense, but professional. "The first number doesn't register anywhere. So it was probably a burner."

"And the second?"

"Registered to Kirill Kushnir. The name matches an ex-Ukrainian military captain who went missing after the coup."

"Sounds like the type who'd be interested in making some easy money."

"The phone shows as being near the waterfront in Ibiza. A watering hole I've driven by. Not the best clientele. Looked pretty rough."

"My kind of place."

"If you want some backup…"

"I'll let you know if I need any," she said. "Monitor the police channels for anything on Mansour. It's a better than even chance they don't call it in," she finished, and switched the call off.

She listened for the sound of approaching sirens, but the night air was still, the only sounds the gentle crashing of waves on the rocks and the echo of the party music from the villa reverberating off the water. After checking to ensure the coast was clear, she set out at a run, hoping to make it back to the Fiat within the hour.

# Chapter 31

The bar was a hole-in-the-wall with a poorly executed sign depicting a rotund mermaid, and the exterior looked like the bottom of a spittoon at quitting time. Jet waited across the street rather than going in, Dov having obliged her by sending a service photo of the man to her phone. She saw no reason to risk alerting him by drawing attention to herself in a place where the only women would be drug-addled pros on their last legs, so she stuck to the shadows in a doorway across the boulevard, waiting for the man to show himself.

Dov had patched in directly with HQ and was watching the Ukrainian's cell phone. He'd agreed to call Jet when it started moving, leaving her little to do but cool her heels in the seediest neighborhood in Ibiza. All port towns had the same sorts of bars for the locals, and Ibiza was no different, the patrons invariably fishermen, sailors, waterfront laborers, along with grifters, thugs, lowlifes, and thieves of every persuasion. Jet had seen more than her share of the worst, so the district didn't faze her, especially armed with a 9mm and short on patience.

A stray dog, teats hanging from weaning a recent litter of puppies, had decided to keep Jet company, and she passed the time scratching behind her ears and murmuring soothing words, the dog a kindred spirit who'd been batted around by the world and just wanted a few moments of kindness. Just after she'd arrived, a pair of bums had shambled by her position and checked Jet out, but neither had decided she looked like anyone they wanted to tangle with, and they'd moved on.

Two men walked out of the bar, both wearing knit seamen's caps and smoking cigarettes as they made their way down the sidewalk.

When the phone trembled in her pocket, Jet was more than ready for the news.

"They just left," Dov said.

"I see them."

She replaced the phone and began tailing the men, allowing sufficient space between them so they wouldn't realize they were being shadowed. The dog insisted on accompanying her, and she was glad for the company – few professionals on surveillance brought their pets, so a trained eye would dismiss her rather than be drawn to her.

The men turned the corner, and Jet picked up her pace. There was a trade-off between subterfuge and the possibility of losing them, especially on turf she was unfamiliar with. When she rounded the building, she spotted them a half block ahead, walking briskly, in a heated discussion, judging by their body language and waving of hands. She followed for two blocks, and then they turned again, this time into a smaller tributary between two ancient buildings. Jet gave it a few seconds and then trailed them into the alley, her senses on alert in the gloom.

Movement from behind a dumpster startled her, and then a pair of strong hands gripped her arms, locking them in place by her sides. One of the men stepped from a doorway on her right and glared at her with expressionless eyes.

"Why are you following us?" he demanded, his Spanish heavily accented.

Jet's answer was to stomp down on the foot of the man who was holding her, cracking the bones in his arch and sending him stumbling backward in pain. The dog took off at a run, frightened by the sudden violence. The man in front of Jet moved toward her, and a knife appeared in his right hand, its wicked blade shining in the dim light. He held it like an experienced fighter, thumb over the butt and the blade extending downward, and when he slashed at her, he moved with blinding speed and abrupt force.

She barely avoided being gutted, freed the pistol from her waistband, and swung it against his forearm. He grunted in pain but didn't drop the knife, his eyes locked on hers as he tested for an opening. Another slash nearly connected with her torso, but she sidestepped it and spin-kicked him in the head, sending him staggering against the brick wall.

The other man threw himself at her from behind, but she'd heard him coming and leapt aside. He'd also palmed a knife, but unlike his partner, he dropped it when he slammed facedown against the pavement, and she kicked it away before clobbering him with the gun. He groaned and she stepped away, but the first man had regained his footing and was hurtling at her, leading with the knife. Jet dropped into a crouch and sweep-kicked his legs out from under him, and when he hit the ground, she heard his head smash against the asphalt like an overripe melon.

When he didn't stir, she stood and approached him. A pool of blood was spreading behind his skull, and his fingers were twitching. He looked older and harder than his photograph, but she had no problem recognizing him as the Ukrainian, and she shook her head in frustration. He was either going to be in a coma for a long time, or he wouldn't make it at all. Either way, her goal of cornering him and learning where he'd taken the girls was moot – she'd get no more out of him than she would a brick.

Jet moved to the other man, who was trying to crawl away, and held the pistol against his neck. "Where did you take the girls? What did you do with them?"

The man stopped moving and Jet prodded him with the gun. "Last time," she said. "Where are they?"

"I got nothing to do with any of that," he protested in accented Spanish.

"That's a shame. I guess I have no choice but to kill you."

"No! Wait. I really don't know."

She exhaled in frustration. "Who are you? What's your name?"

"Dmitry. I'm Kirill's friend. That's it."

"Kirill kidnapped two very important people. They sent me. Make me want to believe you, Dmitry, because otherwise this isn't going to end well."

"I…he told me he did a job, so he was flush. He didn't say what it was."

"Then you're useless to me."

"I can tell you who he did the job for."

"I already know."

"You know about the General?" The surprise was genuine.

"Tell me about him as though I don't, and maybe you'll live to see morning."

"He lives over on Formentera. Has a place on the water. Kirill and he are tight. That's who he was working for. If he kidnapped anyone, it was for the General."

"And he's called the General because…?"

His kick came out of nowhere and knocked her off balance. Her left leg went numb and buckled, and then he was on her, a steel pen in his hand a dagger aimed for her throat. She blocked the strike with her arm and the pen gashed her skin, and she slammed the pistol into his skull with the other. He winced at the blow but used his superior weight to drive the pen at her chest, and it was all she could do to knock it aside with the gun before he punched her wrist.

The gun skittered away, and he grinned in triumph as he drew the pen back to skewer her. He didn't register the snick of the stiletto blade springing into place, and never saw it coming when she drove it through his left ear and into his brain.

The pen clattered against the alley floor as he slumped against her, and Jet pushed his dead weight from her with considerable effort. Her arm stung where he'd gouged her, but it wasn't bleeding too badly, and she could attend to it once she was clear of the fight scene. She stood and regarded the dead man, and then walked over to Kirill, who was still twitching but going nowhere soon. Jet went through his pockets and retrieved his phone, wallet, and keys, and did the same with Dmitry. With any luck, it would look like a robbery gone violently wrong.

She tested Dmitry's weight and then hefted him into the dumpster. Kirill was heavier, and it took her three tries to manhandle him in. When she finished, she closed the lid and looked both ways along the alley, and then walked calmly onto the deserted street, holding her bleeding arm with her free hand as she fumbled for her phone with the other.

Jet stopped at the next corner and called Dov. "Kirill was working for someone he referred to as the General. Has a home on the water on the nearby island – Formentera. That's the likeliest place they would have taken the girls."

"I'll see what HQ can come up with. There can't be that many homes on the water. I've been out there. It's mostly beaches."

"I also have his cell. I checked the call log, but most of the outbound calls are to phones whose numbers don't appear onscreen. Any way to hack that and see who he called?"

"If you can get it to me, I could send it to HQ. But no, no quick way."

"We don't have days to wait. While you're working on locating the General, I need to bandage up my arm and find a boat."

"That's going to be impossible at this hour."

She looked at the keys she'd taken from Kirill. The ring was attached to a float. A name was emblazoned on it in red ink.

*Papanek.*

"I didn't say I wanted you to hire a boat," she corrected. "I need to find a specific one the owner isn't going to be using anytime soon."

A hesitation, and then a sigh. "Ah. The Ukrainian?"

"Bingo. Meanwhile, have the techs go to work. We need to find a general."

# CHAPTER 32

It took three hours of roaming the various harbors to find the *Papanek* at the smallest of the pleasure-craft marinas, but when Jet did, she liked what she saw. The boat was a power catamaran, fifteen meters in length, and the twin hulls beachable, which explained how the kidnappers had gotten the girls on board without the use of a pier or a dinghy.

Jet was the only one on the docks at the late hour, although music from waterfront clubs boomed and pulsed across the harbor. The marina security guard was happily asleep in his security shack, and it had been child's play to sneak past him.

Her arm throbbed where she'd bandaged it after finding an all-night pharmacy whose primary trade seemed to be erectile dysfunction medications and hangover remedies, and she'd bought a bottle of rubbing alcohol, a stitching needle, stitch material, and antiseptic ointment in addition to the gauze and surgical tape.

Once on the boat and after verifying the keys fit the ignitions and the cabin hatch, she lowered herself inside and went to work on her arm, using the light of her phone as she closed the gash one-handed. When she was done, she rebandaged the wound and moved to the helm, where she powered on the instruments and verified that the boat had half-full fuel tanks – more than enough to get her to Formentera, which was only fifteen kilometers away across flat seas.

Her big problem was that once she arrived, she had no plan. Without a fix on the General's villa, she'd be wasting her time cruising around the island.

She called Dov, who sounded fatigued for the first time.

"Anything?"

"They're working on it."

"It'll be light in a few hours. We lose any advantage at that point."

"You don't need to tell me."

"I found the boat. I'm getting ready to power her up, so we're down to the wire."

"I know. But I can't make the computers work any faster."

"Anything on the police channels?"

"No chatter. So your instinct was correct, at least so far."

"They'll find the Ukrainian whenever they pick up the garbage, so that won't last."

"If there were no witnesses, you'll be fine," he said.

She didn't respond that she'd have to be alive in the morning to worry about it.

"I'll leave my phone on," Jet said. "I'm not sure about cell coverage once I'm off the island."

"Should be okay between Formentera and Ibiza. They both have towers, so worst case you might have spotty service in the channel."

Kirill's phone bounced on the table in the cabin with a cheery samba ringtone, and Jet ran down to retrieve it. She eyed the incoming number, but the caller ID was blocked. She answered in Spanish, her voice playful.

"*Sí?*"

"Where's Kirill?"

"He's…indisposed."

"Put him on."

"Who is this?"

"Put him on," the voice repeated. Jet noted the accent. Ukrainian.

Jet set the phone down and waited a full minute, and then lifted it to her ear again. "He's out cold. Too much rum."

"Shit. Who's this?"

Jet laughed. "Cinderella. Who do you think?"

The caller hung up. She called Dov back. "Any way to trace a call that just came in to his phone?"

"Maybe if I had the phone."

"Can't you check the towers like before?"

"You're on the water, right? Every club in Ibiza is there. So there would probably be hundreds, or thousands, of calls to filter through. Sure, it can be done, but it'll take a long time. And we have to wait for business hours, so our connection at the police can put in the request to the phone company."

"Crap. Well, at least it's a fallback."

"You going to stay put or head to the island?"

"If they find the Ukrainian's body tonight by some fluke, it'll probably raise a lot of ugly questions if I'm on his boat. So I'm headed to the island."

"I'll call as soon as I have anything."

Jet returned to the helm and switched on the blowers, which made a faint humming sound beneath her feet. After a few minutes, she depressed the starter buttons, and the Yanmar diesels roared to life. She cast off the deck lines and hurried back to the helm, and then shoved the transmission levers into gear and coasted away from the long line of yachts, moving toward the breakwater at the mouth of the harbor.

Once outside the marina entrance, she gave the engines throttle and the boat surged forward, the twin hulls slicing through the moderate chop with ease. She checked the time and frowned as she set a course for Formentera. If Dov took much longer to get her the information, dawn would be breaking, making it impossible for her to do much until darkness fell again. The alternative was to send in an assault squad and storm the General's place, but if they didn't have confirmation that the girls were there, the director would never approve it, nor would Jet make the recommendation.

The seas kicked up in the middle of the channel, but the catamaran tracked straight, and soon the rise of the island was looming ahead, mostly dark except for the lights of an occasional beach hotel. She throttled back when she was a half kilometer from shore and checked her watch again, biting back frustration. She'd accomplished the impossible in just a few short hours, and now was literally dead in the water, waiting for faceless wonks in Israel to work their technological magic.

Sailboats bobbed near the beach, anchored within skiff distance, and Jet backed off the throttles still further and put the transmissions in neutral. The island was larger than she'd supposed from a distance, and the impossibility of circling it, looking for suspect compounds, struck her with the force of a blow.

Her phone rang and she answered on the first ring.

"Yes?"

"I tried you a half hour ago. You must have been in the channel."

*Shit.*

"You have something for me?" she asked.

"I'm sending coordinates and a map image of the house. It's on the windward side of the island. Where are you?"

"Just off the beach on the leeward side." Her phone pinged. "Hang on."

She thumbed the image live and studied it, and then memorized the coordinates and returned to the call. "Got it. Looks like it has a dock."

"It's a big estate. Several buildings in addition to the main house."

"Anything else?" she asked.

"We got an ID on the owner. He's an ex-Ukrainian general named Yuri Tanasov. Suspected of war crimes and crimes against humanity. On record as rabidly anti-Russian, which would explain why he'd be a willing participant in the kidnapping of an oligarch's daughter. Nasty piece of work all around." A hesitation. "That's all I have. Good luck."

"Thanks."

She engaged the transmissions again and twisted the wheel before entering the coordinates into the onboard GPS. The device informed her that she was seven kilometers from the villa as the crow flies, but twenty-five by water. She considered beaching the boat and trying to reach it overland, but rejected the idea – if the girls were there and still alive, she'd need to be able to get them out of the area quickly, and she wouldn't be able to on foot, especially if they were drugged or hurt.

Jet accelerated until she was doing twenty knots, and resigned herself to losing another precious hour rounding the island.

Once close to her destination, she powered back and went below. A quick check in the cabin yielded a pair of crusty binoculars, which she brought up to the helm. The GPS blinked when she neared the compound, and she raised the spyglasses and focused on the target, which had several exterior lights burning but all the windows dark.

She was far enough offshore not to draw scrutiny, and she took her time putting along parallel to the shore, the catamaran's hull dampening pitching from the beam seas. Jet could make out a dock extending into the water, with a twenty-meter sports fisherman lashed to one side and a guard sitting in its cockpit, an assault rifle in his lap.

The compound was situated on a cove, and she continued past it until its lights had faded, and then steered the boat toward the beach. She picked up speed as she approached the sand, and cut the engines before the hulls skidded onto the slope. The boat stopped, and Jet walked along the deck to the bow and hopped off, one of the bow lines in hand. She had no idea what the tides were like, but she didn't want to break the girls out only to find that their escape had drifted away. Jet lashed the line to a thatched shade element supported by a post jutting from the sand, and then took off at a jog up the windswept dunes, conscious of how precious little time she had left before sunup.

She crept through scrub toward the villa grounds, binoculars hanging from her neck, and stopped periodically to look through them. When she was a hundred meters away, she spotted another guard, this one patrolling the perimeter, also with an assault rifle. She watched as he meandered along, in no hurry, and hoped the duty was so boring that the staff wasn't paying close attention.

The guard moved out of sight behind a row of bushes, and she surveyed the buildings: a large two-story main house, a separate garage, what looked like a stable, and a guesthouse. Jet remained motionless as she inspected the layout, and was preparing to move when the back door of the main house opened and a man emerged carrying a plastic jug and a tray. He walked to the guesthouse and opened the door. The interior was dark. He shut the door behind him, and two minutes later emerged empty-handed and walked back to the house.

A glance at her watch reminded Jet that she had maybe forty-five more minutes of darkness. She waited until the man disappeared into the villa, and then trotted in a crouch toward the grounds, her footfalls nearly silent on the sand. She stopped at a low wall and did another scan of the area and, when she saw no guards, vaulted over the barrier and ran to the guesthouse, gun at the ready.

The door had a deadbolt on the outside, and she could see from the shiny screws that held it in place that it was a recent installation. Jet worked the bolt loose, the steel shaft squeaking against the metal bracket, and pushed the door open and stepped inside, head cocked for any sounds of the guards.

She left the door open a crack and switched on her phone lamp to sweep the interior.

Two young women lay on the floor, their clothes torn, their arms and legs bruised, their hair filthy and matted. The room had a fetid odor, and Jet recognized the smell of fear, sweat, and something more ominous. When the light drifted across the blonde's face, she gasped and drew her knees to her chest in terror, and Jet could instantly see that the girls had been badly abused.

"Tanya, don't make a sound. I'm going to get you out of here," Jet whispered in Russian.

The Russian girl moaned, her eyes wide and panicked, clearly not understanding or believing what Jet had said. Jet tried again.

"Tanya, your father sent me. I need your help so we can escape."

"I…escape? Who…?"

Jet approached her and studied her by the light of the phone. Her eyes looked drugged, and her face was discolored and bruised, her lip swollen and split.

"What did they give you?"

"I…I don't know. Pills. They made us take them."

"How badly hurt are you? Can you run when you need to?"

Tanya looked over to the other girl. "They…broke something

inside her. She's been bleeding for…at least a day."

"We'll deal with that once we're off the island," Jet said and looked to the other girl. "Liv, right? Can you hear me?"

Tanya visibly relaxed and reached over to poke her friend. Liv groaned and blinked in confusion at the sight of a woman holding a gun in one hand and a phone in the other.

"What…"

"Liv, I know they hurt you. Can you walk?"

Liv looked to Tanya, who nodded. Liv raised her eyes to Jet. "I think so. Is this…is this real? Are you?"

"Yes. Tanya's father sent me. We're going to get out of here. I have a boat nearby, but you have to be able to make it there."

Liv struggled to sit up, but barely managed. Jet frowned as Tanya got to her feet. "We may have to leave her."

Tanya shook her head. "No. Either she goes with us or I stay. You need to do something. You have no idea what they…"

"I can guess. But it's only me. I can't carry her, and you're in no shape. If she can't make it under her own steam, she isn't coming."

Tanya was obviously unsteady, but went to Liv and helped her stand. "We'll do whatever it takes." She hesitated. "Why did my father send only you?"

"Any more and they would have spotted us. So I'm it."

"There are at least a dozen guards. They have machine guns."

"Which means we need to be quiet so they don't know we've escaped."

Tanya was forming a response when Jet flicked the phone off and hissed a warning. "Shh. Voices. Someone's coming."

"Oh, God…" Liv whispered, and Tanya hugged her close.

"Be quiet," Jet said, and eased the door closed, her gun trained on it in the darkness as she stepped aside so the open door would hide her.

# Chapter 33

*Tel Aviv, Israel*

The director glared across the conference table at the assembled analysts, who fidgeted beneath his withering gaze. He tapped the ash off his third cigarette of the predawn, inhaled deeply, and then blew a gray cloud at the exhaust vent in the ceiling, which sucked the offending smoke away in a blink.

"Thank you for coming in so early," he said. "I realize many of you never left last night, and I appreciate the sacrifice. Unfortunately, I have more bad news. We received a communication from the extortionists just before midnight, threatening another demonstration. That took place an hour later, when the entire air traffic control system went dark. All flights in and out of Israel have been suspended since. We've declared a state of emergency and issued an official statement that it's part of a surprise drill that will last one day, but we're already getting pushback from the international press, who are justifiably skeptical. Add in all the furious travelers whose flights have been suspended, and this is a major problem, as I don't need to explain."

Reuven nodded. "I saw it on our internal briefing. At this point we have to assume that everything they've threatened is going to take place unless we pay."

"I thought you said you were closing in on the command and control servers," the director snapped.

"We should have the locations of two of the three by midday, based on the traffic we've seen from some of the nodes. But the third is going to be the problem – it's proving more elusive than the other two. We analyzed the data your operative sent us from Estonia, and we now recognize the signatures and have been able to follow them back through the dark web. But the third…we thought it might have been in Tallinn, and then we modified our assessment and placed it in Helsinki, but right now our confidence level isn't high."

"Which is a fancy way of saying we don't know where it is." He coughed. "Where are the others?"

"One's in Latvia, and the other in Ukraine. But we don't have exact locations yet. Just regions."

"Once we do, we need to move teams into position, and that will take some time. Do we have operatives on the ground?"

"We will shortly. They're being moved as we speak. Demolitions experts, tech specialists, the works."

The director shifted his attention to Adam. "You know by now that this Kalda isn't in Helsinki any longer. Are we making any progress on tracking him down?"

"I wish I had better news to report, but no. He's invisible for now. We're monitoring all communications in and out of his Tallinn facility, and there's been nothing suspect since he left. It's as though he doesn't exist."

"Which we know isn't the case. Obviously." The director took another drag and tamped the butt out in his ashtray. "Are we still of the opinion that we have to take out all three command and control servers simultaneously?"

Reuven massaged his forehead and looked up. "Yes. No question that if we don't, a distress signal will trigger all the rest of the nodes to shut down. We've seen the result with the airports. We're having to rely on mobile radar units for military applications and threat detection, which, if that stretches more than twenty-four hours, will invite an attack. Rumors are going to circulate, and if Hezbollah or Hamas or the Iranians think that we're blind, it could mean Armageddon."

"Will we be able to replace the affected systems by the end of the day?"

"Some. Not all. But enough to be able to patch together a workable network. We're airlifting in servers to all the major airports and should be able to start by late this morning."

"I thought nothing was flying in or out."

"The airlift is coming into military facilities," Adam clarified. "With nothing in the air, there's nothing to avoid once in our airspace."

"Can we air gap the new systems?"

"We'll have to. But it will mean a significant delay in threat identification and response."

"Will that be obvious to anyone without a classified rating?"

"Theoretically no, but we all know nothing stays secret for long."

The director sat back and rubbed his face with his hand. "The communiqué gave us forty-eight hours to pay. Which begs the question, why two days, and not one? There must be some reason on their side for not holding our feet to the fire."

"They might still be populating the malware," Reuven said. "That's the only thing that makes sense. Either that, or they know it takes time to put together four billion liquid for transfer."

"We've had over a week, so that isn't likely." He looked around the room. "There will be a cabinet meeting this morning at ten. I want to have another meeting here at eight thirty so you can update me on any progress. Right now we're dead in the water, and I don't want to be the one to tell everyone we have to start liquidating assets to pay a criminal who's outsmarted all of us."

"Once we find the third server–" Adam started, but the director cut him off.

"You mean *if*. Right now you haven't pinpointed any. Is there some nuance I'm missing for why you expect to accelerate the process now?"

"The Tallinn data was material in identifying them. We anticipate that it should go faster from here."

"But you can't guarantee it, can you?"

Reuven frowned as he shook his head.

The director rose. "You have three hours. Work a miracle," he said, and then left the room, leaving his subordinates shell-shocked and glum.

# Chapter 34

*Formentera, Spain*

Seconds ticked by and Jet stood frozen in place, and then an annoyed voice spoke just outside the door. "That idiot left it unlatched. Jesus. Tanasov should shoot him and get it over with."

"This time I get the blonde," another voice said. "The other one's half dead."

The door swung open and two guards stood framed in the doorway, a flashlight beam playing over the girls, who didn't have to fake their fear. The men stepped inside, and Jet closed the door behind them with her foot and smacked the nearest in the base of the skull with her pistol. His knees buckled and he dropped the flashlight as the other spun toward her with his weapon raised, but he was too slow, and she smashed the gun into his jaw with a vicious uppercut that sent him to the floor. Jet kicked him in the head for good measure, and he released his hold on his gun. She scooped up the aluminum flashlight and brought it down on the first guard's head. The light blinked out, and she continued to bludgeon him until his face was ruined, and then moved to the other and broke his jaw with it.

Jet switched the flashlight back on and studied her work – both men were unconscious and bleeding profusely. She glanced at Tanya and Liv as she slid her pistol into her waistband and collected the two rifles – Kalashnikovs, obviously older, but serviceable.

"Do either of you know how to shoot a gun?" she asked.

They shook their heads. Jet ejected the magazine from one of the rifles and slipped it into her back pocket before moving to the first guard and bringing the wooden stock down as hard as she could on his throat. He spasmed, and she stepped to the other and did the same, and then turned to the girls. "We need to get out of here. They'll be missed. You ready?"

They both nodded, and Jet flicked the flashlight off. "Let your eyes adjust. It'll help once we're outside."

A sob escaped Tanya's lips. "They took turns on us. They…like…animals. One of them used his rifle on Liv. That's…that's the problem."

Jet's expression softened. "I'm sorry. But you're going to have to rally if we're going to make it."

Jet moved to the door and pressed her ear against it. When she heard nothing after several seconds, she opened it a crack and looked out. The grounds were empty. Jet pulled the door wider and whispered to the girls, "Follow me."

She ducked from the guesthouse and crossed to the low wall, and only stopped when she reached it. She twisted to confirm that Tanya and Liv were behind her, and frowned at how slowly they were moving. Jet was sympathetic to their plight, and they'd obviously undergone horrendous treatment, but that didn't change the fact that if they didn't pick up the pace, they would all be in jeopardy.

"Come on!" she urged in a low voice. Tanya was supporting Liv with her arm around her, but they weren't moving fast enough, and every second they were out in the open reduced their chances of making it.

They reached the wall, and Jet helped Tanya get Liv over it. She was gritting her teeth and sweating through her dress from just the short walk, and Jet's fear that she was going to be a liability grew with each step.

As if reading her mind, Liv stumbled over a root and cried out as she pitched forward. Tanya broke her fall but went down with her, and Jet spun at the sound of them hitting the ground.

A dog barked from inside the house, and a moment later, lights went on in the lower-floor windows.

"That's it. If she can't make it, leave her," Jet ordered Tanya, who looked up from where she lay with pleading eyes.

"No. I told you—"

Two guards ran from the beach toward the house, and the door opened and three more spilled out, all with guns in hand. Moments later a shirtless older man with the stiff military bearing of a soldier stepped from the entryway, a pistol gripped in his hand. Spotlights flickered on at the corners of the villa, and the grounds were flooded with blinding halogen light. One of the guards pointed at the guesthouse and yelled, but Jet didn't wait to hear the aftermath – she'd seen enough.

She reached down, yanked Tanya to her feet, and squeezed her arm hard enough to make her whimper. "Listen to me," Jet hissed. "They know you're gone. If you want to live out the hour, stop fighting me and do exactly as I say. Clear?"

Tanya nodded, her eyes moist with tears, and Liv struggled to stand. Jet pushed Tanya ahead of her, helped Liv up, and then took off ahead, moving slower than she otherwise would have because both girls were struggling to keep up.

Another cry echoed from the house, and Jet increased her pace, survival now at stake rather than stealth. The guards knew they were gone, and it wouldn't take them long to fan out and search for them – the only question was how many would be on their trail before they could reach the boat.

Liv moaned again and clutched her stomach, and Tanya slowed to help her. Jet wheeled around and glowered at the Russian girl, but she was already almost to her friend and so didn't register Jet's anger.

Rifle fire exploded from back at the wall, and rounds shredded through the bushes around them. Tanya froze in panic and Jet dove at her as another volley tore through the foliage. Liv cried out and tumbled forward. Jet's tackle knocked Tanya to the ground, saving her life, but a glance at Liv told Jet it was too late for her – her sightless eyes stared at faint ribbons of peach and rust coloring the predawn sky.

Tanya gasped with her hand to her mouth, and Jet whispered a warning in her ear. "We're both dead if you don't move your ass. It's too late for your friend, but not us. Stay down and crawl in the direction we were going. Don't stand or you'll get cut down. Understand?"

Tanya nodded, her face pale and luminescent in the last of the starlight. Jet placed her rifle on the dead girl's body, using it to stabilize her aim, and waited for a target to present itself as Tanya crawled away through the brush.

More shooting from the grounds eventually petered out, leaving the area around Jet in an uneasy silence. She waited patiently, secure that someone would appear, each minute that went by buying Tanya a better chance at survival.

The first guard who showed himself moved like a seasoned fighter, ducking and weaving as he approached. When he was seventy meters away, Jet squeezed off a three-round burst that knocked him backward, and waited for the inevitable answering fire. Two shooters opened up on her position, but they were guessing in the dark, and the rounds didn't come close. She barely breathed, ears ringing from the shots she'd fired, and loosed another six rounds at movement in the brush ahead of her before rolling away from the dead girl and crawling a half dozen meters backward and to her left.

More shooting pummeled the spot she'd just vacated, and she hesitated until she had another gunman in her sights before rattling off a burst. The man screamed, confirming she'd struck pay dirt, and she used the distraction to retreat farther, aware that if she stayed in one place too long, the smart tactic would be to flank her, which would put Tanya in greater danger.

This time the shooting didn't resume, which told her that the gunmen were regrouping and would try to be more strategic rather than running into gunfire. They had no way of knowing who was doing the shooting, but the number of men they'd lost would have told them that it wasn't a pair of badly impaired party girls. That unknown would work for her, but not forever, so she had to use the lull to put some distance between herself and the General's men while she could.

Jet rose and sprinted through the brush, thankful for the trees that grew along the dunes. A couple of minutes later she caught up with

Tanya, who was breathing like she'd run a marathon. Jet took her hand to reassure her and led her closer to the water and, when they broke through the brush and were on the beach, pointed to the boat in the near distance.

"You just have to make it that far and you'll be safe," Jet said. "Go to the boat. I'll stay here and hold off anyone who follows until you're on it."

"But what about—"

"Just do it. Go. Now," Jet snapped, cocking her head and turning back toward the trail they'd left in the dirt.

Jet lay down behind a rock outcropping on the land side of the dunes, replaced the half-spent magazine with the fresh one, and bided her time. At the rate Tanya was going, she'd be at the boat in three minutes, which meant Jet didn't have to stave off pursuit for long. Then again, with only forty or so rounds left between magazines, three minutes could be an eternity, and she hoped that the newfound caution she'd instilled in the kidnappers would last until she could make a break for it.

Jet didn't have to wait long to find out. Two gunmen materialized out of the darkness and she opened up on them, expending nine of her precious rounds in under a second. She switched the firing selector to single fire and peered down the sights at the fallen men, her pulse thudding in her ears.

A tense stillness settled over the dunes as the eastern horizon began to glow pink. Jet glanced at her watch and frowned; it wouldn't be long until her advantage turned into certain death with dawn's arrival. She had to get off the dunes and onto the water before the General could bring his boat to bear, because the big cruiser could easily do a third more than the catamaran, at which point without a sufficient lead it would be a matter of simple math before they were on top of her.

Jet's only chance was that there was a limit to how far the Ukrainian would go in terms of overt lawlessness. At some point the Spanish authorities would become involved, and they had more weapons and men than some disgraced general living in the sticks.

Her hunch was that if she could get close enough to Ibiza, the Ukrainian would lose interest in the chase and would back off. If she was wrong, then it would be a cage fight to the death.

A head popped up over the sand, and Jet waited for more of the man to appear before snapping off a single shot. Her effort was rewarded with a spray of blood and bone, but she didn't have time to congratulate herself on her marksmanship before two more gunmen opened up on her outcropping with their weapons on full auto. Jet figured that was laying down cover for someone to rush her from her flank, and scanned the brush in anticipation. Sure enough, another shooter's muzzle flash signaled she was correct, and chips of rock geysered a foot from her head.

She popped off four rounds in quick succession at the new threat and then returned her focus to the others, whose weapons had fallen silent, their magazines expended. When no more flanking fire assaulted her, she backed away from the rocks and dog-crawled through the brush to the beach, where she took off at a sprint, covering the hundred meters to the boat in a personal record.

Tanya was standing by the hulls, and Jet growled at her as she arrived. "I told you to get on the goddamned boat!"

"I heard all the shooting…I didn't want to be stranded on it if they–"

Jet untied the line from the shade pole and threw it over the bow railing. "Up. Now."

Tanya was still trying to clamber onto the hull as Jet pulled herself up in a single movement. She extended her hand to help the Russian and was hoisting her to the deck when gunfire broke the silence and several holes appeared in the fiberglass below them.

"Get out of sight in the cabin. Follow me," Jet ordered, and hurried to the helm. Tanya had the sense to keep her head down as the shooting continued, and Jet started the two engines and threw the transmissions into reverse. The boat surged backward, and sprigs of water fountained the surface around it, and then they were far enough from shore to execute a slow-motion turn.

A round ricocheted off the stainless steel stern railing as Jet slammed the transmissions forward and firewalled the throttles, and she ducked as the boat straightened out and picked up speed. More bullets pocked the stern as diesel smoke clouded her view of the shore, and then they were moving out of range, the hits fewer and farther between. Two more minutes and she dared to straighten and eye the speed indicator, which read twenty-six knots, the engine revs close to redline.

Jet removed her phone from her pocket and called Dov, shouting over the roar.

"I've got her. There was a firefight. Her friend didn't make it. We're headed back around the island at speed, but the General has a fast boat that could catch up to us. What are the chances you can get the locals involved if he chases us down? We're dead in the water if he does."

"I'll call it in. Give me your exact position. It could be dicey, though. Technically, you're on a stolen boat."

She read off the coordinates. "What about an extraction if we ditch on Formentera?"

"Possible. But there's no airport. So it would mean another boat, or the ferry, and we have no idea what kind of resources he has. We have to assume he's connected on the island, and if you ditch, it's anyone's guess on how long until they find the boat and realize you're still there."

"Figure something out, Dov, or this will have all been in vain."

"How is she?"

"Bad shape, but alive. Do something. My battery's running low. I'm signing off."

"I'll call when I have a solution."

"We're on a short fuse."

"Roger that."

Jet switched on the radar and was watching the screen with laser intensity when Tanya poked her head out of the cabin. "We're sinking," she said.

Jet punched on the autopilot and moved to the hatch. "Show me."

Tanya led her below and pointed to water sloshing around on the teak veneer floor. Jet pushed past her and tore cabinets open, and when she didn't spot the leak, removed flooring until she did: a couple of bullet holes below the waterline she could fit her thumb through.

She straightened and looked around the cabin and pulled drawers free, checking for anything with which she could plug the leaks. When she reached the last cabinet in the kitchen, she almost laughed, and returned to the holes armed with a couple of wine corks the owner had saved. She jammed them into the holes and then stomped on each with her foot, and then smiled at Tanya.

"We aren't sunk yet."

Tanya looked at the corks dubiously. "Will that hold?"

"Don't see why it wouldn't." Jet brushed past her. "You look like you could use some rest. Lie down and get some while you can."

"God. Poor Liv…"

"Yes. But don't beat yourself up. She's in a better place now – at least not in agony anymore," Jet said, the mandatory lie hollow to her ears.

"Bullshit. She's dead because those animals killed her. She was my age, and now she's gone…"

"I need to focus on driving the boat, Tanya," Jet apologized.

"Where are we going?"

"Either Ibiza, or someone will pick us up on Formentera."

"What's that?"

"The island we just left."

"Oh," Tanya said, and yawned. Jet could see she was still drugged in spite of the adrenaline rush from the escape, and she clearly wasn't processing. Either that, or she'd thought they'd been taken to the mainland, which was possible since they'd been kidnapped at night.

"Try to rest," Jet repeated, and turned to go.

Jet climbed back up to the cockpit and busied herself with loading the half-empty rifle magazine with the remainder of the other, watching the radar as she methodically thumbed in cartridges. When she was finished, she snapped on the safety and set the rifle beside her, watching the sun transition from a red ember in the east to a fireball rising from the sea. She squinted at the spectacle, tired but still amped from the run, and then her brow furrowed when she saw a blinking icon on the radar screen, moving from the direction of the villa at high speed.

# Chapter 35

Jet switched the range back to twelve kilometers in order to more accurately track the bigger boat's progress. She watched as the screen refreshed several times, and saw that it was closing on them at a decent, but not critical, rate. She calculated when it would be within visual range, and determined that it would be after she'd rounded the point and changed course toward Ibiza – which gave her an idea. The catamaran's draft was far shallower than the big sports fisherman, so she could get in close to shore without running aground. If she could hug the coast, it was possible that she would disappear from the big boat's radar, or at least be impossible to differentiate from the shore clutter.

A red light on the console drew her attention, and she saw it was the bilge pump indicator; no doubt pumping out the water that had entered the boat from the holes she'd plugged. She pressed the throttles as far forward as they would go, the gesture futile since they were already wide open, and continued to monitor the chase boat on the radar as it closed from nine kilometers to seven and a half.

An alarm sounded from the helm, and an LED on one of the engine temperature gauges flashed. The temp was pegged in the redline.

Jet moved to the hatch for the starboard engine. She opened it and saw that the engine was a quarter submerged in seawater, and streams of water blasted from a firehose-sized cooling line where bullets had torn through it, which explained why the bilge pump was working constantly.

She stood and looked over the bow to ensure there were no craft she was in danger of hitting, and then darted down into the cabin to find something with which she could fix the hose. Tanya watched her digging through the drawers and cabinets again and sat up on the bunk where she was lying, clearly frightened. "What is it?"

"I need some tape or something. Some rounds punctured one of the engine lines."

A minute of ferreting yielded nothing, and Jet cursed out loud. She moved to the bathroom and checked beneath the sink, and found a coil of rope, but nothing else serviceable. She grabbed a towel from the shower enclosure and made her way back to the deck with the towel and the line, trailed by Tanya, who was eyeing her with concern.

"What if you can't fix it?"

"That isn't going to happen. Hang on. We need to slow down."

Jet backed off the throttles and the boat coasted to a near stop. With the revs down, the engine wasn't in as much danger of seizing, which it might if she shut it off, and the cooling water wasn't under severe pressure. Within moments the solid streams diminished to spurts.

Jet lowered herself into the engine compartment as the bilge pump dropped the water level, and doubled over the towel before placing it around the hose. She held it in place with her foot and cinched the cord around it, and continued wrapping the makeshift repair until the entire length of towel was covered with line. She finished by tying another knot so the coil remained in place, and then pulled herself out of the cramped space and moved back to the helm.

Jet eased the throttles forward and watched for water spraying from the engine compartment as the boat returned to speed, and was heartened when she saw none. The bilge light blinked on and she turned to Tanya. "Hold the wheel straight."

Tanya moved next to her and gripped the stainless steering wheel while Jet moved to the stern to inspect the engine. Water was seeping through the towel and into the bilge, but at a reduced rate the pump was keeping up with. She closed the hatch and returned to the helm to eye the temp gauge, which had dropped from the red to the higher end of the green range.

Tanya stayed by her side when she took the wheel back from her. "Did it work?"

"For now. We should be fine." Jet looked at the radar again. The delay had allowed the chase boat to gain on them, and it was now only six kilometers off.

"Why do you keep staring at that?" Tanya asked.

"The General has a boat." Jet tapped the screen with her forefinger. "That's it."

Tanya's eyes widened. "So it isn't over? They're coming for us?"

"They're chasing us. But we're moving pretty fast," Jet deflected, unwilling to scare the younger woman further.

Tanya twisted to look behind them, where there was nothing visible but azure sea and diesel exhaust. She reached out to grab Jet's arm, and her hand was shaking. "This is a nightmare."

Jet regarded her. Bruises blemished her face, and where it wasn't discolored, her skin was sallow and pale. To Jet she looked like she was going into shock from the ordeal. "When did you last eat?"

"I...I don't know. A while ago."

"How about water?"

"The same."

Jet nodded. "Go below and lie down. If you can find anything down there to eat or drink, do so. You can't do anything up here. Try the tap. The tank may have water in it."

Tanya looked back at her vacantly and then stumbled back to the companionway. Jet exhaled in frustration and turned back to study the radar. The General's boat was less than six kilometers away now and gaining fast. The catamaran speedo read just over twenty-three knots, the extra water in the bilge and the less than optimally operating engine slowing them.

The point they were on course for grew larger as they neared it. Jet gave it a wide berth as she steered around it, fearful of submerged rocks she couldn't see. She wished in her digging around downstairs that she'd found a chart to help her avoid ripping the bottom out of the hulls, but Kirill had apparently seen no need for any. Once the catamaran was headed north, the radar image changed and the island obscured the blips behind her – which meant that she was now as invisible to the chase boat as it was to her.

Jet twisted the wheel and pointed the bow at the rocky bluffs and, when she was fifty meters offshore, turned so they were running parallel with the coastline. Flying fish leapt ahead of where the twin hulls cut through the sea, sailing along with the catamaran before plunging back into the water after a brief but exhilarating flight. Jet smiled at how idyllic the image was, and told herself that she would take Hannah sailing when she got home.

Her phone vibrated. Dov's voice sounded strained.

"I'm working on a solution, but I need an hour," he said.

"We don't have an hour."

"I'm doing the best I can."

Jet struggled to remain calm. "I've got a girl who's been repeatedly raped and beaten, who's at the end of her rope and is going into shock. One of the engines has a problem, and the boat with the bad guys on it will be on top of us within no more than forty-five minutes. So don't tell me you're doing your best. Make something happen."

Dov didn't say anything for a long beat. "Here's what I've got."

She listened for a half minute and then nodded. "I'll give you my coordinates. Call when we're closer to pickup. The phone's about to die, so I have to make it quick."

Jet switched the call off and shook her head. She needed to buy them just a little more time, but didn't see how she could. Unless her ruse of staying close to shore worked, they were out of luck – the General's superior speed made it inevitable.

The bluff arched around and she edged away, intending to cut across the half-moon bay created by a second point ahead. By her reckoning, the General's boat would be in radar range on the northern side of the first point within ten to twelve minutes. If she timed it right, she would be rounding the second point right around the time his boat rounded the first, and she could begin skirting the shore from there. The natural assumption for whoever was piloting the chase boat would be that she'd continued on a straight course for

Ibiza. If they lost time trying to pick up her signal again on the open sea, instead of closely studying the longer route that followed the coast, that might buy her sufficient edge so they would never catch up.

The only wild card was how good their radar was, and whether it would pick up the catamaran only a few meters offshore.

A sailboat anchored to port answered the question for her. Even though it was nearly on the beach, it appeared on her radar as a blip. Whether that was due to a radar deflector mounted on the top of its mast or because it wasn't solid land, she didn't know, but she didn't like her odds.

The bilge pump switched on and off intermittently, and as she neared the second point, it went on and stayed that way. Her eyes flitted to the temperature gauges and she saw that the problem engine was inching back up into the danger zone. She engaged the autopilot, opened the hatch again, and was greeted with six inches of water in the bilge, the soaked towel pouring a substantial amount, its porous nature no match for the high-pressure streams.

Jet left the hatch open and moved back to the helm. She needed to keep pushing until she could turn the corner at the next point, and then could risk a few minutes to adjust her repair. She counted the distance in her head as the craggy rocks came into view, and once around the bend, cut power to idle and raced back to the cabin to scrounge for something else to augment the towel.

A roll of plastic garbage bags beneath the galley sink caught her eye, and she tore off two and made for the deck, pausing by where Tanya was unconscious on a bunk, her exhaustion having gotten the better of her. At the engine, Jet untied the cord and released the coils and, when the towel was loose, pulled it free, wrung it out, and unfolded it. She spread the towel on the deck and laid the garbage bags on it before refolding it, her bet being that the waterproof plastic would adequately slow the seepage so they could continue without losing the engine.

Jet rewrapped the hose and tied everything back in place and, after revving the engines back into the redline, returned to inspect the fix.

The leakage was still significant, but no more than a third of what it had been, so she closed up and focused on steering the boat.

The speed increased to twenty-five knots and Jet hugged the shore, only veering away to dodge anchored boats. Tanya poked her head out of the salon and asked if everything was okay, and Jet assured her that it was, even as she kept one eye on the radar.

When a blip appeared on the screen from around the second point, Jet knew she'd have her answer on the quality of the bigger boat's radar soon. Her breath caught in her throat as it continued on a trajectory that would take it straight to Ibiza – the course she would have been on had she not opted for the scenic route.

"Keep going," she whispered to herself, willing the sport fisherman to stay on track and miss her completely.

Jet got her wish for five minutes, and then the blip slowed. She could imagine the scene on the bridge, with gunmen studying every speck on the radar. Jet backed off the throttle and allowed the boat to slow to a crawl. Tanya called out from below. "What's going on?"

"Nothing."

The other option that had occurred to Jet as she'd considered the alternatives was to pretend to be moored off the coast. With at least a dozen other boats anchored along the shore, on the radar she would appear indistinguishable from those if she was immobile. If the ploy bought another ten or twenty minutes, that could be the difference between a successful evasion and capture.

Her phone rang. Dov's voice was distorted, the cell tower on Formentera on the other side of the island. "Where are you? Coordinates?"

Jet read off the GPS latitude and longitude. "They're only five kilometers off. At the speed that boat moves, that's seven or eight minutes if we're not underway. Twenty if we are."

"It'll be close. I'll call in fifteen to get a final fix."

"Is someone coming to rescue us?" Tanya asked from the salon doorway. Jet studied her for a moment without speaking. She looked terrible, if anything paler than earlier.

"That's the plan." Jet paused. "How good a swimmer are you?"

Tanya looked at her like she was mad. "What?"

"You heard me."

"We're going to have to swim out of here?"

"We may."

"I can't swim. I never learned how. Living in Moscow, it—"

"Damn," Jet exclaimed. The General's boat had changed course and was heading for the island. Jet calculated how long it would take to get close enough to be dangerous. It would be tight. The smartest play would be to remain still and watch the course, and only take off when it was obvious that they'd sighted the catamaran's distinctive profile. She had to assume they had binoculars, so that could happen when they were a few kilometers out.

Not good.

If the big boat could sprint wide open at thirty-five knots, and the cat did twenty-five with a tailwind, the math wasn't in their favor. If she waited until they were three kilometers off, they could close that distance in less than twenty because of the angle – she was limited to a line along the coast, whereas they could adjust their course from far farther out, shaving time off their interception.

"What's wrong?"

"They spotted us. Get below, and put on a life vest."

"I don't know how!"

"Stick your head through it and tie the straps around your waist. Go. I have to concentrate."

Tanya looked ready to argue, but Jet's expression made her reconsider, and she disappeared below. Jet goosed the throttles forward until the catamaran was skimming along the surface at top speed. The big boat altered course and adjusted until it was on target to intercept them. Jet allowed it to close the distance, watching the time as it did, and then swung the catamaran around and reversed course, using the sports fisherman's trajectory against it. The same geometry that had worked for it now worked against it, and she'd increased their lead by at least a few minutes.

Her phone jarred her from the screen, and when she answered, she had to yell over the engines.

"Tell me something good. They've got us in their sights."

"Give me your position."

She did as instructed, and heard Dov speaking to someone in the background before he returned. "Okay. He has you on visual. This will be close, but it should work."

"My battery warning is blinking. We'll see."

Jet pocketed the phone and slowed to fifteen knots. The General's boat moved faster on the screen, and she reached for the AK-47. It wouldn't be long until they'd be in range, and she'd be damned if she'd allow Tanya to be taken without a fight.

A humming turned into a roar, and a seaplane dropped from the sky and landed a hundred meters from the boat. After decelerating, it executed a turn and headed toward them.

Jet maneuvered the throttles to help get closer to the plane, and half a minute later it was bobbing a few meters from the boat. Tanya came when Jet called and stood on the stern as Jet backed toward the plane, careful to avoid clipping the wing with the radar arch.

The pilot emerged from the cockpit and held out his hand.

"Tanya!" Jet called. "Grab him and step onto the pontoon."

Tanya looked like she was ready to run in the opposite direction, but she clenched her jaw and leaned out to the pilot, who latched onto her arm and pulled her to safety. He helped her into the cockpit and waited for Jet.

"One second," she called, and disappeared into the cabin. When she reappeared, she closed the cabin door and moved to the helm. Jet entered a course setting on the autopilot and slammed the transmissions forward, and then rushed to the stern as the boat began moving away from the plane, and leapt across the gap, latching onto the wing strut to avoid slipping into the water.

The pilot nodded to her. "Nice."

"Let's get out of here. Company's on its way, and they're not friendly."

Thirty seconds later, the aircraft was beginning its run across the water. Jet removed her phone from her pocket as the plane bounced on small wind waves and took off, eyes locked on the catamaran moving north. The sports fisherman raced toward it, throwing a rooster tail of water at least ten meters high, and she waited until the big boat was pulling alongside the catamaran before pressing her phone's call button, automatically dialing the number she'd entered.

There was a pause before the line connected. It rang once and went dead.

The catamaran exploded, the fireball an orange fist that punched into the sky, and the lateral fire blast enveloped the bigger boat.

Jet allowed herself a small smile and turned to where Tanya was sitting in the rear. "Won't have to worry about them anymore."

"How…"

"Propane tank for the stove. I left the captain's phone in the cabin. They warn you about using a cell at a gas station or when a plane's refueling." She shrugged and sat back. "They aren't kidding."

# Chapter 36

*Nice, France*

Jet and Tanya walked to a waiting ivory sedan double-parked at the private terminal of the airport. The seaplane had flown them to Valencia, where a doctor had done a quick examination of Tanya at a safe house while Jet bought her a loose jogging outfit at a store down the street, and then they'd had a late lunch while they waited for a private jet that headquarters had chartered to take them to Nice.

The doctor's expression had been grim when he'd finished his exam, and when Jet returned from her shopping, he'd taken her aside to give her his assessment. "She's been badly abused. Raped repeatedly. Sodomized. Beaten. I can't say definitively she doesn't have internal injuries, but she claims that she's not passing blood in her stools, so at least that's something. She needs a thorough workup, though – more than I can do here. CT of her skull, MRI of her organs, bloodwork. She told me that there wasn't any part of her that they didn't brutalize, and I believe her."

"But with time she'll be okay?"

"She's young and strong. So physically, I'd say yes, barring something that turns up on the scans. Mentally is a different story. You don't just walk away from something like this. It's going to scar for life. The only question is how badly."

Jet gave a small shrug. "I'm not surprised. She's been to hell and back."

The doctor looked at the agent standing mute by the entry door, avoiding eye contact with all of them as instructed, and then back to Jet. "She should be in a hospital."

"I agree. But it's not my call. Any idea what they drugged her with?"

"Probably benzodiazepine or some kind of barbiturate. There's a big illegal market in Spain. Could have even been Quaaludes. They still make them in underground labs in North Africa and in the former Soviet republics. Whatever they were, they're still in her system. She's groggy, dehydrated, and seems to drift in and out of full consciousness. That makes Quaaludes the likeliest. They'll stay in the system for up to a couple of days. Which is only one reason she needs to be hospitalized."

"I'll pass that on."

The doctor left, and the agent ordered take-out food.

Jet was ravenous, but Tanya only picked at hers and spent most of her time staring into space or at the television, which was turned low in the sparsely furnished living room.

"Where are we going next?" Tanya asked. "I want to see my father."

"That's where I'm taking you. He needs to see you're safe."

"Were the men on the boat the only ones involved in the kidnapping?"

Jet's eyes narrowed. "Why?"

"I want them all to die. Slowly and horribly. My father will see to it."

Jet could certainly understand her Old Testament-style demand for revenge, but didn't respond. Tanya was a pawn in a far larger game, as was her father. How they decided to exact retribution was between them and the kidnappers, and no concern of Jet's.

They'd ridden in silence to the airport, where a Learjet 35 sat on the tarmac, its two pilots already seated in the small cockpit, no flight attendant for the short hop to Nice. Air traffic had been delayed for two hours, and when they'd finally been cleared for takeoff, the day had mostly gone by.

Tanya was still unsteady on her feet, and Jet helped her into the sedan and then climbed in beside her. The driver didn't talk as he drove through town; the only words he spoke were when he stopped in front of an anonymous apartment building high in the hills, its only redeeming feature a breathtaking view of the sea far below. Two men were waiting by the entrance, their windbreakers in the muggy late afternoon a giveaway that they were armed beneath the jackets. Jet opened the door and stepped out, and guided Tanya up the steps to where the men were surveying the street from behind mirrored aviator glasses.

"Third floor. 3C," one of them said, and stepped aside. Jet led Tanya to the elevator, and they waited on the lobby floor, its marble floor cracked and chipped, the building long past its prime, as the conveyance descended from the top floor.

The third floor was as dingy as the first, and the hall smelled of cooking and mold. Jet knocked on the 3C door and, when it opened, escorted Tanya into the apartment, where two more agents were waiting along with the head of station, who Jet had been told was named Laurent.

"This way," Laurent said, and Tanya followed him to the bedroom on the ocean side of the building.

Karev was lying in bed, his vital signs monitor beeping, eyes closed. When they entered, his eyes opened. "Tanya!" he exclaimed, his voice rough.

"Papa!" she cried, and ran to him.

She hugged him and he held her in his arms, the cast and IV line an afterthought, and then she pulled away.

"Are you all right? Who are these people? Where's Sergei?"

Karev frowned. "I'm a guest of these…people. We made a deal. They find and rescue you, I help them. But don't worry about any of that. I'm fine. Just a little beaten up." He looked her over. "My God, baby. What did they do to you?"

She looked away, her eyes brimming with tears. "They…they killed Liv."

"What about you?"

"I...I don't want to talk about it."

He took in the bruises, her split lip, her dull gaze and monotone responses, and his eyes hardened. "Of course. You don't have to." He looked to Jet, as though seeing her for the first time. "You!"

"She belongs in a hospital," Jet said in Russian. "She's been through hell. The sooner you tell us what we need to know, the sooner she can get the help she needs. And she's going to need a lot of it," she finished, emphasis on her final words.

"You're responsible for saving her?"

Jet shrugged. "It was a team effort."

"But I thought you...the attack on the boat..."

"I'm a good swimmer."

His eyes flitted to the bandage on Jet's arm. "And the men who did this to her?"

"The ones who were holding her are dead or wounded. We'll give you all the information you need to deal with any survivors in your own way. That isn't our affair."

"You tried to kill me."

Tanya looked to Jet, her mouth forming an O. "What?"

Another shrug. "It wasn't personal."

Karev's lips tightened. "It was to me."

"You have bigger problems. You made a deal. It's time to deliver."

"Once Tanya is safe at a hospital. You need to allow me to provide security for her. You have no idea what you're dealing with. This man...Kalda...is superhuman. He'll stop at nothing to have his way."

Jet looked to Laurent. "Not my concern. I've done my part. Good luck with your daughter." She turned to Tanya. "I'm sorry about your friend. And for what they did to you. But don't let it break you."

Tanya just stared at her. Jet took a step back, and Karev threw her a final ugly look.

"I appreciate what you did for my daughter, but you people slaughtered my security team, and you tried to kill me. I won't forget. This isn't over. Not by a long shot."

Jet held his stare. "Maybe for you. For me it is."

Laurent moved toward the bed. "Time to honor your commitment. Tell me everything you know about Kalda. No more stalling."

"When my daughter is safe, and I'm in a public place where you can't harm me. Not before."

"That wasn't the deal."

"I'm changing it."

Jet shook her head and left the Russian to Laurent. She was bone-tired, and she needed a shower and some sleep. She expected the director would want her involved in finishing the Oliver episode, and she wanted to be rested and alert to do so. Whatever Laurent needed to do in order to convince Karev that he couldn't renege on his deal, she had no part in it, and would wait to receive new instructions.

"I need a hotel," she said to one of the agents.

"There's one down the hill on the left. St. Marin. You have money?" he asked.

"Plenty. Tell Laurent that's where I'll be." She spied a phone-charging cable on the breakfast bar. "Can I commandeer that?"

The agent nodded. "Sure. We have more."

"I'll be at the St. Marin."

"I'll let him know."

Jet unplugged the cord, verified it fit her phone, and then left the apartment, the only sound in the hallway her footsteps on the cracked stone floor. The elevator indicator showed it was at the lobby level, and she glanced at the fire stairs at the far end of the hall while she waited for it to arrive. It had been a long few days, and she hoped that the hardest part was behind her, but until they found Oliver or were able to disarm his servers, she feared the worst was yet to come.

The two agents who'd been stationed outside were gone, or at least concealed well enough so she couldn't spot them. The sedan had taken off, leaving Jet to walk down the hill, the exercise feeling good after so many hours on boats and planes. The sign for the hotel was coming into view as twilight painted the sky purple and salmon, and she picked up her pace, anxious to finally get some well-deserved rest.

She'd nearly reached the hotel when the evening was shattered by the distinctive sound of suppressed gunshots from the apartment and the squeal of tires on the hillside pavement.

# Chapter 37

Jet pirouetted and raced back up the hill, her legs burning from the exertion. When she arrived at the apartment complex block, there were three SUVs parked in front with their engines running. She ducked into the underground parking area and ran to the elevator. The panel showed it on the third floor, and her stomach sank – any doubts she'd had about what was taking place evaporated at the certainty that someone was attacking the safe house.

She swung the fire door open and listened, and then started climbing the steps, taking care to make as little noise as possible. At the third-floor landing she paused, ears straining for any sounds of a fight. After several moments of not hearing anything, she inched the door open, looked through the gap, and stepped from the stairwell.

When she reached the apartment door, which was hanging from one hinge with the lock shattered and the doorjamb splintered in pieces, she paused again. The only thing she heard was a stuttering gasping coming from the master bedroom. She entered and stepped over the obviously dead form of one of the agents, and reached down for the 9mm Sig Sauer P229 Nitron Compact pistol lying by his head. Jet chambered a round, taking care to do so as silently as she could, and flicked off the safety before continuing into the apartment, leading with the gun.

Another agent was slumped against the living room wall, the plaster behind him painted with blood from where he'd slid to the floor after being shot twice in the chest, the exit wounds accounting for the red swatch behind him. Jet's eyes narrowed at the sight and she took cautious steps, one foot slowly in front of the other, peering down the gunsights as she made her way toward the bedroom.

The door was open. The gasping noise was coming from Laurent, who lay on the floor of the otherwise empty room, the crimson trail on the floor testament to his having dragged himself from the other bedroom after being shot. A bloody hole in his chest made a wet sucking sound each time he struggled for breath, explaining the gasping she'd heard when she entered. He looked up at her through glassy eyes and tried to speak, but only managed a wheeze.

Jet knelt beside him and leaned over him to better hear. "Who? Kalda?"

He managed a single shake of his head and mouthed a word. "Russian."

She stood and moved to the window to look down at the street. The doors of the SUV were closing. Jet threw open the window and drew a bead on the hood of the first vehicle and fired four times, her intent to disable the motor, but the truck lunged forward and tore away. The other two vehicles raced off, zigzagging as they went, and Jet emptied the pistol at them, knowing that the gesture was futile – the 9mm slugs wouldn't do much damage at that range.

Jet turned to Laurent, but he'd stopped breathing, his eyes wide as though in disbelief even in death. She leaned over and closed them, and then felt in his jacket. Her fingers found a cell phone, and she removed it along with the twin of her gun and an extra magazine. The immediate threat was over, but that didn't mean that the Russians wouldn't return to finish the job, or that they hadn't left a few shooters behind to mop up.

She tossed her empty pistol aside and pocketed the extra magazines before returning to the entry. Jet hesitated there, weapon in hand, and ducked around the doorjamb in a crouch, scanning the hall with the gun. She caught a glimpse of a frightened woman's face at one of the other apartment doors before it slammed shut, but nothing else. The hall was clear.

None of the operatives would have any ID on them, so Jet didn't need to linger to clean up the scene. Now her imperative was to get clear in one piece and report the attack to headquarters so they could take appropriate action – not that there was much they could do now. If the Russian hadn't broken in the short time Jet had been gone, Laurent hadn't learned anything of value, so the entire drama on Ibiza and Formentera had been for naught, and her country was still in the same ugly predicament as before.

Jet made her way back down the stairs, moving slowly, gun at the ready. At the ground floor she stood, scarcely breathing, trying to sense the presence of anyone lying in wait. After a long pause she cracked the door open and scanned the lobby. There was nobody there, and no signs of violence, just the same cracked marble and poorly swept floor.

She stepped from the landing and slowly walked to the door. Jet fleetingly wondered what the assailants had done with the two agents who'd been outside, but decided it didn't matter. That they were dead was a given, and nothing she did would change that.

At the entry, she jammed the gun into her pants at the small of her back and exited the building. Out on the street, she saw fluid on the pavement approximately where she'd shot the lead vehicle, and she ran over, dipped a finger in it, and sniffed it.

Oil.

Maybe she'd done some damage after all. The thought gave her no pleasure. Jet had fired out of frustration, not because she'd believed that a few pistol rounds would stop an SUV. Still, she felt strangely satisfied she'd drawn blood, if only from the bastards' car.

Sirens ululated from down the hill, and Jet took that as her cue to leave. There was nothing more she could accomplish, and to risk being caught was pointless. As she walked toward the hotel, her mind pored over how the Russians could have found the safe house, and she concluded it either had to be an internal leak or some sort of tracking device on Karev that a search had missed – likely sewn into his clothes or implanted somewhere on him. The latter seemed most logical, but the hindsight didn't do anyone much good other than to teach them all a lesson. That Laurent had been careless was also a possibility. The question was why the Russians had taken so long, if that was the case, to break Karev out.

"Probably to plan the logistics and get reinforcements from Russia," she whispered, the answer obvious to her once she voiced it. That Jet had managed to achieve the impossible and locate and rescue the daughter had simply been coincidental timing, if the tracking hypothesis was correct.

The more ominous possibility – that they had a leak – perfectly accounted for it, though, which, try as she might, she couldn't dismiss. In the end it would be the director's problem, not hers, but even so the thought that someone in the Mossad had sold out an entire cell chilled her to her core.

Jet snuck a glance back over her shoulder at the apartment complex and saw half the units now had lights burning in the windows. She could make out at least four faces looking down the street at where emergency vehicle roof lights were winking off the buildings down the hill.

The sirens drew nearer and she increased her pace, anxious to get clear of the scene. She couldn't stay at the hotel now, but she'd find another. She had her passport and enough cash to last for a month, and nearing the end of the season, there would be plenty of rooms. A police car growled past, followed by two more, and she turned off the main street and onto a tributary.

When the sirens had faded, she fished Laurent's phone from her pocket and called the director's private number as she ambled unhurriedly down the hill, to any observer a young woman out for her evening walk who couldn't stay off her cell.

# Chapter 38

After finding a suitably middling hotel well off the water and paying cash to a clerk who didn't bother asking for her passport, Jet retired to her room, plugged her phone into the wall to charge, and stripped off her clothes. She took a quick shower, luxuriating in the hot water even if the gashes on her scalp and arm stung from it, and then lay down naked on the bed to sleep for as many hours as the director allowed her before calling back with an update.

He hadn't been happy to hear Jet's report, but like a professional, he'd absorbed the information, asked several pointed questions, and then signed off with a promise to reconnect later. Jet hadn't asked what the status of the malware extortion scheme was, and he'd volunteered no information she didn't already know, which was fine by her – she didn't need visions of her country in ruins to keep her from getting some badly needed sleep.

When the phone rang two and a half hours later, it was like broken glass in her ears. She rolled over and answered, instantly awake.

"The short version is that we've got nothing on the third server or Kalda," the director said. "Which is another way of saying we're screwed. We've located the first two and have teams in place, but without the third, we're nowhere."

Jet considered the information, which was far more than she needed to know. "Why are you telling me this?"

"We're down to the wire. I'm asking if you have any ideas."

"Don't you have a room full of the biggest brains in the world?"

"Humor me. Do you have anything or not?"

"Let's run this down. Kalda disappeared. You can't find him. He isn't at his Helsinki place, and he hasn't communicated with his company. Right?"

"Correct."

"Nothing in these servers or the traffic that led you to them points at where they're being monitored or controlled from?"

"No."

She thought for several moments, something at the back of her mind tickling her consciousness but not springing to the forefront.

"Do you have any more background on him? Any siblings?"

"Only child. Parents and grandparents are dead. He doesn't seem to have any connection to anyone."

"His banks? Follow the money?"

"Swiss and Austrian and Cayman. Might as well be talking to a rock."

Jet snapped her fingers and sat up straighter. "What about the girlfriend? The ex. Anna. He was in a serious relationship with her. Maybe she knows something or can give us some clues as to where he might have gone to ground."

"We haven't been able to locate her. Can't get into the company's records – their security is more elaborate than the Pentagon's. And with just a first name, it's a nonstarter."

Jet eyed her clothes. "What do you know about cosplay?"

"Is that a band? I need ideas, not a pop culture quiz."

"It's relevant. How soon can you get me a computer? I need to do some digging."

"In about an hour. Any special kind?"

"As long as it's got wireless." She gave him the name of the hotel and told him she'd meet the courier in the lobby. "Call when he's downstairs. Oh, and I could use a change of clothes, too. It's too late for me to get anything tonight," she said, and told him her size.

"Is there anything else?"

"I need to think. There's something I'm missing. It could be nothing. I don't know."

"That's it? You want a computer and some clothes, and maybe you know something, but you can't tell me what?"

"Kalda and his ex were into cosplay." She explained the concept to the director, who grunted when she was finished.

"And?"

"I can't remember the character she loved. It was kind of obscure. But if there are cosplay groups online or conventions in Europe, maybe something will jog my memory."

"Sounds like a long shot," he said, in a voice that made clear he was regretting he'd called. "We only have one day left. If we don't pay by midnight tomorrow, it's lights out."

"How are they going to collect the money? You can track it."

"Negative. They want bitcoin."

"There'll be a record of the address."

"Our people tell me that within ten minutes of the transfer, it'll be converted into five other currencies and disappear into the ether."

"Can't you force the miners to back out the transaction once it's done? If they all agree to void it, it's like it never happened. At least that's my understanding."

"One of our team already proposed it, and it was shot down as impractical. Apparently someone stole four hundred million in bitcoin from an exchange called Mt. Gox, and to maintain the integrity of the blockchain, the miners let them get away with it. The problem is that if a majority of the miners can decide to void a transaction if a government applies enough pressure, then there's no integrity to it, and the value of the blockchain drops to zero. That's the opposite of what the people involved in it stand for, and we'd need to be able to convince over half the miners to void the transaction, which isn't going to happen. So no. Not an option. Once the money's converted and gone, it's gone forever."

"Then hurry up and get me the computer. I'll see what I can come up with."

"I'd hoped you might have something more solid."

"I wish I did."

She disconnected and walked to the bathroom, where she inspected her wounds. Her scalp was healing nicely, but the arm was still an angry red. She made a mental note to get some antibiotics if it continued to flare up, and returned to the bedroom, where she donned her clothes and sat on the bed to wait for the director's call.

Forty-five minutes later she was downstairs accepting a cheap red nylon suitcase from a middle-aged woman outside the hotel. Neither of them spoke, and Jet waited until her car drove off to go back upstairs and inspect her delivery. The laptop was a few years old but in good shape, and the clothes were acceptable, but not much more. The woman had thought to provide two pairs of underthings, and Jet stripped off her dirty clothes and slipped on a new pair of panties before sitting down at the computer and beginning her internet search for cosplay information.

It boggled her mind that there were conventions all over the world for those who enjoyed playing dress up and role-playing. In Jet's lexicon, where each day could bring real-world death and chaos, the notion of pretending to be some comic-book character for stimulation seemed absurd – the hallmark of cultures with far too much time on their hands and too much money in the citizenry's pockets. Yet website after website featured thousands of cosplay enthusiasts, some in outfits that had cost small fortunes, the men generally nerdy, some of the women incredibly beautiful, if nothing more than male-inspired caricatures of real females.

Two hours into her research she found a blog that revolved around cosplay in Norway, Sweden, and Denmark, and clicked through countless photographs of conventions and smaller get-togethers in clubs and bars. She stopped at one, which featured six women in colorful attire, the names inscribed below. The second from the left in particular caught her attention – not because of the neon wig and elaborate corset, but because of the woman's moniker: Charlotte, from *Galaxstar 3*.

The discussion with Piia came back to her, and Jet enlarged the photo and studied the woman in detail. Not a waif by any means, strong arms on full display and a round, pretty face with eyes that radiated good humor and intelligence.

The more she looked at the woman, the more she could picture her with Oliver. He was a swine and a disgusting mess, but she might have been attracted to his mind or his money or both. Certainly not his physique. Jet couldn't pretend to understand why anyone would want to be in the same building as him, much less the same bed, but she'd long ago recognized that there was a universe of complexity to human emotion, and relationships often defied logic.

The photo had been taken in Stockholm six months earlier at a costume contest. Jet typed in the pseudonym *Charlotte* and the words *cosplay* and *Sweden*, and spent another half hour going through the results. The woman appeared in at least a score of photos from different events, so it was safe to assume that she was living in Stockholm, or had been until recently. The oldest one she could find dated back less than two years. Before that, nothing. Also in keeping with the timeline Piia had described.

Jet jotted down the names of the venues that were mentioned, as well as the names of as many of the other cosplayers in the photos that she could find, and then called the director to tell him what she'd learned. When she was done, his response was immediate.

"I want you on the next plane to Stockholm."

"I figured you'd say that. I already checked. There's one in the morning."

"That's cutting it close. See if you can do a connection in Paris or Germany. We're out of time. You still have your passport?"

"Yes."

"Get on a plane to wherever. Make it happen. I'll notify the Stockholm head of station you're on your way. He'll supply whatever you need."

Jet sighed. "This isn't the week I'm going to catch up on my sleep."

The director sucked in a lungful of smoke and exhaled loudly before responding.

"I'll bet you a hundred shekels you've gotten more than me."

# Chapter 39

*Stockholm, Sweden*

Morning was breaking as Jet's flight from Berlin banked through a carpet of low clouds hanging over Stockholm and the city's fourteen islands came into view. The plane straightened as it continued its descent on a flight path over the Baltic Sea toward Lake Malaren, and the attendants prepared the half-empty cabin for landing. Jet sat back in her seat as the aircraft shed altitude, and then it was bouncing on the runway and slowing.

The terminal was lit up like a parade float, and Jet was one of the first passengers off. She carried her cheap bag to immigration, where she was waved through with a smile by a tall man who could have appeared on a billboard for the Swedish people, and continued through the terminal to a coffee shop that had just opened.

She normally didn't drink stimulants, but hadn't gotten much rest on the planes, so she ordered a tall coffee with cream and dialed the number she'd been given for the Stockholm Mossad station chief. A baritone voice answered, and she spoke her code phrase. The man responded correctly, and she glanced around as she spoke in Hebrew.

"I'm in the terminal."

"Very well. I have an operative who will meet you outside arrivals. How long will you be?"

She sipped her coffee and checked the time. "Ten minutes."

"She's in a black Volvo S90." He recited a license plate number. "Her name's Alva. She's been instructed to be at your disposal as long as you need her."

"I appreciate it."

"It isn't often I get a call from the director in the middle of the night. He was very forceful in ensuring we rolled out the red carpet."

"We're to meet this morning?"

"Up to you. I'm working on your schedule. You're the priority."

"I'll contact you when I have something."

"I can offer you as many operatives as you need. Just say the word. I was told to provide every resource."

"Hopefully that won't be necessary. I work alone."

"As you wish." He paused. "Good luck."

The coffee helped revive her, and she easily spotted the Volvo in the nearly empty arrivals area. Jet walked to the car and got in, and Alva smiled a greeting.

"Good morning," she said. "Where would you like to go?"

"What time do the stores open in the city center?"

"Depends on the type. Mostly ten. Restaurants earlier, of course."

"Do you have a hotel recommendation?"

A traffic cop blew an ear-piercing whistle a few meters from them and motioned for Alva to move. "Near there? Sure," Alva said, and put the car in gear.

Early rush-hour traffic into the city slowed their progress, and it took twice as long as Alva had indicated to reach the hotel, which was a charming boutique lodging in an antique building. Alva waited for Jet to check in and drop off her things, and when she got down to the parking area, raised an eyebrow as Jet slid back into the passenger seat.

"Where to?"

"I have a list of places. But they won't be open yet. Is there a good place for breakfast? Someplace quiet where I can get online?"

"Several." Alva's brow crinkled as she thought. "There's a great one near the water. Is this your first time in Stockholm?"

Jet didn't feel chatty, nor inclined to share that she'd carried out operations there years before, so simply shook her head. Alva got the hint and remained quiet until they pulled up in front of a bright, overly cheery restaurant, all chrome and glass and white porcelain tile. Jet showed Alva her list and asked whether she was within walking distance of the venues, and Alva nodded. "Most of them. All within…ten minutes of here."

"What's your number?" Jet asked.

Alva recited it, and Jet entered it into her cell and dialed it. Alva's purse beeped, and Jet hung up. "I'll call if I need anything. Might want to stick around the area."

"I can take you wherever…"

Jet unbuckled her seat belt and opened the door. "I want to walk. Need the exercise."

The restaurant was efficient and pristine, and the waitress spoke good English, as did most of those working in areas that saw tourist traffic, Jet remembered from her prior assignment there. She ordered the special and another cup of coffee, and took her time surfing the internet on her phone and pinning the locations she wanted to visit on her map application. She switched to cosplay-related sites over her second cup of coffee, and read everything she could find, again marveling at how seriously many appeared to take the odd hobby. That some would build their entire identity around pretending to be an anime or gaming character baffled her, and for a moment she wondered what kind of world Hannah would grow up to inherit.

Eventually she paid the bill and went to her first destination – a coffee shop that was heavy on bohemianism and neck beards and hippy attire. She showed the cashier and the barista a photo of Charlotte, but got nothing but blank stares in return. Apparently the morning shift wasn't part of the cosplay world; it was more of a nocturnal pursuit than a diurnal one.

Jet next visited a comic-book store and had better luck with a heavily tattooed young man dressed entirely in black, his face elaborately pierced and his earlobes distended, who weighed less than she did. He greeted her inquiry with a condescending sneer and rolled his eyes when she showed him the picture.

"Yeah, sure. I've seen her around. We sponsor some cosplay nights at the local clubs. She's a big favorite."

"Do you know her name? Or how to get in touch with her?"

He pursed his lips like she'd just asked for his email password. "No. They just come to the events, you know? That's like their entire thing. Most don't talk about who they are in real life. The whole point of cosplay is to be something special, something extraordinary, the center of attention. Who wants to tell people they're a babysitter or a waiter?"

"When did you last see her?"

"Maybe a month ago. But never in the store."

"Do you know any places where they congregate during the day?"

More eye rolling. "Most people have jobs. Cosplay is like playing in a garage band. Something you do after work, you know?"

The store a dead end, her next visit was to a nostalgia boutique that sold vinyl records, VHS tapes, cassettes, and pulp paperback novels in both English and Swedish. Her questions were met with much the same responses by the owner, who was a nice enough young woman with a gap-toothed smile.

"I wish I could help you. Why do you want to talk to her?" she asked when Jet had exhausted her questioning.

"Oh, I'm writing an article on cosplay for a New York paper, and she's been identified as one of the more popular Charlotte players."

"Wow. Well, if you want to give me your number, I can ask around. I get a lot of people who know folks in that crowd. How long are you in Stockholm for?"

Jet scribbled down her number. "Just today."

"Bummer. Well, if I hear anything, I'll give you a call."

"That would be great."

Four more shops, and Jet hit pay dirt with a woman in her forties whose long curly mop of hair was fringed with the beginnings of gray.

"Sure. I know her," the woman said. "Name's Anna. You want me to call her for you? I'm sure she'd love to be in an article on her cosplay thing."

"Would you?"

"Let me see if I can find her number."

The woman disappeared into the back of the store, and when she returned, she had a cordless phone in her hand. She held it out to Jet with a grin.

"Anna?" Jet asked into the handset.

"That's me. Lora says you're writing an article about cosplay in Europe?"

"That's right. It's a lifestyle piece for the *New York Post*. I'd love to interview for it if you have time."

"Over the phone?"

"Better in person."

"I…I look kind of dumpy today. No pictures, okay?"

Jet put a smile into her voice. "I promise."

"My lunch break is in an hour. It'll take about twenty-five minutes to get here from there. Do you mind waiting?"

"Not at all."

"Cool. There's a restaurant on the corner, near my office." Anna gave her the name, and Jet repeated it.

"I'll see you in an hour."

"Awesome."

Jet thanked the helpful shopkeeper and left, wishing she could accelerate time so the meeting could happen sooner. Instead, she played tourist on the way to the restaurant, admiring the historical buildings and their rainbow hues, as well as the overall impeccably clean streets and handsome population. The breeze off the waterways that threaded between the islands was chilly, but not as frigid as the blasts off the Gulf of Finland she'd been treated to in Tallinn and Helsinki.

The restaurant was unremarkable in appearance, a typical neighborhood family-owned place where most of the customers and service staff seemed to know and like each other. Jet was shown to a booth near one of the windows by a young blonde woman who could have been a catalog model, and sat patiently waiting for the appearance of Anna/Charlotte. Within a short time she'd know whether her hunch had been a good one or not, and she tried to forget the fact that the fate of her country might be relying on her judgment.

Anna entered right on time, and Jet easily recognized her from the photos. Jet waved and stood, and Anna walked over to her, as statuesque and well padded as in her images. Jet shook her hand and introduced herself as Kimberly and took her seat, and Anna sat across from her, a sunny smile in place.

"I have to admit this is all kind of thrilling," she said. "I've only been interviewed for local magazines."

"Why don't we order, and then we can talk?"

The waitress came over and beamed at Anna before taking their orders. When she departed, Anna sat forward with her hands folded in front of her, obviously excited. "So how do we do this?"

"Couldn't be easier. I ask you questions, and you answer." Jet took her phone out and activated the audio-recording feature. "Ready?"

"Shoot."

Jet spent ten minutes asking about Anna's history as a cosplayer, how she became interested in it, what she liked best about it – all questions designed to relax her and confirm her background. When she was absolutely sure that the woman was Oliver's ex, based on her timeline of living in Stockholm and a few comments about a boyfriend who'd been into the scene encouraging her to take it more seriously, Jet dropped the pretense and narrowed in on her actual interest.

"Tell me about this boyfriend," Jet said.

"Oh, I don't discuss old flames. I'm sure you understand."

"Maybe in broad terms? I'm curious about how you met. You say it was a cosplay event?"

"Yes. He had a wicked costume, really elaborate and obviously handmade. We started talking and found we had a lot of common interests."

"But it didn't work out?"

Anna frowned for the first time. "In the end, no. But we had a great time together."

"What did he do for a living, if you don't mind me asking?"

Another frown, and uncertainty beginning to show in her eyes. "Computer stuff. Technical."

*Bingo.*

The waitress delivered their lunch. Jet pushed her plate aside, sat forward, and lowered her voice. "Anna, I have a confession to make. You're not going to be happy with me, and I don't blame you. But I need your help."

"I...I don't understand."

"I'm not a freelancer for the *Post*. And as interesting as it is, I didn't want to meet you to discuss cosplay."

Anna looked like she'd been gut-punched. Her mouth worked, but no sound came out.

Jet sighed. "I'm with a foreign intelligence agency. We tracked you down because there's a crisis unfolding, and your ex is behind it. Oliver. If we can't find him, millions of people are going to die." Jet figured it wouldn't hurt to raise the stakes so Anna took the situation seriously.

She stared at Jet like she'd spit in her food, and moved to stand up.

Jet shook her head. "Don't. If you won't speak with me voluntarily and do the right thing, you'll be grabbed off the street. I don't want that. I think you're sweet and basically good, and you don't want to get involved in something ugly. But my group doesn't have any choice. They need information on Oliver, and they need it fast."

"You...you're threatening me?" She looked over at the waitress. "We'll see what the police have to say about this."

"The police won't be able to help you, Anna. Don't do it. It won't end well. At least listen to what I ask before making a decision." Jet paused and saw hesitation in the big woman's glare. "Your ex is blackmailing my government. Threatening to shut down the grid if he isn't paid a fortune by midnight. That would leave the country defenseless and in chaos. We need information that could help us find him. That's all. Cooperate, and you'll never hear from us again."

Anna took a bite of her food and chewed as she thought. "What country?"

"Does it matter?"

"What country?" Anna repeated.

"Israel."

Anna slammed her hand down on the table and looked around the restaurant before fixing Jet with a dark stare. "That bastard. This is all about getting back at me. What a prick. I mean, seriously."

"What are you talking about?"

"We used to argue all the time about Zionism. Oliver views Israel as an abomination – a colonial decision by the British to give the Rothschilds what they wanted with the Balfour Declaration. The Rothschilds owned the Bank of England at the time and were big Zionism supporters, and the Balfour Declaration was addressed to Lord Rothschild. It basically agreed that Zionists could established a state in Palestine, which was instrumental in how Israel came into being." She took another bite of her meal and shook her head. "He says that the British had no right to carve up the Middle East as they saw fit, and to force people who've lived on land for thousands of years to move based on some religious text."

Anna took a couple of deep breaths before continuing. "Obviously I disagreed. Not with his basic point, that the British had no right to do it, but with his statement that the Jewish people didn't have a right to a homeland where they could be safe from persecution. Whether or not the Brits should have or morally had the right, they did, and that's history. It's settled. It happened, and there's no putting the toothpaste back into the tube. I would always go back to how to make it work from here, understanding that plenty of countries came into being by taking other people's territory. I mean, the U.S., for example. Ask any Native Americans if they're happy Europeans came and took their land. Or Mexico. Or Central America. Or South America. Or Europe. World history is one group confiscating resources from others and taking what they want. So while maybe he had a historical point, it was naïve and didn't solve anything moving forward."

Jet had allowed her to expound, even though she was growing impatient – given the deadline, she didn't have time for a dissertation on Zionism and the history of Israel. "Why was it such a big deal between you?"

"I'm Jewish. Not all militant or anything, but that disagreement was a way for him to sort of pick at me when he wasn't happy. We got along well, but he grew more and more surly as we stayed together, until it became a daily fight. So I said screw it and left." She sighed. "He was into some seriously sketchy shit. That was another problem I had. We didn't talk about his business, but I'm not an idiot, and I saw enough to know he was involved in…bad stuff."

"So it doesn't surprise you that he would try to blackmail the country?"

That drew a laugh. "Not at all. He's got a serious God complex. The cosplay is just a way to act that out. But he truly believes he's superior to just about everyone. I mean, he's really smart, no doubt, but he's borderline pathological about it. It took me years to understand the truth, but once I did, it was harder and harder to live with him. He views people as ants. Disposable. He's the center of the universe – his plots and schemes, his wants, his needs. Everyone else is just a walk-on in his movie."

Anna put down her fork. "When we first met, he wasn't rich. He was just starting out. And he was a lot thinner. He got nothing but worse as he became more successful. Maybe he was always that way and was just hiding it. Over time I realized he's a complete sociopathic narcissist with delusions of grandeur. One day, I found some, uh…kiddie porn…on his system and decided I'd had enough. I never looked back. I'm glad I left."

"He's a pedophile?" Jet asked, even though she'd seen the footage herself.

"No. I believe he uses it for blackmail purposes. I think that's part of the way he built his fortune. Some of the people in the videos are famous industrialists and politicians."

The answer didn't surprise Jet. Anytime she'd heard of a great fortune built quickly, some sort of criminal activity was usually lurking behind the scenes.

Jet spoke quietly but deliberately. "He isn't in Tallinn anymore. He took his helicopter to Helsinki and then disappeared. The reason I'm here is to find out where else he could have gone. Do you have any idea?"

"Disappeared? I would have said Helsinki. He loves that house."

"Does he have anyplace else?"

She took a sip of her drink and frowned as she thought. "Not that I know of. I mean, it's been a while, so he could have bought something. He's rich enough."

"Nothing shows up on any of the databases."

Anna laughed without humor. "It's child's play to get around those. You create a shell company or a trust. It holds the deed. Simple. I learned a lot looking over Oliver's shoulder."

"Think, Anna. Please. There has to be some place."

"I'm afraid I can't help you. I really don't know. I would if I did."

Jet smiled sadly. "I believe you."

Anna glanced at her watch. "I need to get back to work."

"It's going to be a catastrophe, Anna. All his doing."

"I know. I'm sorry I can't help. He's...evil."

Jet eyed her uneaten meal. "I'll pay the check. Least I can do."

"Thanks." Anna slid from the booth and stood. "No team's going to grab me?"

"I'll see that they don't."

Anna walked away, and Jet's shoulders sagged. Another dead end. This one their last resort. She switched the phone on and thumbed through to the director's number, and her finger was hovering over the call button when Anna's shadow darkened the table again.

"You know, this may be nothing, but in the early days we used to go camping in Umeå. He used to love the fishing lodges there. Some were pretty incredible. Maybe he decided to buy himself one? That's the only thing I can think of other than Helsinki."

Jet put the phone down. "Umeå? How often did you go?"

"Maybe...seven times?" She fiddled with her purse. "Now I really have to get back to work. Good luck. Sorry I couldn't do more."

Jet pulled up a map of Sweden on her phone. She zoomed in on Umeå and saw that it was a smallish city on the Ume River, about eighteen kilometers to the coast and surrounded by verdant expanses. After studying the area, she switched to a site that described the locale, including weather, history, economy, and such. It had been a university-driven economy until the last five years, when it had become a hub for information technology and cryptocurrency mining, and now featured a number of large data centers and mining operations due to plentiful availability of cheap power from the nearby hydroelectric dam.

This time when Jet thumbed to the director's number, she had a completely different discussion in mind. One that might just turn out to be worth four billion euros if her gut was right.

# Chapter 40

*Umeå, Sweden*

Jet squinted through the Volvo's passenger window at the industrial park where the data centers were located – long, low, single-story buildings that were unremarkable other than for the guard gates and huge nearly empty parking lots. She turned to Alva, who looked frazzled after four hours of high-speed driving from Stockholm up the E4 highway.

"Slow down."

This was their second time around the park, and Jet was particularly interested in one facility that was obviously newer than the others, but more strikingly, had security guards not only at the entry to the parking lot but also patrolling the grounds. Given that the crime rate in Sweden was lower than most places in the world, and that the data centers only had servers in them – which would be hard to sell on any secondary market and, more importantly, wouldn't justify the risk of prison time to steal – the presence of the guards was unusual.

Jet had had a long discussion with the director about her interrogation of Anna, and he'd concurred that they had nothing better to go on than the possibility Oliver had relocated to the wilds of Sweden and was running his extortion scheme out of a data center he'd set up specifically for his criminal operations. The Stockholm head of station had equipped Alva with a backpack containing explosives and a timer, as well as a pistol, a set of lockpicks, and a host of other items Jet had requested, but even so she didn't have a high level of confidence.

The director had reported that the Mossad tech team had narrowed the IP addresses of two of the three command and control servers to locations in Latvia and Ukraine they could pinpoint, but they were still working on the third, and had underscored that taking out two would serve no purpose. He'd said he hoped to have the third any minute, but that discussion had been three hours ago, and she'd received no update since.

He'd also mentioned in passing that the tech team had identified all of the men in the pedophile sex tapes, but that a close examination of the footage had shown some irregularities that were consistent with computer-generated images, so it looked like Anna's fears about Oliver blackmailing politicians and high-net-worth individuals had been valid – only with videos that weren't actually them.

All of which pointed to a ruthless sociopath who viewed others as prey. It was only natural, then, that he would escalate to extorting entire economies, given his tech capabilities. And if the rumors of his having done work for the Estonian clandestine agencies were true, he had a good feel for what spy networks could and couldn't do, so wouldn't fear their retaliation if he'd insulated himself sufficiently.

Although it was a dangerous game he was playing, she could see how it would be worth it from his perspective – if he was successful and pocketed four billion euros from Israel, the Mossad would be desperate to keep the fact a secret forever for fear of being targeted by every hacker group in the world, so the country was likely to never say anything. Just the fact he'd done so would be almost as devastating as if he'd triggered the full-blown shutdown.

In many ways, it was a perfect crime, and one that might actually pay off.

Her phone rang.

"We nailed down an IP for the third server," the director began. "Your hunch was prescient. It's near the dam. Congratulations."

"Have you been able to narrow it down any further?"

"Negative. The IP isn't like a residential IP. It simply terminates in a district. We can't get any more granular than that."

"I'm staring at a data center that has armed guards patrolling it in an industrial park near the dam. I'll give you the address. See if you can find the ownership information. It might be a government-funded installation. No point wasting our time if it is. But if it's private, it's a likely candidate." She read off the numbers on the side of the building. "It would be nice if they could get the location of the IP address a little closer. There are at least twenty server farms in this area."

"You now know everything I do. I'll call back as soon as we have a trace on whose facility it is."

Jet hung up and looked to Alva before turning back to the building. She'd counted four guards on the perimeter of the huge building she was interested in – easily eighty thousand square feet under one roof. The other data centers had none. That in itself was a red flag, although not definitive.

"You think that's it?" Alva asked.

"It's possible."

"What if it is?"

"One step at a time."

"You could probably cut the fiber optic going into the building," Alva suggested. "Into the whole district, if you can't narrow it down."

"Which assumes no microwave or wireless backups. Centers this size would have those in place. So it wouldn't work."

"Cut their power as well?"

Jet sighed and turned to Alva. "No offense, but I think better in silence."

Alva was properly chastened and looked away. "Just tell me where to drive."

"One more time through the park. We might have missed something."

An hour later, they had accomplished all that Jet felt they could, and she instructed Alva to go to a hotel she'd found on the web that was located nearby. She couldn't do much more until she heard back from the director on the ownership of the suspect facility, and didn't want to draw unwelcome scrutiny circling the area repeatedly.

They checked in, booking different rooms, and Jet flirted with the clerk, who spoke excellent English and was friendly. She asked about fishing lodges in the area, and the clerk's eyes lit up.

"Oh, yes, we're rather known for them. Some are spectacular — really, they aren't lodges so much as rustic mansions with every amenity. Why? Were you interested in some fishing? It's a lovely time of year for it."

"No, someone told me I should try to get a look at them while I'm here, that's all. How far out of town are they?"

"They vary. There are hundreds of lakes, some privately owned."

"Oh, I didn't realize. Sounds exclusive."

"Some are simple one-room cabins, but it's become fashionable for the wealthy to build extravagant places with many bedrooms, saunas, and gourmet kitchens. Like vacation homes, you know?"

"Sure. Although I have a feeling I'll never see the inside of one. I know all the wrong people."

The clerk laughed sympathetically. "Me too."

The room was sterile but serviceable, and Jet lay down to snatch a little sleep before the director called back. She was painfully aware that she only had seven hours left before Oliver shut down the grid, but there was little she could do until nightfall, and there was no point wearing her nerves out with worry absent the information she'd requested.

It felt like she'd just nodded off when the phone awakened her.

"It isn't a government facility. It's registered to a company located in the Seychelles. No ownership information besides a registered office. So it has all the earmarks of a shell."

"With that kind of security, it's probably the place. Nothing else stands out like it does."

"The only way to know for sure is to penetrate it and identify the server. If it's there, you know what needs to be done."

"Yes."

"Do you think you can do this?"

"What's the alternative? Can you get a team here in time? I have the charges if you want me to hand it off."

"What's your take? Do you think you'd do better on your own, or would a team be capable of penetrating the facility?"

Jet thought for a moment. "With the guards, I'd say a lone operative would have higher odds of success, unless you were ready to shoot your way in and risk an early triggering of the malware."

"Then there's your answer. And for your information, no, I don't have anyone more qualified than you I could put into the field on such short notice."

"Then why even ask?"

"I wanted to hear that you're our best shot."

The director's uncharacteristic lack of confidence was a troubling distraction she couldn't afford. She hung up and put the phone down and rummaged through the backpack Alva had given her, and removed the C-4 charges and timer. She inspected the explosive device, which she was familiar with from training and countless other operations, and set it aside. Next, she examined the lockpicks and finally the LED flashlight, a couple of flash-bang grenades, and rappelling line with a grappling hook cinched to one end.

The pistol was an Israeli-manufactured BUL M-5 Ultra-X compact 9mm. She dug out a paper clip and fieldstripped the gun, and was happy to see that it was well lubricated and spotless.

Jet reassembled the weapon and slid bullets into the three twelve-round magazines, and then slotted a magazine into the butt before admiring how light the weapon was, even with a full mag. It was small enough that it wouldn't be noticed in her waistband, unlike the larger 1911 version, and had adequate stopping power when loaded with hollow points, as she'd just done.

She returned everything to the backpack and moved to the window to part the curtains. The sun was setting, signaling that her time was growing short. Because of the deadline, she couldn't wait until three or four in the morning, when the guards would be at their groggiest, another long night of unending boredom drawing to a close, so she'd have to compensate by being extra careful…and lucky.

With the fate of Israel hanging in the balance, something she definitely didn't feel.

## Chapter 41

The industrial park was deserted after dark, the parking lots of the data centers barren except for the night shift's vehicles, the streets empty and still. Jet moved like a wraith along the sidewalk, the overcast sky contributing to the sustained gloom; there were no lights other than those of the security lamps on the buildings and the guard shacks. The industrial park was new, the streets freshly laid, and the Umeå city lights in the distance were a lifetime away from the antiseptic symmetry of the area's design.

Jet paused beneath a tree at the corner of an intersection a block from her target and took in her surroundings. The night air buzzed with the hum of climate-control compressors maintaining the server farms at frigid constancy. She checked her watch, and her brow furrowed – she only had three hours to go before the fat man's threat would become reality.

She hadn't had time to do much in the way of formulating a plan. Headquarters had hacked into the city and pulled up the building's construction blueprints, so she had a good feel for the location of the control room: the vault that housed the computer that tracked the identity and status of every server for maintenance purposes, and the Achilles' heel she was hoping to use to her advantage.

But first she needed to breach the secure facility without being intercepted by the security contingent. Ordinarily she would have spent days watching the data center, logging the shift changes and the timing of the patrols, planning her entry with the precision of a Swiss watch. Now she'd be forced to wing it, which in Jet's business was a surefire recipe for disaster unless Fate smiled on her.

Jet shrugged off the doubt and crept toward the building, her jaw clenched in determination. Four guards patrolling the exterior, with one at the gate, was nothing – she'd gone up against far longer odds and come out on top. Still, a stir of anxiety tightened in her gut, and for a fleeting moment she imagined Hannah and Matt sitting stunned at the dining room table as one of the director's flunkies explained that Mama wasn't ever coming home.

She crouched behind a row of bushes near the parking lot wall and watched the guards, timing their passage with her watch. After half an hour she felt sure she had a good feel for how many minutes she had on her side of the building without any security in sight, and she prepared to make her move.

The guard at the southernmost end rounded the corner and disappeared, and Jet tossed the grappling hook at the top of the parking lot wall and pulled the rappelling line taut. She was up and over in moments and then ran to the building as fast as she could, the cord and hook in her left hand and a pistol in her right. She made it a few seconds faster than she'd calculated, and threw the hook into the sky. Its prongs bit into the side of the roof and she heaved herself up, scaling the sheer wall with ease. At the top, she made for one of the air-vent covers in the center of the roof, tar paper crunching beneath her boots.

The housing lifted easily. Jet dug the hook prongs into the corner of the housing and lowered herself into an oversized duct. She shimmied down into the interior, lifted a ceiling ventilation grid out of the way, and dropped to the linoleum floor, the rappelling line dangling from the vent opening like a black snake.

Jet pulled up the blueprint on her phone and oriented herself. She was on the north side of the enormous building, and there were rows of server racks stretching for a hundred meters, their lights blinking, the only sounds the whir of thousands of fans and the hum of the climate-control system that kept the interior as cold as a refrigerator.

She crept toward the southern end of the facility along an aisle between two rows of racks, where the drawings had indicated the computer control room was situated. Jet paused occasionally, listening for any sounds of life, but heard nothing. On the blueprint there was a security room for the guards on the west wall, but given the temperature, she was sure they would stay inside and not venture onto the main floor.

Jet located the control room, but the door was locked. She extracted the lockpick wallet from the backpack, knelt by the door, and went to work on the tumblers, taking her time, the lock more complicated than most. After several minutes the lock clicked open, and she twisted the lever while turning the locking mechanism with one of the flat picks.

Once inside, she used her phone's flashlight to locate the central computer terminal and activated the terminal screen. The system listed all the servers in the data center and would automatically alert an operator of any mechanical or electrical faults before they could become critical. She thumbed her phone to the IP address the director had given her, and began combing through the list, looking for a match.

Three hundred servers in, she spotted the IP and pulled up a schematic that indicated where the server was located. It was in a rack on the far end of the building, near the security office and the hub where the data center's power transformers were situated. She memorized the location and then took a photo of the schematic for good measure before returning to the home screen so there would be no trace of her search. When the screen went dark, she raised the phone to her lips and placed a call to the director.

"I found it," she whispered.

"We're down to the wire. You know what to do."

"I'm on my way."

"Confirm time synch," he ordered. She eyed her watch and read off the time, and when the director confirmed synch, removed the digital timer from the backpack and entered the numbers into the display. It blinked twice. Jet next entered a detonation time of 11:45 p.m., and it blinked again. She inspected the device to confirm that it was armed, and then slipped it back into the bag.

"Synched and set for eleven forty-five," she said. "Confirm."

"Synch confirmed," the director said, and the line went dead. She returned the phone to her pocket before stepping away from the terminal and creeping to the door.

Back on the floor, she made her way along a side aisle, gun in hand, until she reached the server rack she'd identified. She checked the number at the top to verify it was the correct one, and then shrugged the backpack off and removed the explosive charges. Four one-kilo bricks of military-grade C-4 were sufficient to take out a quarter of the building, but the Mossad planners had wanted to ensure there would be nothing left of the server when the explosives detonated, and so had supplied her with serious overkill.

Jet opened the front of the rack and placed the bricks behind the server, their bulk hidden by the servers above and below it. She retrieved the timer and placed it by her side, and uncoiled a length of wire with leads on one end and contacts on the other. She inserted the leads into the timer and then affixed the contacts to four detonating caps, and then pressed the caps into the C-4. Her final step was to conceal the timer high above the explosives, where the LED display wouldn't be visible, before she closed the rack with a soft snick.

If all went to plan, the timer would detonate the C-4 simultaneously with two identical timers at the server locations in Ukraine and Latvia, and all three command and control servers would go dark at the same time. In Israel, hundreds of workers were standing by to shut down the various grids of the most critical infrastructure in case some sort of dead man's trigger was activated, and to replace the power station, airport, and national defense hardware before the night was through. The rest of the servers would be checked and replaced before being returned to service, with stopgap systems standing by until duplicates of the specialized hardware could be obtained. Many of the networks would run slow, but excuses would be made, and the population would deal with glitchy stoplights and delayed trains with typical stoicism.

The only problem was if any of the three teams failed in their mission. Then all bets were off.

Jet couldn't worry about that. She'd done her part, and now all that remained was to get clear of the data center without being gunned down.

She walked back to where the rappelling cord dangled from the ceiling and hoisted herself up into the duct, taking care to make as little sound as possible. Once inside, she dog-crawled up to the roof end of the ducting, removed the grappling hook from the housing, and carried the rope to the roof lip. She wedged the prongs behind a pipe fitting and coiled the line beside it, and then returned to the housing to close it. Jet was lowering it into place when the hinges groaned, and she froze, the sound amplified by the housing so it sounded like a trumpet from where she stood.

Jet eased it the rest of the way shut, pushing against the side in an effort to silence the hinges, and then ran to the line and peered over the roof lip. She didn't spot any guards and, according to her earlier observation, would have to wait five minutes from the time they showed themselves to when they'd circle the building and be out of sight. She crouched in the darkness and waited for the sound of boots, willing herself to be patient now that she was so close to a successful mission conclusion. Jet frowned when minutes went by and nobody appeared, and was growing anxious when a voice called out from the far end of the roof.

She looked up to see three guards with assault rifles pointed in her direction, the door to the roof access stairs standing open. Jet didn't need a Swedish translator to clarify the warning or the seriousness of their intent, and she slowly raised her hands as the men approached with their guns trained on her head.

# Chapter 42

Jet bounced in the back of the van, cuffed to a ring on a steel bench, seated across from a pair of stone-faced guards. She'd demanded to know where she was being taken, but nobody had spoken to her, and her captors had ignored her protests as they loaded her into the van and got underway.

The tires hit a particularly ugly run on the gravel road they'd taken once outside the business park, and Jet winced as the cuff cut into her wrist. The vehicle slowed and made a sharp left turn, and then bounced along for thirty seconds before drawing to a halt. The driver killed the engine and the back doors swung open, and Jet found herself facing three heavily muscled men with pistols in shoulder holsters.

One of them barked an order, and the guard nearest Jet unlocked her from the bench and cuffed her wrists in front of her before pushing her toward the doors. Two of the goons lifted her out, and she resisted the urge to break their noses with a head butt as they groped her.

A guard tossed her backpack from the van and the third man caught it, and then the doors closed and the engine restarted and the van drove back down the trail, leaving Jet standing with her new friends in front of a two-story cabin fashioned from raw timber, the windows blazing with light. A lake stretched from the back porch as far as she could see, the area dense with conifers and foliage. Down the drive, she could make out the lamps of the industrial park no more than a kilometer away.

When the sound of the engine died, she looked the men over and waited for them to speak. Nobody did. Instead, they half dragged her into the cabin, where Oliver sat in the large living room, his cart near a rustic stone fireplace with the heads of elk and a moose mounted over it.

His eyes widened when he saw her, and then he chuckled. "So we meet again, Miss Mendez. If that's even your real name."

The bodyguards sat Jet in a wooden chair opposite Oliver and stood beside her, awaiting instructions.

Oliver studied her for several beats. "What were you doing at the data center?" He paused. "Never mind. I can guess. Very clever of you. Your people obviously were able to track the IP to this area. But what I'm curious about is how you knew which building was mine."

Jet shrugged. "Only one with a bunch of guards."

"What were you planning to do?"

"What does it matter? Your men stopped me before I could get inside."

"They sent a girl to sabotage the site? I expected better. It appears they've cut way back on their operational budget. Or I overestimated my adversary."

"You'll never live to spend the money."

He smirked and shook his head. "Tut-tut. Threats are unbecoming, especially given your situation."

"It isn't a threat. It's a statement of fact."

Oliver pursed his lips and waved the guards away. "My dear girl, it was never about the money. Money's just a way of keeping score."

Jet didn't respond.

He smiled. "You're wanted for murder in Estonia. I have to decide whether to ship you back and turn you over, or deal with you here in my own way. I could keep you around for my amusement for a while. Would you like that?"

"When was the last time you saw your dick or were able to wipe your ass without a squeegee and a mirror?"

He laughed again, although his eyes hardened. "You're a tough one, aren't you? Well, let me tell you what's about to happen, tough girl. Your government won't pay me. I know that. As a penalty, I'm going to shut down a third of the country. Just enough to paralyze it, but not enough to destroy it. Then I'm going to give it twenty-four hours to come up with ten billion euros instead of four. This time they'll do so. That will make me one of the richest men in the world, although I can't pretend to compete with guys like Bezos or Gates. At least, not yet."

"Guess kiddie porn doesn't pay as well as you thought. Have to resort to extortion?"

"Let me guess. You kill people for a living, right? You murder them without a second thought because your country tells you to. And you dare judge me? Please. The hypocrisy is sickening."

It was her turn to study him. "I'd kill you if I had the chance," she said.

"Why, my dear, I believe you would. Instead, you're going to be my sex slave. I can't promise you'll enjoy that, but I know I will. For the record, I prefer it if you struggle and fight."

"That's the only way you can get a woman, you disgusting blob. I feel sorry for you," Jet said, stalling for time.

"I think I'll let the guards have you for a few hours before I bother. Maybe I'll film it for posterity, or for my enjoyment long after you're dead and buried." He regarded her. "How does it feel to know that everything you worked for was in vain?"

"Probably about like you feel trying to roll out of bed every morning. Assuming you don't sleep in that asinine cart."

He motioned to the man by the door to bring him the backpack. The guard placed it on Oliver's tray, and he proceeded to unpack it, stopping to inspect the pistol.

"Nasty little piece of work. Rather like you. Israeli, I see."

The lockpicks interested him, and he touched the stainless steel implements with bloated fingers. "I always wanted to learn how to do this. Perhaps that will be my next challenge."

"Right after gastric bypass surgery."

He looked over her phone and placed it beside the pistol. "I wonder who I'd get on the line if I pressed redial."

"Try it. I've got all night."

"Maybe later. The camera looks suitably high definition, so I can stream your rape and torture live."

"One thing I'm curious about," she said. "Why go after the Russian?"

"Tying up loose ends. He reneged on his part of a deal to sabotage a natural gas pipeline from Nigeria after I adjusted the pricing to reflect the actual level of difficulty. Ultimately he's of no consequence. A bit player with an overly high opinion of himself." He held the backpack up to his face and sniffed.

Jet smirked. "I didn't keep my dirty underwear in there, if that's what you're after."

Oliver's maniacal grin faded and he looked over at his guards. "Where was she captured?" he snapped. "Exactly?"

"On the roof. She'd just climbed up and was trying to get a vent cover open."

He threw the backpack at the men, who stepped back. "Pick it up, you morons. Tell me what you smell."

One of the guards retrieved the bag and sniffed it. He looked at Oliver, puzzled. "I don't know. Maybe…motor oil?"

Oliver drew his phone from his breast pocket and barked his orders into it. "Search the facility. She was inside. Go for server 327 first. That's where you'll find the bomb."

He hung up and frowned at Jet. "C-4 is made with motor oil. It leaves a distinctive odor."

She didn't speak for a moment. When she did, her voice was calm. "What time is it?"

His eyes widened in realization. "You bitch!"

Her smile was genuine. "You're out of your depth, you fat prick, and you're about to find out just how badly you overestimated your abilities."

An explosion from the data center shattered the night, and a few seconds later, the lights in the fishing lodge went dark. The guards threw open the front door and stared at the fireball, the interior of the cabin now pitch black. Oliver howled in rage as Jet tipped over her chair, and it broke apart when it hit the floor.

She threw herself onto the hearth and grabbed for a poker. The first guard rushed at her and fired blindly, the room too dark to make her out, and Jet swung it at his legs and knocked them from under him. He hit the timber floor hard. His gun skittered toward her when she stabbed the end through his eye, and she grabbed the pistol and rolled away as the second guard began firing into the room.

Jet squeezed off two shots at the guard's muzzle flash and then rolled away. The third guard was framed in the doorway, his pistol clutched in a two-handed combat grip, and she put three bullets into his chest before spinning to where Oliver was fumbling with her pistol, his hands too big to easily work the safety or trigger.

"It's over," she said. "You lose."

He raised the pistol, and Jet emptied half her magazine into him at point-blank range. He grunted at the impact of the rounds and then groaned hoarsely as he slumped over his tray, his beloved computer screen shattered from the shooting.

The guard she'd neutralized with the poker groaned, and she turned and put two shots into the back of his head. She checked the others to confirm they were dead, and then dropped the gun on the floor, walked back to Oliver's cart, and felt for her phone. She switched on the light, found the lockpicks, and freed herself of the cuffs. Jet rubbed her wrists and then checked Oliver for a pulse. He was dead. She glanced at her watch and gathered up her phone, the BUL and the extra magazines, and the lockpicks, but left the rappelling line and grappling hook where they had fallen during the fight, their purpose served.

Jet found the backpack beside one of the dead men and placed her things inside, and then exited the cabin and dialed the director's number as she walked down the drive. When he answered, she spoke so softly he could barely make her words out.

"It's finished. Kalda's dead, and the data center's destroyed."

"Kalda? How?"

"He had a house nearby. I allowed myself to be captured. The explosion caused a power spike that took down the local grid, including his place. The rest was easy."

"I sincerely doubt that."

She looked over at the data center, which was blazing in the distance, and let out a heavy sigh. "Get me on the first plane out of here. First class. I think I've earned it."

"No question. Consider it done."

Her next call was to Matt. When he answered on the fourth ring, he sounded half asleep.

"Hello?" he croaked.

Her eyes moistened, and when she spoke, her voice was tight.

"Tell Hannah…Mama's coming home."

# Chapter 43

*Tel Aviv, Israel*

Jet, Matt, and Hannah entered the playground and walked to one of the benches that ringed the area. They took a seat, and Jet tousled Hannah's hair and lightly spanked her bottom. The little girl ran off to play with the other children, her long hair trailing behind her like a flag, eyes glittering with excitement. Jet smiled at the sight and squeezed Matt's hand.

He shifted beside her and grinned. She snuck a peek at his profile, the lines at the corners of his eyes lending him an air of distinction, his skin weathered sufficiently to give him character, she decided.

"To be young again," he said.

"Speak for yourself, grandpa."

"I'm ever grateful that you're willing to tend to me in my dotage."

"Part of my penance to the universe."

"Because of how bad you've been?"

She laughed. "I was thinking about how bad you've been. But it'll do."

They sat together on the wooden bench, the weather balmy in the late morning, and let the sun warm them as a gentle breeze dented the surrounding treetops. Peals of laughter and glee rang from the slide, where Hannah and two other little girls were running around it at manic speed, and Jet leaned into Matt and rested her head on his shoulder.

"I'm thinking of retiring."

Matt didn't say anything for several beats. "You think they'll allow you to?"

"I just saved the frigging country. They'll have to. After this, I feel like I'm done, you know? Let someone else take the bullets and save the day. This is what I want. Not…that."

Matt took her hand and gave it a squeeze. "I don't blame you. I'm just questioning the practicality. The director…everything you've told me about him, and how he's played you, says *snake* in mile-high letters. I find it hard to believe he'll really let you go."

"I'm not going to give him a choice. We're rich. If we have to, we can move somewhere else. Maybe it would have to be Lapland or Nepal or Sudan, but there have to be places where my enemies can't find us."

"Didn't we try that already?"

Hannah came at a run and interrupted them. "Mama! My new friends are having a party tomorrow! Can I go? Please?"

Jet threaded her fingers through her daughter's hair and glanced at Matt. "I don't see any reason why not. Where are their mommies?"

"Over there," Hannah said, pointing at a pair of women on another bench, one of them with a stroller in front of her.

"Okay. I'll talk to them in a couple of minutes. Be careful on the slide and the monkey bars. And stay away from those boys," she said, indicating three tykes about Hannah's age who were roughhousing by the sandbox. "They're playing too rough."

"I will."

Hannah scurried off, and Jet sighed. "Do you ever think about having another one?"

Matt turned to her. "We're not exactly the most stable family right now, given the circumstances. That said, sure I do. But…"

He didn't have to point out the implicit threat their pasts had created, which would always be with them, at least until all their enemies were dead.

"It was just a question. I'm not saying we should. At least, not immediately."

He shrugged and offered her a lopsided grin. "I suppose we could always practice. I mean, for when the time comes. To make sure we're doing everything right."

Her smile grew. "You're a thinker. I like that."

"I'm willing to sacrifice if I must."

Jet kissed his cheek and whispered in his ear. He pulled back in mock surprise and looked at her with raised eyebrows.

"Why…I never!"

Jet elbowed him and slid closer. "Then it's about time, big boy. Don't know how many more summers the old bear has to come out of the cave."

"Or go in."

"Exactly."

# Chapter 44

*Moscow, Russia*

Karev lay in a bed in a private room with Tanya next to him, her breathing uneasy as she slept in a narcotic haze. The doctors had diagnosed her as having a concussion but no internal injuries that wouldn't heal, although her psychological prognosis was more tentative. The abuse, rape, and murder of her friend would require a long and tortuous road to put behind her, and she was currently sedated, the IV in her arm feeding vitamins into her.

The door opened a crack and Sergei's head poked in. Karev motioned for him to enter, and he took a seat at Karev's bedside.

Sergei glanced over at Tanya and shook his head. "How is she?"

"About as you might expect."

"A news report from Sweden broke yesterday. A prominent Estonian technology baron was murdered in what appears to be a gangland slaying. Judging by the report, he went hard."

Karev frowned. "Not hard enough for my liking. I'd like to dig him up and kill him all over again for what he did to Tanya."

"I can understand. But he's dead, so there's nothing else to do on that end."

"What about the Ukrainians who held her prisoner?"

"I've got men on the island as we speak. They've been instructed to film it."

"Good. Make them suffer."

"They understand."

Karev narrowed his eyes to slits. "And the woman?"

"That's going to be harder. We have contacts in Israel, but we have to tread lightly. She's Mossad, and they take care of their own.

She won't be easy to locate, much less get to."

"There has to be a price to pay for trying to kill me. If I let her get away with it, it sends the wrong message to my enemies."

"No argument. I'm not questioning your motives. Just saying it will be difficult. And expensive."

"I don't care about the money."

"I know."

"Have you gotten anyone to replace the fat pig on the pipeline? No more mafia tactics. We can't have everyone associated with it executed. We need more finesse than that."

"I'm speaking with some people. They come highly recommended. And they're less expensive than he was."

"That's not hard to believe."

They discussed other security matters until Karev tired. Sergei stood and walked to the door.

"No promises on the woman," he said. "That will be a process that won't happen overnight. And it could get complicated. There might well be blowback if it was discovered that you'd put a sanction on one of their operatives. For the same reason you're concerned about your enemies. If it's open season on Mossad operatives, that's bad for their business, and they'd need to make an example out of whoever was behind it."

"I understand the risks. Just make sure I'm well distanced from it. Hire professionals from other countries – no Russians. Use cutouts. Do whatever you must. But I want this done, Sergei. They killed my security detail and snatched me like a schoolgirl. That can't stand. An example must be made."

"Sometimes to win the war, you have to be prepared to lose a battle."

Karev's expression darkened, and when he stared at Sergei, his eyes were dead. "Not this time. No more discussion. Make it happen."

<<<<>>>>

# About the Author

Featured in *The Wall Street Journal*, *The Times*, and *The Chicago Tribune*, Russell Blake is *The NY Times* and *USA Today* bestselling author of over fifty novels.

Blake is co-author of *The Eye of Heaven* and *The Solomon Curse*, with legendary author Clive Cussler. Blake's novel *King of Swords* has been translated into German, *The Voynich Cypher* into Bulgarian, and his JET novels into Spanish, German, and Czech.

Blake writes under the moniker R.E. Blake in the NA/YA/Contemporary Romance genres. Novels include *Less Than Nothing*, *More Than Anything*, and *Best Of Everything*.

Having resided in Mexico for a dozen years, Blake enjoys his dogs, fishing, boating, tequila and writing, while battling world domination by clowns. His thoughts, such as they are, can be found at his blog: RussellBlake.com

☼

Visit RussellBlake.com for updates

or subscribe to: RussellBlake.com/contact/mailing-list

# BOOKS BY RUSSELL BLAKE

*Co-authored with Clive Cussler*
THE EYE OF HEAVEN
THE SOLOMON CURSE

*Thrillers*
FATAL EXCHANGE
FATAL DECEPTION
THE GERONIMO BREACH
ZERO SUM
THE DELPHI CHRONICLE TRILOGY
THE VOYNICH CYPHER
SILVER JUSTICE
UPON A PALE HORSE
DEADLY CALM
RAMSEY'S GOLD
EMERALD BUDDHA
THE GODDESS LEGACY
A GIRL APART
A GIRL BETRAYED
QUANTUM SYNAPSE

*The Assassin Series*
KING OF SWORDS
NIGHT OF THE ASSASSIN
RETURN OF THE ASSASSIN
REVENGE OF THE ASSASSIN
BLOOD OF THE ASSASSIN
REQUIEM FOR THE ASSASSIN
RAGE OF THE ASSASSIN

*The Day After Never Series*
THE DAY AFTER NEVER – BLOOD HONOR
THE DAY AFTER NEVER – PURGATORY ROAD
THE DAY AFTER NEVER – COVENANT
THE DAY AFTER NEVER – RETRIBUTION
THE DAY AFTER NEVER – INSURRECTION
THE DAY AFTER NEVER – PERDITION
THE DAY AFTER NEVER – HAVOC
THE DAY AFTER NEVER – LEGION

*The JET Series*
JET
JET II – BETRAYAL
JET III – VENGEANCE
JET IV – RECKONING
JET V – LEGACY
JET VI – JUSTICE
JET VII – SANCTUARY
JET VIII – SURVIVAL
JET IX – ESCAPE
JET X – INCARCERATION
JET XI – FORSAKEN
JET XII – ROGUE STATE
JET XIII – RENEGADE
JET XIV – DARK WEB
JET – OPS FILES (prequel)
JET – OPS FILES; TERROR ALERT

*The BLACK Series*
BLACK
BLACK IS BACK
BLACK IS THE NEW BLACK
BLACK TO REALITY
BLACK IN THE BOX

*Non Fiction*
AN ANGEL WITH FUR
HOW TO SELL A GAZILLION EBOOKS
*(while drunk, high or incarcerated)*

Made in the USA
Coppell, TX
05 December 2022